Tamburlaine

by

Gregory A. Kompes

Fabulist Flash Publishing

Las Vegas, NV

ISBN: 978-0-979361272

Editor: Leslie E. Hoffman

Cover Design: Gregory A. Kompes

Fabulist Flash Publishing
PO Box 570368
Las Vegas, Nevada, 89157

For more books by Gregory A. Kompes,
please visit www.Kompes.com.

This project is funded, in part, by a grant from the Nevada Arts Council, a state agency, and the National Endowment for the Arts, a federal agency.

Dedicated to:

Rusty Warren.

Thanks for the inspiration and the laughter.

Tamburlaine

by

Gregory A. Kompes

One

Disappointed with the bar's take for the day, Chris Marlowe closed the accounts book and locked it in the safe with that evening's receipts. "Your time is coming," he said to the painting of streetwalkers on the wall. An image of Jimmy sitting in the boss's chair flashed into his mind. Chris breathed deep, pushing those memories back into the depths; he turned away and left the office, locking the door behind him with a series of turns to the combination-lock doorknob.

The short hall, lit only by the dim shadows of red light from the emergency exit sign, led to the red-dark dining room and into Tamburlaine's main barroom with the piano and small performance stage, a dozen chipped Formica tables, most of which wobbled, and a long wooden bar that had aged incredibly well. A neon beer sign cast yellow dimness over the room. After a sigh that only he heard, Chris placed the chairs, one after another, upside down on the worn table tops. He questioned again why he even bothered taking them down in the afternoon when he arrived; no one sat in them anymore except the occasional stray who wandered in and, after realizing where he found himself, wandered out just as quickly, head ducked low in embarrassment, maybe his own, or maybe for Tamburlaine.

Benny, the part-time bartender, had already upended the barstools. Those balanced atop the long bar and the chairs, with feet in the air, like of turrets and fences, not that there was a need for barriers to keep folks out, or protection for those inside, for that matter.

The old tile floor, chipped and cracked and worn with the movement of thousands of feet, lay cluttered with napkins and debris. How could so few patrons make such a mess?

He considered one more drink; he considered gasoline and a match; he considered walking off the nearby pier into the dirty water of the Hudson River. Chris shuddered at the thoughts.

"Snap out of it, old man," he said to his reflection in the long mirror behind the bar. His lipstick was smeared, his wig slightly askew. His image was one of those tired drag queens he'd made fun of in his youth.

He had been beautiful, once. He'd had suitors, once. People who were famous now, important now these twenty, okay, thirty years later. He'd used his wiles to build a career...and Tamburlaine. With both hands, Chris straightened his wig. What had happened? How had he fallen when all he believed in was happening now, equality, openness, positive laws. So far had they all come from those early days, scraping and clawing, defending against nightsticks and blackmail. And yet, he, a community leader in his own right, at the time, was now earning a pittance. But, still he kept it open, Tamburlaine. He'd promised all those years ago. He'd always kept his promises.

Chris offered himself that signature wink, oversized with a dramatic turn of the head. "No tears."

A light tapping at the glass door pulled his attention. It was that young fellow from earlier. Another stray hoping for... tap...tap...tap.

Chris waved and pointed toward the side alley; that's where he'd exit. The boy with the strong, aquiline nose nodded, his unkempt auburn curls bounced in rhythm, but then he didn't move. Chris studied his reflection for another moment before turning with a click of his heels. He strode across the barroom, through the dark dining room, and into the dismal kitchen; he pushed the panic bar, exited into the alley, and slammed the door closed.

The cool evening air caught up with him. Chris pulled his crimson wrap tight around his shoulders as he passed the Dumpsters. There the man stood. What was his name? Did it matter? They were all the same, these boys on the street. Boys. They all seemed like children to him. Chris chastised Benny to check identification before serving these men in training. Yet, the vast majority were of legal drinking age. This one had been drinking at Tamburlaine, hadn't he? He was there; Chris remembered that. For some reason, he thought the guy might have actually spoken to him, but frankly, after his nightly bottle of bourbon, all bets at memory games were off.

"Hello," he said.

"Hello." Chris smiled at the thought of waking up next to this one. How old must he be? Twenty, twenty-two, nineteen?

"Buy me a drink?"

"The bars are all long closed. The sun will be up soon." How many times had he heard and said these lines? It was like some bad Logo movie. Imagine that, a gay television station. Drag queens on screen every week. Difficult to believe all the fighting after Stonewall had come to that. Television reality shows for queers; looks like they'd made it.

"Take me home with you." The young man ran nimble fingers with well-manicured nails through natural auburn locks. He smelled of tobacco and whiskey.

"Is that really what you'd like?" Chris barely had the energy to flirt. It had all been done so very many times before. Yet, it would be nice to sleep with a warm body next to his. It had been so long since anyone he found attractive had propositioned him. He missed propositions; they reminded him of his youth. They didn't just remind him; they caused him to feel young.

"Yes," the boy whispered.

"What's your name, kid?"

The man's demeanor stiffened. "Don't call me that. Don't call me kid." He took a step closer to Chris. "Understand?"

Unthreatened, Chris said: "Sure. What's your name?" Without waiting, he turned and started to walk away.

"Ingram," he said without attitude, now aligned at Chris' side.

"How old are you?"

Ingram took Chris' hand and slid it into the crook of his arm. "How old are you?" He was back to flirting.

"Is this illegal? That's all I need to know."

Ingram laughed. "Like that would matter to you. Aren't you flattered having a guy interested in you? Wanting to fuck you."

It was Chris' turn at indignity. He stopped short, pulled his hand away from the boy who turned back. "Listen," said Chris in a hissing whisper. "I've been on this planet a long time without you, and I really don't need you now. I make up the rules. I'm the top to all you baby boys who only think you're tops, who only think you're men, who only think you know how to fuck." He wiped spittle from his lipstick-smeared lips. "Now, if you want a place for the night, fine. If you want to fuck, we'll see how it goes. If you expect to get cash from me, forget it."

Squared, eye-to-eye with Ingram, Chris faced off with the slighter man. A game of chicken. It might end in violence. It might end in embarrassment. It might end in romance. No matter the outcome, he would not be the one to blink first.

A harsh wind came off the river. "It's cold," said Ingram, his voice soft and seductive. "Do you live close?" The boy wrapped his arms around his body against the cold.

"Around the corner."

Ingram turned toward home and held out his bent arm. Chris walked up and slipped his hand once again into the warmth of the bend. For a moment, he felt twenty-two. They moved as one. Now, in silence, Chris lead by slight tugs and pulls of Ingram's elbow. The kid knew how to follow someone else's lead. Promising. If he could follow from a tug of elbow, imagine how well he'd do in bed.

At an unmarked, steel door Chris stopped. He freed himself, dug into his pocket, and pulled out a key ring with two keys. In a swift action, he shoved one of them into the industrial deadbolt, turned it, and pulled hard on the door. It opened with a loud creak.

"Is this it?" Ingram asked.

Chris enjoyed his skepticism. He held the door for the kid, and once they were both inside, he pulled the door closed with a bang, taking the time to check that it was secure by pushing against it. The air was warmer here, but not by much. Chris pulled on the shawl, but it was as close to him as the fabric could get. He breathed deep of the mossy, earthy scent of the alley. That smell had whispered home to him for more than thirty years.

"We're still outside!" Ingram pointed to the night sky.

"This way, my little waif." Chris' heels clacked on the paving stones in a self-assured rhythm. Ingram's trainers made a thudding sound as he quickened his pace to keep up.

Down the walk, into a dark, open area, left turn, and another door. This one unlocked. Chris pulled on the door, it opened easily, and he held if for Ingram who entered and stopped. Chris hit a switch near the door and blinked several times as his eyes adjusted to the brutal kitchen light.

"Wow!" As if drawn by an invisible force, Ingram moved a step more inside. Then another. "This is all yours?"

Chris always liked when newcomers took in his home. The twenty foot ceilings, ancient hardwood floors, exposed pipes, duct work, and crumbly brick walls of what was once a motor shop. Some days, there was still a hint of machine oil in the air: the idea of workmen in overalls lingered. He let the door close and moved to the counter, throwing his wrap over a chair. "Coffee? Beer? Something stronger?"

"A beer would be great. What *was* this place?"

"Frizer Motors." Chris opened the fridge, handed Ingram a beer, and twisted the top off his. "They built all sorts of motors and engines, mostly for machinery. The building had been abandoned for years before I bought it. That was—"

"You own the building?"

"Yes."

"How many other tenants?" Ingram took another step and whistled up toward the high ceiling.

"None. It's just me."

"What's upstairs?" He pointed across the room to a large staircase.

"We'll leave that for another time. Come on." Chris led Ingram through a maze of partitions; they arrived at a walled-off area. He spun a knob and soft lighting revealed a large bed, overstuffed dressers with their contents leaking out, and walls covered with large canvases. Among the pieces were Warhol, Pollack, Lichtenstein, and Jasper Johns.

"Are those real?" Ingram pointed a finger at the paintings while turning toward Chris.

"What do you mean? Oh, the art. Of course they're real." Chris thought for a moment of sharing the story, how they'd arrived here, but he'd just met this, damn, what was this kid's name. Chris knew he couldn't.

"Shouldn't they be in a museum?" Ingram's demeanor softened, his shoulders drooped a bit. The ruffian from the street became a smaller, awestruck, wide-eyed kid. "I mean, isn't that where all art ends up?"

"Not all of it." He walked to an open arch and left the room. He had to get the makeup off his face. It felt like a lead mask by this time of the morning. He hated 4:30. Not enough night, but no bagel trucks on the street yet to signify day. Chris sat at the vanity and opened the cold cream, it's cool velvety smell bringing him a moment of joy.

Ingram followed him. Chris watched his face as he entered the massive bathroom. "Wow!"

"You really would do well to come up with something more original to say. Your 'Wow' is almost as bad as the 'Oh, my Gods' on those makeover shows." Chris had already removed his blouse. He took a seat at the vanity, flipped a switch, and a bright light revealed wrinkles and lines caked with makeup. He tugged off his wig and placed it over a wooden head—three similar dummy heads held different red wigs—within moments, he had a coat of cold cream on his face.

"I thought you'd be wearing…"

"What?"

"Well, women's under…a bra." Ingram continued his tour of the bathroom, touching each fixture and tile.

"Not with this outfit. Not on a Tuesday. I don't pull out the big guns until the weekend."

Ingram laughed and turned on the water in the shower. "Do you mind?"

Chris eyed him in the mirror as Ingram kicked off his shoes. "Not at all." And, as he stripped off what remained of the night's makeup, he watched Ingram undress, no seduction now, just the promise of a hot shower. Chris remembered those days, so long ago. They'd all looked like this kid at one point, hadn't they? Flat and hard, mostly hairless, the way men were now. Chris missed hair on men, hairy chests, hairy stomachs, hairy balls. Lately, everyone was…what were the young people calling it these days? Manscaped?—trimmed and shaved and ripped.

Chris wasn't any of those things, anymore. He'd never had much hair, so he never needed to shave his chest. Chris wasn't a hard body by any stretch of the imagination, but he was still thin, except for a little paunch and those horrible love handles. His days of working out daily long gone. He tried to avoid the carbs, but he loved bourbon. Performing nightly, even to an empty showroom, did keep him in shape, more or less. Running the empty Tamburlaine caused enough stress to keep him nearly thin. He thought again about the promise: "Really, I'll keep it running," he'd pleaded with his dying, what was he, friend, lover, boss, an asshole, that's what he was, but it had been a deathbed promise.

As he watched the boy shower, Chris removed his skull cap, then, hairpin by hairpin, he released his head-full of pin curls, his natural hair a sweaty mess. He ran a brush through the curls, pulling them back out to a normal length. Was that another new wrinkle in his brow?

Just before Chris joined Ingram in the shower, the water turned off and Ingram luxuriated in a large, thick bath towel. Chris held out a plush robe, which Ingram slipped into; he left it open, his dick, now slightly hard, was smaller than Chris had imagined based on the kid's foot and hand size. He quickly removed his slacks and panties and slipped into the shower.

The weight of the day took hold. Chris barely made it through the quick shower without falling asleep standing up. He dried himself and pulled on a silky robe that extended to the floor. He ran a finger over the frayed cuff. Ingram wasn't in the room so he went back into the bedroom. There was the boy, naked, stretched out on the bed, snoring, his cock still exposed, but retreated. Chris was pleased about that. He got what he wanted, a warm handsome body without the effort of sex. He changed out of his Victoria Secret robe and into a long nightshirt with the image of a bear hugging him.

With a small effort, he gathered the boy under the covers and pulled him close, wrapping his arms tight and protectively around Ingram, who moaned softly his acquiescence. Chris felt his own dick stiffen slightly against Ingram's ass, but he knew he'd be asleep in a few moments. All of that would have to wait. For now, it was a last moment of enjoying the warmth of a man against him. It was knowing that he'd somehow survived another day, as he had survived so many others before. He snuggled tighter to Ingram, enjoying his rhythmic breaths and fresh-from-the-shower, Ivory-soap scent.

Two

Chris Marlowe awoke to the smell of bacon. Hungover and momentarily confused about who could be fixing breakfast, he considered that this waking moment might be a dream, but the intoxicating aroma seemed so real. Chris further considered that he might be having a stroke or a drug induced memory lapse. Both might be possibilities.

He pulled himself out of bed, wrapped his favorite silk kimono around his body, folded over the cuff with the frayed edge, and slipped into a pair of flip flops; their unmistakable sound followed him along the polished floors. For just a moment, Chris regretted giving up cigarettes. The first one of the day had always brought clarity.

Oh, it was him. Chris couldn't conjure the young man's name. It was something old-fashioned. Slender, naked under that open, plush robe. He remembered *that* from the previous night. "You really should close up your robe while frying bacon. Most don't like to suck a cock with burn scars."

"Bacon flavor. Don't knock it till you try it," he said with a wink. "Bacon and eggs? Toast and coffee? Sit. I've made plenty. It's my cure for a hangover."

"At least I'm not the only one feeling a little rough this morning." Chris took a seat at his kitchen table and allowed the man to serve. "Have we actually met? I'm Chris Marlowe." He held out his hand to the handsome exposed stranger in his kitchen.

"Ingram," said the boy. "We did meet last night. It was the end of a very long day."

"You don't know the half of it." Chris added a spoon of sugar to the coffee mug, stirred. He watched Ingram beat eggs in a bowl, add some salt and pepper, beat some more, his cock and balls bouncing in the rhythm. It was nice having someone take care of him, even if it was only bacon and eggs.

The kid flipped the bacon, placed paper towels on a plate, beat the eggs some more. As his wrist worked the scramble, his small dick and balls once again bobbed.

Chris wanted to comment, to make fun of the guy, but he didn't want the scene to change. "Why did you come home with me?"

Ingram, silent, plucked bacon out of the pan and placed it gently on the paper towels. He lowered the flame under the pan and poured the eggs into the grease.

Chris watched as his cholesterol silently protested. He gave the kid more time to answer, enjoying another sip of good coffee and the ongoing eye candy. He wondered if they'd fucked the night before. Not remembering sex was never a reason to believe or think it hadn't happened in some form or another.

The kid worked the eggs, gently pulling from the outer rim of the frying pan into the center with the spatula. He'd obviously done this before.

"I needed a place to crash. I liked your act, your energy. Your jokes are like old, but still funny. My dad could never manage that—his jokes were never funny, but old. So, I figured," he portioned out the eggs onto the plates. "I thought, from the look of you, that you might like some company."

Chris held up his coffee mug for a refill. After placing the plates heaped with food on the table, the boy obliged, then placed the coffee pot on the table, covering a place where the Formica had long-ago chipped.

"Well, I do enjoy young men. And, as time has passed there have been fewer and fewer of them." Chris threw all caution to the wind and added more salt to his eggs.

"It was nice sleeping with you. Your arms around me. Your wonderful bed. And, then to wake up to this amazing kitchen." Ingram, his butt now leaning against a counter, plate in his hand, shoved a forkful of food into his mouth, followed by a large bite of buttered toast.

Chris had forgotten how much boys ate. He'd be broke before the weekend if this one stuck around.

"Listen, I have an appointment this afternoon. An audition. But, then I was hoping to come back. Maybe do a number or two at your club. Not a paying gig, of course. But, I don't like to be a freeloader. I'd like to return your kindness and hospitality."

"How long do you plan on staying?" Chris asked amused at the cojones of this, what was his name? This Ingram.

The boy blushed. "Well, if I get this part, I'll have a paycheck again very soon. I've also got resumes in at several places around town. And most days there's a cater-waiter gig."

"What's your day job?"

"I'm a cook. Not a chef, mind you, but a short order variety cook. Breakfast all day, diner food, you know. That's how I paid for college, cooking eggs at all hours of the day for hungry stoned students."

Chris savored the food, and the boy, in silence. After another sip of coffee, he began to feel a bit better. "Where's your stuff?"

Ingram pointed to a small backpack. "That's it."

Chris was curious, but didn't ask. "Tamburlaine opens at four. I get there about three or half past."

Ingram pointed to the *Playbill* covers papering the walls and partitions. "Have you seen all these shows?" He finished his heaping portion of food. Chris thought Ingram might actually lick the plate.

"Yes. It's one of the great joys of living in New York City, seeing the shows. I used to see them all."

"Not now?" Ingram moved back to the table. "Finished?"

Chris nodded and Ingram picked up his plate and took it to the sink. Chris followed. "You wash, I'll dry." Once they got their rhythm together, Chris said, "Well, my fortunes aren't what they used to be."

"Really? You live in this cool place. Your club is classy and clean."

"Well, business has been slow the past few...years. The Great Recession and all, you know?"

"Hmm," Ingram murmured. "Do you mind if I take a quick shower? Bed head," he said, running his damp hand through his full head of curly hair.

"Help yourself. Do you need clean clothes? We could probably dig something up that isn't too...feminine."

"No, thanks." He turned into Chris and pressed himself up against his host-ess.

They kissed. It was a small kiss at first. Just a brush of the lips. Chris let the boy lead. He parted his lips and Ingram slipped his exuberant tongue into Chris' mouth. They played tongue tag for a moment. Chris dropped a hand and slid it into Ingram's crotch. The boy's little dick was at full attention, its size not much improved. He adjusted his grip and worked the boy hard and fast. It only took a few, quick moments until he shot with a gasp.

"Oh, I've…"

"Shhh," whispered Chris. "Just go take your shower and get ready for your audition." He watched Ingram leave the room, his cheeks flushed, head hung a little low, and a hand over his crotch. Chris smiled to himself as he quickly toweled away the cum on his robe and then washed his hands, scrubbed the frying pan, and wiped the counters. A voice drew him into the loft. The kid was still in the shower; the water ran and steam rose above the partitions. He sang. A tenor voice the likes of which Chris hadn't heard in years. Like his name, the kid's voice was old-fashioned, too. It reminded him of Eddie Cantor recordings. Soft, lilting, stylized. Then, suddenly, Ingram changed tunes and he was modern pop.

Chris sat on the unmade bed. Ingram sang a bit of a lyrical ballad Chris had never heard before. It was moving and powerful and the tones brought tears to Chris' eyes. He'd had a voice like that once, decades ago, when drag queens actually sang instead of lip-synched.

When the shower stopped, so did the concert. Chris sat for a moment longer, listening to the boy clear his throat and then throw off a few quick scales.

"What are you auditioning for?" Chris called into the bathroom as he stood up and began making the bed.

"What?" Ingram came to the doorway, naked, drying his hair. His flat body all muscle and sinew.

"What's the audition for?"

"Oh, it's a callback for The Great Jericho Taylor's revival of *Godspell*."

Jericho Taylor. Chris had known him for years. Many, many years. It had been a long time since they'd talked. Jericho's career took off, Chris' hit the skids. It's life in New York. People come and go. Clubs are in one day, out the next.

"A callback?"

Ingram went to the sink; water ran; teeth were brushed. Chris finished making the bed. He quickly changed from the robe into a fresh, pressed pair-of-slacks and flowing blouse. No makeup, no wig today. He wasn't feeling it.

The kid emerged, ruddy and handsome in a boy-band sort of way. Chills ran through Chris' body as the amazing talent and future of Ingram embraced him.

"What? Is my cowlick out of control?"

"No, you look wonderful. Very handsome. Star quality."

"Thanks." Ingram blushed.

"And, about what we almost talked about. Earlier. In the kitchen? You can stay with me as long as you'd like. I want to do all I can to support the arts." He held out his hand, the beautiful red tips made Chris happy. "A little lunch money." He palmed five twenty-dollar bills into Ingram's hand.

"I can't," the kid protested.

"No, you should have a few dollars in your pocket. You can pay me back later. Or...no, later. When you're on your feet again."

Ingram practically fell into Chris' arms. "You don't know what this means to me." The words were barely audible.

"Yes, I do." He thought about giving Ingram a key, but instead said: "Come by the club when your day is over and I'll put you to work."

He waved to the boy as he left the building. What are you doing? Another stray. Another out-of-work actor. Are you insane? Have you learned nothing after all these years?

Chris puttered around the house for a bit before he picked up his phone, searched the contacts for the coded name and number. He pressed the phone icon and listened to it ring.

"Uh, hello. Chris Marlowe calling for Jericho Taylor...no, I'm not kidding. If you'll just tell him my name, I know he'll take the call." Chris heard muffled conversation. "...Yes, it's me. After all these years." He listened. "Well, Tamburlaine is still up and running. Although it's been quiet lately...I would love for you to stop in, it's been a long time....Of course...no, what I called about is a boy you have coming in for a callback today." Chris realized he didn't know the kid's last name. "A young man I've come to know, Ingram—." Thankfully, Jericho cut him off. "Yes, he's incredibly talented and I was hoping I might nudge you into seriously considering him...I do. He's a bit green, but has an amazing voice. He's more versatile than you can imagine...of course. Yes, I know this was an inappropriate call, but that's how this business works, right? We all take care of one another. We all have our agendas, right?...Yes, I'd love to see you. Still seven nights a week. Sure...I'll buy you and your friends a round...okay...yes, soon." The call ended.

Chris wandered into the bathroom. He picked up a towel from the floor, hung it on a hook; he took Ingram's toothbrush from the counter and placed it in the holder next to his own. A sigh escaped his lips.

What are you doing? You can't even take care of yourself and you're getting a gig for some kid you just met. He added a little lipstick, which led to eyeliner and mascara. Are you insane? Of course, you are. A touch of rouge next and finally a little powder. Jericho remembers me. Chris turned his head and winked in his over-sized manner. "There, now you look like yourself."

Chris ran his manicured fingers through his ringlet curls, tucked keys and wallet into his pockets, and headed for the door. He wanted to be out in the world. He felt, for the first time in a long time, that there was actually hope that somehow, someway, he'd be okay, and so would Tamburlaine.

Three

Chris Marlowe enjoyed a coffee at a sidewalk table of the small café. The crisp air announced fall's arrival. The neighborhood welcomed fall: trees turning from dirty green to copper and brown before they'd lose their leaves all together; time to air out the cable knit sweaters and fake fur wraps. At one time they'd been real fur; thankfully, those were out of fashion now, passé; he'd needed the cash.

The men who passed paid no attention to the aging queen in makeup and heels drinking coffee. If Chris had passed a drag queen on the street in daylight thirty years ago, he'd have chuckled to himself. No one noticed. The times had changed. Having a bar where it was okay and acceptable to be like him was no longer necessary. It was embarrassing, even. The young queers weren't hiding themselves away in alleys and basements. They were out and proud. They were running for political office. They were simply out, going to proms, kissing on the street, fighting for the right to marry and adopt children. Chris shuddered at the thought. Children? He had no interest or desire.

"Chris? Chris Marlowe?"

He glanced up to see the handsome Jericho Taylor standing before him. Chris got up and hugged his old friend.

"Let me get a coffee and we'll sit and talk for a moment." Jericho smiled.

Chris waited. His heart pounded. When they'd known each other, when they'd met, they were boys. Life was new to them. Possibilities existed for them. All of New York awaited them. A star: a commodity; a Tony Award winner; The Great Jericho Taylor they called him. He'd become everything he'd ever said he'd be. Chis looked down at his flowered blouse and realized he'd become nothing over the past decades but a frumpy drag queen. The world passed him by while he'd been inside Tamburlaine. But, now, here, in the light of day...

Jericho emerged onto the street, steaming cup in his hand. He sat down, still smiling. "Wow. We haven't seen each other or talked in ages. Then, twice in one day. It must be fate."

"What are you doing here?"

"Well, we're working in the new rehearsal studios that just opened around the corner. I didn't realize this neighborhood was the same as it had always been. These great old buildings and warehouses haven't changed a bit."

"Still the same, no more blood running in the streets in the afternoons. But, little-by-little, the city encroaches." Chris gestured with his coffee cup to the green logo on the shop window.

"So, how are you? What are you doing these days?" Jericho asked.

"Tamburlaine. Still singing there nightly. Thinking about reopening the kitchen. But..."

"But what?" Jericho focused on Chris' eyes.

Tears rose and Chris flushed at the sentiment. He brushed away a tear and hoped his mascara hadn't been ruined. He wanted to...what? If he told Jerry everything, that's what he wanted to do, but if he did Chris feared Jerry's response.

"What?" Jericho pressed, taking one of Chris' hands into his own.

"Oh, Jerry, I'm about to give up on the club. I've been bleeding cash for years. It's not that I don't have money, Jimmy took care of that; but no one is coming. It's empty most nights. A few local drunks. I spend my evening singing to myself. Oh, listen to me, going on and on. I guess my time is done. The city has changed. The kids are different today. No one hides in dark clubs anymore." Chris raised his head to find those friendly eyes intently locked on him. Chris filled the space to cover his embarrassment by speaking: "Not like they did when we were kids."

"What can I do?" He hadn't wavered.

Chris played with the green plastic coffee stirrer. "No, that's not why I—"

Jericho repeated: "What can I do? We have a long history, Christopher, and I would be happy to do whatever I can to help you. I remember Tamburlaine. A lot of us do. It was fun and safe and wild. There aren't many of us left who remember, are there? But, that doesn't mean we can't bring some of that spark back to the city."

The steam from their coffee cups filled the silence between them.

"I don't know," Chris finally said. "I just don't know how to save my club."

Jericho's phone rang. "Sorry," he said to Chris as he answered. "Okay, I'll be back in five." He closed his phone and tucked it into his coat. "Listen, I have to go. But, I'll be at your club tonight and we'll come up with a solution...or at least a few ideas." He stood and Chris followed. They hugged. "I really do appreciate our history," Jericho whispered into Chris' ear. He turned. Chris stood on the street with tears ruining his mascara as The Great Jericho Taylor walked away.

Four

Chris sat at the far end of the bar, away from the facing doorway. His spot. A metal plaque signified the designation. That brass plate with his name had been there for over four decades. Long before he owned Tamburlaine, he'd been first a regular, then a performer, and then a headliner. Moments like these, just him and a bartender, Chris missed cigarettes. Not that he wanted to take up the habit again, or would ever consider it, but it had always given him something to do with his fingers. Of course, to smoke these days he'd have to go out on the street, so uncivilized.

He flipped the page of the *New York Times*. The bombings and terror acts had returned. There had been a brief break, after that Flash Mob event at the train station. They'd broken up the ring of bomb builders. But, here they were, once again blowing up military installations, or at least, the gates of military installations. This time, they were further south. Not that Chris wished such problems on anyone, but better somewhere else than New York or New Jersey, like before.

Ingram entered, a stream of daylight following him into the club. The door closed. The kid practically skipped across the room. "How was your day?"

His exuberance was lovely.

"It was…quiet."

Ingram scanned the empty Tamburlaine. "I can see. Do you want to go for an early dinner? I could whip something up for us lickity-split."

"You're sweet." Chris turned his attention to the bartender who was cutting a lime. "Benny, put Ingram here on the VIP list. Anything he wants until further notice."

"Oh, you really don't—"

"It's done. Have you ever really been here before last night?" Chris knew he hadn't.

"No. I've walked by a few times. There's a rehearsal studio around the corner."

Chris uncrossed his legs and slipped off the bar stool. "I'll give you the penny tour. It used to cost a nickel, but the recession and all. How was your day?"

"Amazing. I'm, well, I'm pretty sure I got a part. I've got another callback at least. And, Mr. Taylor paid a lot of attention when I sang. And, they had me sing with one of the girls, so that's got to be good. I'm flying. I can't believe he stopped, asked my name, scrutinized my resume, and had me sing several different songs. I guess that makes sense, you know. *Godspell* is full of styles and options. Anyway, listen to me go on and on like a fool. I'm just so excited!" He hugged Chris.

As the kid talked, Chris pointed to the dining room, the small stage, the showroom doors, the door to the kitchen.

"I'm sorry, I haven't really been paying attention to you. Did you say a kitchen?"

"Yes." Chris pointed again to the door.

Ingram led the way into it. "Where are the lights?"

Chris hit a bank of switches revealing a dusty professional kitchen.

"Holy smokes! You serve food here?"

"We used to. Still have all the licensing, although we barely passed our last inspection because the equipment hasn't been well maintained."

"What happened, Chris? Why did you..."

Chris twirled away, tears stinging his eyes. Damn, another ruined mascara job. "It's been a tough few years." Like ten.

"Well, with a little effort, you could be serving food again. I would love to be your chef. Like I said this morning, I'm not a gourmet cook, but I can serve comfort meals. We could—sorry."

"What?" Chris appreciated this man, so full of energy and excitement. It gave him a sense of hope for the future just being near him. How could the world not spin with so much youth and enthusiasm to spend? At that moment he fell in love with Ingram, whose last name he still didn't know.

"I was going to say we could get this place on its feet with a great comfort kitchen. Sorry, I didn't mean to be presumptuous."

Chris looked into Ingram's eyes for a long moment before he spoke. "I love that you're presumptuous. And, that might be something we'll try. I'm going to meet with an old friend this evening to talk about a few ideas for the place."

"That's great." Ingram's disappointment was palpable.

"In the meantime, why don't you go out with a few of your friends and celebrate?" Chris reached into his pocket.

"No, I have money. I...I."

Chris pulled out a key. "It's for my place. You remember which door?"

"Oh. Gosh. I'm...I do remember.... Are you sure?"

Chris tugged Ingram tightly to him. "Yes. I told you this morning, you've got a place with me as long as you need one. But, I need you to take off for a bit so I can talk to my friend."

"Your lover?" Ingram turned his face toward his feet. The pout seemed real.

"No, just an old friend. We did have a romp or two, but that was a long, long time ago." He wanted to say, "before you were born," but refrained. "So, go out." There were a lot of other things that could be said. "Celebrate. Enjoy your evening with some people your own age. And, I'll see you at home."

"At five in the morning?"

"Probably." Chris turned off the kitchen lights and led the way to the bar. He walked Ingram to the door, kissed him on the forehead, and then wiped the trace of lipstick off with his thumb. "Bye." He watched Ingram sulk down the block. The kid turned, saw Chris watching him, and he did a pirouette and gave a wave before disappearing around the corner.

"Who's the kid? Son from some tryst of yours while on a bender?" Benny laughed.

"Just a kid. An actor. A stray. You know the type."

"The city is filled with the type. Bourbon?"

Chris returned to his spot at the end of the bar. "How about a cup of coffee. It's a fresh pot, right?"

"Will be in five." Benny went to work.

Chris suddenly felt antsy. He walked to the stage, went behind a curtain, and flipped a few switches. "It's Raining Men," blared. "Not now, girls." He turned it down and pushed a few levers, colored lights came up on the stage and around the room. If he squinted just right, with the lights and music, it was the Tamburlaine of his youth. It was filled with queers dancing, drinking, a cloud of cigarette smoke over the room tinged by a hint of poppers. The mirror ball spun bouncing specks of light off all the surfaces and people. Drag queens, dozens of them, performing and entertaining. Singing their own songs. Magical. A spectacular fantasy come to life.

When he returned to the bar, Jericho Taylor, tall, handsome, watched Chris.

"You're certainly not seeing me at my best today."

"I'm your friend. You don't have to be at your best with me, ever."

"You're sweet, Jerry." Chris kissed Jericho's cheek.

"No one has called me Jerry in a long time."

"No, you're The Great Jericho Taylor now."

They just stood together, close, gazing into each other's eyes. A flood of memories and history flowed without words between them. The energy caused some cosmic shift and, for just a moment, they were once again the only two on the entire planet.

Chris wanted to question why it hadn't worked with them, but then he remembered Jericho. The cad he was. The cheater. The libido of... a dancer.

"Can we still get a good dinner here?" Jericho asked.

"No, not at the moment. We're between chefs."

"So, let me take you to dinner. We'll catch up. And, I've already got a few ideas that you might enjoy." Jericho placed a hand on Chris' lower back and guided him toward the door.

"Let me just grab my wrap." Chris returned to the bar. Benny waited with a colorful shawl. "You can close up tonight, right?"

Benny shook his head. "I've got plans at midnight."

"Just lock up if I'm not back. Be sure to lock the gate, too. Got it?"

"Yes, boss."

Chris turned to Jericho, now framed by the door he held open as sunlight flooded in from behind him. That sunshine gave him the look of a saint on one of those holy cards, the ones given out at funerals. Something stirred in Chris' heart: a flash of memory; a hint of desire; a tingle of regret.

Five

Jericho and Chris had talked for hours. They'd relived a few old memories and rehashed about the state of musical theater over the past decade. What they hadn't discussed: Tamburlaine.

After folding the linen napkin, Jericho placed it on the edge of their table. He'd already paid the check, after a polite and expected argument between them. "Listen, finish your coffee and then take me to your club. We'll walk through it and I'll share my ideas."

"Fine." Chris wiped his thumb over the lipstick mark he'd left on the cup before he finished the last swallow of coffee. "I was wondering if you really did have ideas to share or if you just wanted my company for a meal." He batted his eyes in Jericho's direction.

"Well, I do enjoy your company. I'm only sorry we fell out of touch all these years." He offered his hand to Chris, who accepted it and stood. It felt so comfortable to Chris, his hand resting in Jericho's, that he panicked. He pulled his hand away, straightened his blouse.

On the street, the wind off the river chilled Chris; he stepped closer to Jericho and slid his hand into the crook of the great director's arm. "I have missed you."

Jericho placed a hand atop Chris' and increased their pace toward Tamburlaine. The place was locked up like a fortress. All the gates were down over Tamburlaine's door and window.

"I told Benny to lock up when he left. But, so early?" Chris led the way into the side alley and the rear door of the club.

"It's almost one."

"Really?" Chris popped the lock. "How time flies." They'd talked about how quickly it was all going by during their dinner. "Here we are." They entered, Chris pulled the door closed behind them, and then turned on a few lights in the kitchen. He let out a gasp. The place was clean, shiny clean. As if some magic elves or one of those reality TV cooking show people had brought in a team of workers.

"It looks great," said Jericho.

Chris just nodded. "The hall here leads to the backstage area." They walked down the hallway; he pointed: "Dressing rooms, bathrooms. Star's dressing room." He turned the corner and pulled a lever, the stage lights came up full and blinded them for a moment. "It needs a good cleaning. We haven't had a show in here for...a while." He really couldn't remember the last production. "It's not very big. Not big enough to do more than a review."

"I remember."

"Of course," said Chris. Just because Jerry hadn't been there in ten years, twenty, how could he forget the place that gave him his start?

"There are some smaller shows that will work here." Jericho walked onto the stage. He clapped his hands a few times, listening to the quick reverberation. He sang a quick scale: "La la la la la la la la la." The notes sounded crisply. "This is a great space. I'd forgotten. Has this ever been used for anything other than drag shows?"

Chris harrumphed. "You never did understand."

"No, I didn't then and don't now. And, at least then the boys sang."

"Well, we agree on that. Queens should sing, not just lip sync." It felt like a repeated record. "I'm not going to defend it again. I'm not going to have this same argument that we had a dozen times thirty years ago. I won't do it." Chris left the stage in tears. How had it happened again. Anyone else could say whatever they wanted and Chris would fight back, viciously if necessary, about the life of a drag queen. But, when Jericho questioned him, it was over. He fell to puddles of tears. He went to the back of the house, in the dark, to nurse his wounds.

"Chris, I didn't mean...oh fuck it." Jericho walked the stage. He inspected lights and curtains and fly space. He walked out through the seating area, tables and chairs, not rows of seats, until the last bit of the theater where five rows of old, velvet-covered seats moldered and decayed. Chris followed him out through the swinging doors at the rear, into the sidebar. There were lights on in the barroom; he moved toward the light.

"Remember being a young dancer, a show boy for the queens? I noticed you leave that gig out of your bio."

"When did you read my bio?" Jericho presented his award-winning smile.

"I went to see *42nd Street*. I managed to get in before the reviewers."

Chris, behind the bar, poured bourbon into two glasses. When Jericho approached, he pushed a glass toward him. They drank.

"Listen," Jericho began. When he set his glass down, Chris refilled it. "I really do want to help you. I know we have a volatile history. But, all the same, I want to help you. This is an amazing space." He gestured with his glass, taking in the small showroom stage connected to the bar. "I can't remember what this building used to be. How is there a full stage with fly space?"

"It was a factory in the twenties. In the late thirties, it was converted to a speakeasy. The big showroom was added in the forties and the place was popular through the fifties. Then, it was shuttered. In the seventies, Tommy inherited the building from his aunt. You remember him, right?"

"Crazy S-O-B." Jericho swallowed the shot and allowed another refill.

"Well, he started this underground drag club that became very popular around the time you and I arrived in the early eighties."

"When did you buy it?"

"Late nineties. Tommy died, like so many." Chris dabbed at the damp corners of his eyes. "We lost so many." He took a sip of liquor. "Anyway, it was in the will, that if I wanted to buy the place, I could, and his estate would carry the note. It was good for a while and then, around the time equality and rights and lip syncing were all the rage, we fell off. I think young people saw me and what I was doing here to be a joke. They wanted pounding music and drugs and, well, not this." He pointed a red tipped finger into the darkness of the room. "I thought about giving them what they wanted, but it wasn't me. I thought about selling, but couldn't. So, we've been quietly limping along for a decade. There's a buyer interested now, a developer, but I just can't let it go, you know? I promised him."

Jericho didn't speak for a long moment, his eyes drilling into Chris'. "Well, I think it's time to change. But, my suggestions include doing something a bit different."

Chris felt his resolve like iron over his wrists. "I'm listening."

"I want to mount a show here, and then maybe a new one every month or six weeks. Small casts. We'll do them under showcase contracts, so they'll be cheap. Young actors. They work for peanuts. Occasionally a name or star who will work cheap because they've always wanted to try a role or because they've always wanted to work with me."

"What is this going to cost?"

"We'll work out the numbers later." He moved toward the middle of the room. "I think you need a piano in here. Get people up and singing. Old stuff. A good piano player. Late nights. And, shows that defy gender. Men and women switching roles. Turning straight plays gay. I've always wanted to try this, but haven't had a venue. If you'll allow me, I want to try it here." He implored. "Really, this can work."

"I don't doubt that. I just...I...I don't know why you're willing to do this for me."

"Not just for you, but with you. I have to tell you, while it seems like you're getting the better end of this deal, I really do think it's me that's getting it. I've always wanted the freedom to do something outside the box on a regular basis. Not just directing revival after revival the way the mainstream expects it. What do you say?"

"I...I..."

"You have to do this. You know you're doing this. Stop playing hard to get. I mean, you have nothing to lose!"

"Another bad investment, perhaps."

"Oh, Chris, you've got more money than anyone I know. Sell a fucking painting."

Christopher Marlowe contemplated his empty glass. Jericho was right, money wasn't the issue. Working with Jerry was. Having his heart broken day after day, that was the issue. Not having anyone to go home with at night and share the success and the failures, that was the issue. "Fine." The word barely audible. "Fine."

"Really? You won't regret this. I've got so many ideas..."

On and on Jericho talked. Moving around the rooms. Talking and drinking and drinking and talking. He inhabited another world. Chris watched him as he passed from the bar to its small stage where Chris performed nightly, from the bar to the dining room and big showroom. Wherever he wandered, Jericho's voice trailed him as he talked incessantly about this idea and that. None of them involved changing anything. Instead, they were all ideas about shows and actors and possibilities.

Chris felt his world evolve in those late hours alone with Jericho. It reminded him of meeting Jimmy that first time, of fucking Jericho—of being fucked by Jericho. Of roses tossed at his feet after completing an aria. It was like...now. Like then, a brilliant moment...with a hint of...of...future. The possibility of a new era: not reliving the past, but creating a new chapter.

Six

Chris entered his kitchen. Lights on. Rusty Warren softly sang "Life is Worth Living," from somewhere deeper in the loft. He dumped his wrap on the kitchen chair, poured a glass of bourbon. He watched the tail wag on his aqua antique cat clock. Three fifteen.

"You're home early," said Ingram, who wore only pajama bottoms.

"Hello." Chris raised his hand and cupped Ingram's face. "You look sexy in those silks."

"I hope you don't mind." Ingram's voice was soft. "I found them in a drawer."

"Going through my things on your second night here?" Chris left the boy and opened the fridge, now filled with food he hadn't bought. Fruits. Vegetables. Their colors blared under the bright bulb. "You've had quite a day. I assume it was you who brought my kitchen up to code? And my fridge."

"I hope you don't mind. I was bored. Benny helped for a bit. No one came into the club the whole evening." Ingram bit his lip. "Sorry."

"Well, an old friend has offered some help with that, so we'll see how it goes."

"Is that *old friend* Jericho Taylor?" Ingram squared himself, facing Chris. "Are you the reason I got that callback?"

"Yes. And, don't be jealous, it was Jericho who has offered to help. And, yes, I called him on your behalf. But, I know him. When you got another callback it's because he likes you, he saw something in you. There isn't anyone who can get someone into Jerry's show just because they're a friend."

Ingram didn't speak. He poured a few fingers of bourbon into a glass. Chris held out his empty glass and, after a long moment, Ingram filled it.

"Listen, in this business, hell, in this town, if someone offers you a hand up, you take it. There are too many of you. Handsome singers who dance, dancers who act, triple threats. You're on every corner in Manhattan. You take help or you perish."

The two drank to the bottom of their glasses. Ingram refilled them both with a smile. "So, you're happy with the kitchen?"

"You know I am, Baby. But, if you become a Broadway star, who will cook in there?"

"One thing at a time. Are you hungry? I could whip something up for you."

"No, Jerry and I had a very nice dinner at Veronica's."

"You had dinner at Veronica's?" Ingram's eyes grew wide as saucers.

"Yes. Jerry suggested it." Chris sat in a kitchen chair and removed his heels. "The food was very good; surprisingly large portions. Most of those uppity places serve you nothing and charge you a fortune. This was an actual meal."

"Jericho and you at Veronica's. You say it like it's nothing." Ingram sat at the table across from Chris. "We went to Veronica's...We went to see the Queen of England..."

"It's just dinner with a friend. The place, the titles, the expectations, they just don't exist for me like they do for you. I've been in this town a long time. You're too young to remember or even know my name, but I was a star when I was not much older than you. A star." The word hung between them. Ingram poured a bit more booze. "So, you want mother to tell you a story?"

"Please, don't invoke mothers."

Chris laughed. "As you wish. And, I'm tired. And, I'm a little too drunk. So, the story will have to wait." He stood, wobbled a bit, and then made his way down the hall to the bathroom.

The boy trailed behind. "You can't drop a word like star and not share a little."

Chris sat at his makeup table and began the ritual of removing his makeup and washing his face. "Be a doll and turn on the shower so it's good and hot." He watched Ingram, the boy's ass was perfect, his stomach flat, his chest strong and wide and hairless with erect nipples in the middle of huge, deep brown aureoles. Instead of licking those inviting bullseyes, he began: "I was born a small black child in Alabama."

"Come on." Ingram's eyes sparked when he smiled. "Don't be a drag queen. Be a storyteller."

"Same thing." Chris offered a head turn and over-sized wink. "Well, I arrived in New York, a confused little queen. My drag was horrible. I didn't know anything about makeup or foundation garments, but I could sing. I made the rounds of all the piano bars and sang. I was laughed out of a lot of places, but the ones that let me in, that let me sing, well, they invited me back. I earned a few tips. I met some men. I slept around. I got known." He let the cold cream soak into his skin a bit. "I met a queen. Mercy Mia. She took pity on me and taught me the ropes. She got me into the lineup at Tamburlaine. Oh, those were the days. Drag queens everywhere, performing, singing, dancing. The crowds and the money. It was amazing. And, me a little girl, just starting, oh how the old men loved me. I rode all their cocks at one point or another and made lots and lots of money."

"You were a whore?"

"I was a kid. One-by-one, those men started to die. We didn't know what it was. No one knew what was killing them. There were rumors. There were conspiracy theories. It didn't matter, our friends, our lovers, our daddy's and boys were dying and we didn't know why. Soon, there wasn't anyone at the club and the owner wanted out. Some of those men who died left us money and paintings and jewelry. We buried them as they died, whether they could afford a pine box or not; we held their wakes at Tamburlaine. Generations of men, young and old, gone."

Chris wiped the cold cream along with his tears off his face and stood up. He stripped off his clothes and got into the shower. While there, he didn't speak; Ingram waited patiently, sitting on a tall stool in the corner of the big room. He handed Chris a towel when he turned off the water.

"Thank you, dear boy." He dried himself. "Well, we buried those men. Buried Jimmy. I kept the club going. There was a rebound in the late nineties. Then, everything fell off. We closed the kitchen. We laid off what little staff we had. Now, it's down to me, a bartender, and a cleaning lady who comes in every morning. I own the place outright, including the building. But, there's a conglomerate who has bought up most of the block, hell, most of the neighborhood. It's just my bar, the deli, Sal's, and an empty lot that they haven't gotten, yet. Part of me thinks I should just sell out and be done with it, but I made a promise." Chris wrapped the towel around his chest.

"What was the promise?"

"Time for bed." Chris turned off the bathroom lights. The two men got in, he naked, Ingram still wearing the silk pajama bottoms.

"Do you want to fuck me or I could suck your cock or—"

"Relax. It's late and I'm drunk. Just find a comfortable spot."

Ingram snuggled up to him until the head of Chris' cock pressed gently against his ass. Within a few moments, the boy was asleep.

"Just like that, the end of a long day." Chris wrapped his arms loosely around Ingram and thought about the possibilities of Tamburlaine. With The Great Jericho Taylor mounting shows there, how could it not be a success?

Seven

"What are your plans for the day?" Chris applied a layer of pale blue powder on his right eyelid while using the mirror to watch Ingram dry off from a shower.

"I'm going to finish taking inventory of your kitchen equipment. Then, I plan on making you a wonderful dinner at Tamburlaine. Do you still have credit with any of the vendors?"

"Oh, I think I might. It's been a long time since it's been used though. Have you searched the executive chef's office?"

"The chef has an office?" Ingram wrapped the towel around his waist and went to the sink.

"Downstairs. There's a prep area down there, too, unless the rats have dismantled it. If we don't have credit, I can give you cash. It's not a problem." Chris had finished his eye makeup and moved down to his lips.

Ingram lathered and shaved. They continued to eye each other, the mirror a convenient tool.

"This is all very domestic, you and I. Like an old married couple." Chris' tone sing-song, but something a little dark lurked beneath the words.

"Is that a problem?" Ingram wiped shaving cream from his ear.

"No, of course not. It's just...it doesn't matter."

"If it's important to you, it's important to me, Baby."

He couldn't remember the last time someone had called him baby—or babe or sweetie or honey or hot stuff. "You're a sweet boy." Chris stood up, went to the closet, and removed a large, padded bra. Within a moment, he had massive breasts with ample cleavage. "The transformation—Just because Rusty is flat as a boy doesn't mean mother must be, too."

"You go through this every weekend, but no one comes?"

"It's what I do. It's who I am. It doesn't really matter if there are only three or four people. I'll do the act for myself. I do that, too. I do it for me. I do it for...well, it's just what I do." Chris stepped into a foundation piece that added a padded ass. A few adjustments. In the bedroom, he selected slacks, a sequined, royal-blue top, and a long flowing jacket with padded shoulders.

"You're a big breasted version of Bea Arthur."

"I'm surprised you know of her." Chris smiled at the comparison.

"Reruns of *The Golden Girls*." He pulled on socks, then a freshly pressed shirt followed by very tight jeans, without any underwear.

"Oh, television. That was never my thing. We had one in the bar for a while, but all the shows seemed insipid so I had it removed. I knew Ms. Arthur from the stage. Brilliant. 'With the way he looks and the way she sees, they're a perfect match.'" He mimicked Bea as Yenta from *Fiddler on the Roof*. The boy raised his eyebrows in question. "A role model for me," said Chris.

"I thought you said you moved here in the 70s?" Ingram stopped pulling at buttons and zippers.

"I'd come for the shows for years and years. Mother used to bring me. Yenta the Matchmaker, Vera Charles... And, then, a few years before she died Bea returned to Broadway and performed her one woman show."

"So, that's why you dress like that?"

"No, there was another woman who molded my appearance. She was a comedian in the '60s and '70s. The biggest name at the time. Joan Rivers is given credit for breaking through the comedy barriers, but it was Rusty Warren who did that first. Rusty paved the way with her raunchy act dedicated to all things sex. By today's standards, she'd be considered tame, even a joke. But, then, it was a new world for a foul-mouthed broad. She was wonderful. Amazing. Funny. And, that's the act I do. It's based on excerpts and pieces of her acts over the years."

"You've been doing the same material for thirty years?" Ingram, dressed and handsome, asked. "Do you mind? I found these clothes in a bureau and they're amazing."

"I don't mind. Those things, well, it's good to see them being worn."

"Where did—"

"It's best if you don't ask too many questions." Chris checked his appearance in a floor length mirror, turning from side to side, inspecting his enhanced ass and grotesque bosom. Two squirts of perfume from an antique, crystal atomizer and he was ready to go.

Eight

They arrived at Tamburlaine just as Benny unlocked the door. He held it for Chris and Ingram. Ingram headed into the kitchen. Benny turned on lights and got to his prep work behind the bar. Chris headed for the small stage.

He turned on some lights. With a few hearty pushes, he rolled the upright piano into position and pulled out the microphone and adjusted the stand. Finally, he positioned the piano bench at the keyboard, sat, ran his hands along the keys, playing scale after scale. It's why he kept his nails trimmed and manicured, so that he could continue to play his own music, just as Rusty had done for all those years.

Chris launched into Rusty Warren's signature tune, "Knockers Up." Such a massive hit for her in the '60s, she built a brand around the song. While he played to the empty room, Chris remembered the crowds of the late '80s who played along with him, who laughed at and with him. He remembered the full tills. The late-night bank drops. The drugs and parties and sex. So much sex.

His hands glided into a lush, romantic Chopin study. He loved music. He loved playing. He longed for the days when he would play from memory anything anyone asked for. He could accompany anyone, no matter what song they chose.

That was done. He hadn't kept up with music. If the request was after 1984, there was no hope. He had little repertoire that didn't involve Broadway ballads or sentimental World War II classics. The old black book, the standards, he could play them drunk or sober, preferably drunk.

And, so he played. An hour passed, then two. He played for no one. Benny had headphones on as he read the *Daily News*. Ingram had taken off with $100 for the grocery store. And, so he played for himself, for the memory. He knew, with each key he pressed and each note expressed on the beautiful black Yamaha upright grand, that he was fulfilling the promise he'd made long ago. Keep the club open, even if just for himself and the occasional regular who hadn't yet died—one more day of a promise fulfilled. When they died, and most of them died, he'd be sure they received a proper burial, a memorial, a remembrance—one more day of a promise fulfilled.

He wondered if he'd see Jerry again. Would he actually come through as he'd said? Would Tamburlaine once again conquer the nightclub scene. Would the restaurant flourish? Would the showroom sell out night after night again?

"What have we here? Madame Sousatzka plays again?"

Chris peered up from his reverie. He despised the developer. "Ah, Mr. Folgate. To what do I owe this displeasure."

"I just wanted to give you a heads up that my friends at the health inspector's office will be stopping by to shut you down. It's time for this rat trap to have the doors bolted."

A few days ago, the threat of the health inspector would have sent chills through Chris. He would have negotiated a fortune in bribes to survive. But, because of Ingram's cleaning binge, the place was in great shape. Ingram's actions had inspired Benny and the old cleaning lady, and the place was brighter and fresher than it had been in ages.

Before Chris had a chance to gloat, the inspector walked through the door and announced himself to Benny. Chris turned to the keyboard and, without another word to Mr. Folgate, began to play the wicked witch's theme from "Somewhere Over the Rainbow," his fingers rapid, light, and precise.

Folgate turned away and went to the bar. He ordered a drink, but Benny just shook his head. The man grew loud. Benny silently refused. Folgate threatened.

Benny pointed at the printed sign on the mirror. "We have the right to refuse service to anyone for any reason."

"It won't be long," Folgate hissed to Benny. "Your days are numbered here!" he shouted toward Chris and then left the room.

The inspector returned to the barroom. "Excuse me, can you turn on some more lights?"

"Of course," said Benny, who walked out from behind the bar and led the inspector into all the nooks and crannies of the place.

In the end, there was a problem with a urinal not flushing properly. The kitchen received near perfect marks. So did the bar and refrigerated areas. It was the best inspection Tamburlaine had ever received. The Inspector, impressed and happy, let Benny and Chris know of the success and accepted a shot as a reward.

Within hours, the club had thirty people in it. They were buying drinks at the bar and taking up seats at the tables around the small stage where Chris continued to play piano, sing, and tell the same stories and jokes that Rusty Warren had told decades before.

The audience, a mix of races, genders, and sexual orientations laughed, applauded, and quickly learned the refrains for the audience participation songs.

By 11:30, the bar was packed. Chris had had no break, not for dinner or even the restroom. He was in heaven, singing and entertaining; a dream come to life. Those fantasies that he often had on the empty lonely nights had somehow come true. And, because this just might be a dream, he wasn't about to leave the stage, not even for the bathroom.

At midnight, The Great Jericho Taylor entered with a group of people. He took in the club and smiled. He said something to the handsome man on his arm. The guy seemed familiar to Chris, but he couldn't place him.

The crowd around them parted, a table up front emptied quickly. Jericho's group immediately began to play along with the act. When Jericho robustly belted out the chorus of "Lay Me Down, Roll Me Over, and Do It Again," people all around the room snapped photos with their phones.

Chris found the flashes annoying, but Jericho remained unphased by the activity, so he followed suit.

At one in the morning, Billy Lake and Hank Miller came through the doors. The "ooos" and "ahhhs" momentarily drowned out the music from the Yamaha upright.

Jericho stood and came over to the edge of the stage and whispered to Chris: "Invite them to sing."

"Really?"

"Yes, really. They know all the classics and they're brilliant." Jericho didn't wait for Chris' response, instead, returning to his table.

Ingram came by with an apron around his waist and cleared the tables of empty glasses and debris. He smiled up at Chris, mouthed "Billy Lake" and made goo-goo eyes.

"We have a few stars in our midst tonight," said Chris as he vamped on the piano. "I would be remiss if I didn't allow my great friend, The Great Jericho Taylor to take a bow. Jerry?"

Jericho stood up and gave a little nod to the wild applause of the group.

He'd figured out where he'd seen so many of these people before. "And, here's to the cast of *42nd Street*, long may it run," said Chris, raising a bourbon glass to the audience. They hooted and hollered. "Finally, I would like to not only acknowledge them, but invite Billy Lake and Hank Miller to offer a little musical experience for you all. Again the crowd went wild. The two boys protested as they made their way to the stage. Chris continued to vamp on the keyboard as the three of them whispered and decided upon a song to perform together. Chris, excited that the boys knew everything he suggested, narrowed down the options to a romantic duet.

As the men launched into their second number, with Chris accompanying their every nuance, the front door of Tamburlaine was open more than it was closed, allowing a steady stream of patrons into the joint.

Jericho stood while the boys were once again in debates about what to sing next. He came over to the stage and got Chris' attention. "This is just the beginning, my friend. You wait and see what I can do for you and Tamburlaine and what you can do for me."

"I'm in, no matter what," said Chris. He wanted to get up and hug Jerry, but there was no opportunity, he began another duet for Hank and Billy.

Nine

Chris sat at the quiet bar, drinking bourbon. His throat hurt. His fingers hurt. His heart sang. He watched as Ingram, singing "Roll me over, lay me down, and do it again," light on his feet, cleaning tables and placing chairs upside down on top of them, a joy-filled young man.

Benny finished counting his till. He handed the bank bag and the long paper receipt to Chris. "Finally, something to put in the books, in the bank."

Chris opened the bag, took out two hundred dollar bills, and handed them to Benny. "Just a little something extra for all your hard work tonight. I really do appreciate it."

"It was nice being busy. I forgot what it felt like to make some money." Benny tucked the cash into his jeans pocket. "I'll finish up these glasses and be out of here."

"Take your time." Chris sipped more bourbon. He pulled another hundred-dollar bill from the bag. When Ingram came up with the last tray of glasses, he tucked the bill into the kid's shirt pocket. "Thanks for all your help tonight."

"It was amazing. You were amazing. The fun, the energy. I had a good time."

"You're a great waiter." Chris filled his glass again, and a second one, which he handed to Ingram.

"Well, I've done this for a few years. But, cooking is really my thing. Too bad we didn't have the kitchen running and a waiter or two. Could've really done it in."

Chris watched Ingram's eyes. They sparkled and glowed, his pale grey, nearly blue eyes. It had been years since anyone expressed such happiness in Tamburlaine.

"And, Jericho Taylor was right there." Ingram pointed toward the spot where Jericho had sat. "The stage manager. Billy Lake. Hank Miller."

He continued to point out the spots where each had sat. "All of them. I joked with them and..." He absently spun an empty tray. "I don't want to be their waiter. I want to be on stage with them."

"You will. You're gorgeous. You're talented. You should have gotten up there and sung tonight. You really could have shown off." Chris spoke in his soft, motherly voice.

"Maybe tomorrow night. Tonight was all about them."

Chris downed the last of the bourbon in his glass. "Yeah, tomorrow it may be only the three of us, again."

"I like that." Ingram glanced up from his thoughts right into Chris' eyes. "What do you like?"

"Being here with you and Benny. Feeling like I'm a part of something. And, knowing that, in a short time, this place is going to once again explode back onto the circuit. The scene. Drag queens everywhere!"

"I'm done, boss," said Benny, wiping his hands on a bar towel.

"Great. We'll all leave together." Chris stood up, wobbled on his heels, gained his balance, and headed for the door, the bank bag under his arm. He stopped Ingram. "I'm glad you're happy. You're always welcome here. Got it?"

Ingram hugged him tight, or at least attempted. The big boobs between them were a great obstacle.

Ten

Chris and Ingram left Benny at the corner and walked the quiet street to the steel door. He wobbled a few times and Ingram gently took his elbow and guided them home. "You're such a help, such a dear," said Chris as he handed Ingram the key.

The two walked down the dark alley to the rear of the building; Chris braced himself on the crumbly brick walls. He felt far more drunk than he'd realized and barely made it into the house. He stumbled and landed in a kitchen chair.

"Are you okay?" Ingram dropped down on his knees next to Chris.

"I don't know. Water might help." He was so weak he couldn't really move. A stroke? His greatest fear, that he'd suffer a stroke, but survive it as a needy dependent old queen. Death would be better than some nurse wiping his ass twice a day.

Ingram held a glass of water to Chris' lips. Most of it dribbled out of his mouth. "I'm going to call nine-one-one."

"I think that's a good idea."

Ingram produced a phone from somewhere and dialed. Chris fed him the necessary information, address, side streets. The boy hung up.

"I need you to...two things." His words were slurred. "Put the cash in the freezer." Ingram did as Chris said. "Help me...my my my blouse off."

"What? I don't—"

"Ingram, I don' wan...see...w-w-wiff tits." He sounded like an old person who hadn't put in their teeth.

"Gotcha."

Together, although mostly Ingram, they got the blouse off, unhooked the brassiere and removed the breasts, and then got the blouse on again.

"I'll just have to suffer through the ass padding."

"You seem so together, so with it." Ingram was kneeling again, listening for the ambulance.

"My my my mind seems to be to to to be working. It's my my my mouth that's not."

Time stood still. He heard sirens.

"Go, you'll have to let them in."

Ingram jumped up and bolted from the room.

Chris felt a fuzzy feeling in his brain and throughout his body. It wasn't an unpleasant sensation. He focused on his trusty cat clock, ever vigilant, ever watching with those tick-tock eyes. It might be five; he wasn't sure. Voices rose through the fog. Metal banged and rattled. Hold on, he encouraged himself, but it was futile. Everything went white, bright white. He could hear the men

Eleven

"They're going to move me to a different room later this morning. That's what they said, anyway," Chris said to Jericho who had talked his way into Chris' room.

"And, you're feeling better?"

"Yes, Jerry." Chris took his friend's hand. "It's really strange, but the best they can tell, there was aconite in my bourbon; it's really rare; but you didn't get sick?"

"No, I was fine. And, so was Ingram. He'd had bourbon with you, too. It's a poison?"

"Yes a poison. How do you know about Ingram?" Chris batted his eyes. "Have you been checking up on me?"

"Well, the police questioned all of us. And, the kid has been sitting out in the waiting room since you were brought in here. I talked to him. We compared notes. He's worried sick about you."

"That's sweet, isn't it?" Chris ran a hand through his curls, loosening them. He pulled out a hairpin he'd missed. "I feel like a fright, so I must appear that way."

"You're gorgeous." Jericho squeezed his hand.

"Now, I know you're a lying flirt. Thank you." He smiled and took his hand back. "I need a manicure and a fresh coat of face. Or, maybe some big sunglasses, a scarf, and a floppy beach hat."

"Mona Desmond you're not."

"Oh, Jerry, it was feeling like that until you strolled back into my life." Chris adjusted himself in the bed and took a long sip of water from the straw in a plastic cup. "It was feeling like the long goodbye."

"Well, I think there's still plenty of third act, not to mention a fourth and fifth." Jericho paced the room. "I've got so many ideas. I can't wait until you're out of here and we can work together in the club. I need to walk the stage. Get a feel for the place. See what type of choreography will work there."

"The stage really isn't that big. I remember being cramped with just two or three dancer boys. And, you know how small you were!" Chris cackled. His response seemed disproportionate, even to him.

"Have the police talked to you about any leads?"

"No. They said it was the bourbon. It's the last thing I had. But, no one else got sick from it. So, it doesn't make any sense." Chris again adjusted in the bed.

"Are you okay? You seem fidgety." Jericho stopped pacing and returned to Chris' side.

"I'm ready to get the hell out of here. They want to observe this and test for that. I don't get it. I feel fine. But, I'm connected to all these tubes and wires. Can't get up to pee. Can't go for an easy walk. I'm ready to move on, to get on with it."

"And, that's our thought, too." The doctor's eyes widened at Jericho Taylor standing there. "This is a family only—"

"Oh, Jerry's better than family," said Chris with a smile followed by a flirty wink. "He's, of course, welcome."

"Okay. Well, we're releasing you. A nurse will be by to remove the IV and all that other stuff. She'll give you some papers to sign and some discharge instructions." The doctor poked and prodded Chris a bit. "Yep, you're set to go. Good luck." He turned and shook Jericho's hand.

"How about that?" Chris said.

"I have a meeting, but I can cancel it and wait for you, if you want." Jericho checked his watch.

"No, it's fine. Can you let Ingram know that I'm being released and he can take me home. He'll get a kick out of that."

"Of course. I'll go now." Jericho bent over and kissed the top of Chris' head. "Listen, you call me as soon as you're settled in again and we'll get to work on our project, okay?"

"You bet." Chris waved at Jerry as he departed.

A few moments passed and a big nurse entered the room. Chris could spot a transvestite at a hundred yards. He smiled at the woman who professionally removed the IV needle and the electrode wires with their sticky ends. She went through the paperwork, and after a bit, returned with a wheelchair and escorted Chris and Ingram out to the street where the boy hailed them a yellow cab.

Twelve

"Honey, I'm home!" Ingram bellowed from the kitchen. He raced down the hall and into the bedroom where Chris was propped up in bed, reading. "I got everything you asked for."

"Aren't you a sweet boy!" Chris put down Virginia Woolf's *To the Lighthouse*. "What did you bring me?"

The words fell out of Ingram's mouth in a rush. "Magazines, gum, nail files, the *Times*. Are you okay? Do you want anything else? Something to eat?"

"What is it?" Chris took his hand; forced him to stop.

"The final callback is this afternoon. I got called for it." Ingram turned away.

"Well, that's wonderful news. You should be preparing, not acting like a nanny for the old lady."

Neither of them spoke for a long while. The silence grew uncomfortable.

Chris broke first. "What?"

Ingram played with the bedspread fringe. "I'm afraid that I've only got the callback because of you. I saw Jericho at the hospital. We talked for a moment. Not about the show, but about you. Still, the hospital, the club, your call."

Chris slapped playfully at Ingram's hand. "I don't understand. What's the problem?" He adjusted himself, adding another pillow behind his scarf-wrapped head.

He looked into Chris' eyes. "I don't want this part if I'm getting it because of you or my connection to you. I want things to happen for me based on my own abilities, my own merits." Tears sprung to Ingram's eyes.

"Listen, in this business, in show business, you take every break and opportunity you can drum up. No matter how you get through the door, you still have to perform the part. It's your performance that matters in the end, not how you got into the audition. And, look at me." Chris reached up and, with two fingers to the boys chin, he turned Ingram's face toward his own. "I know Jericho better than a lot of people. If you weren't his best possible choice, you wouldn't get a call back. And, the fact that there's been so many call backs, he's deciding between you and someone else. You're only going to get the role if you sing and act circles around the other guy."

Ingram let out a deep breath. "Well, then. I have to go."

"Change your shirt. That one is all wrinkled."

The boy did as instructed, choosing something from a rack of vintage, '80s shirts. "Okay, I'm off." Ingram bound down the hall and left with the bang of the door.

Chris got up and went to the bathroom. He felt better, more like himself, but still not a hundred percent. Instead of standing to pee, he chose to sit. With an empty bladder and clean hands, he made his way to the kitchen and drank two tall glasses of water. That was the doctor's advice, two or three glasses of water every hour. It made for a lot of trips to the bathroom, but Chris understood that cleaning out the kidneys and liver was the most important thing.

He debated food, but wasn't really in the mood. Nice not to be hungry.

The police said they tested everything he'd come in contact with, his cosmetics, soap, toothpaste, clothes, the piano, his keys, the bottle of bourbon. None of them had any traces of the poison. From tests done by the hospital, they were certain it was the powder form of the drug, not the sap or leaves. He'd definitely ingested the stuff. The only possibility then was that the powder was put into the glass he drank the bourbon from and then the glass was washed clean. Benny and Ingram were the only two in the bar when he drank that bourbon. Or, someone had randomly put the powder into the glass and anyone could have gotten it. Making Chris just the "lucky" recipient. That didn't seem to make sense.

Chris realized that the only two people he'd been able to trust, Benny and Ingram, were the prime suspects in the attempted murder. Neither one really had anything to gain from his death. Without him, they'd both be without income.

He thought about his will. It hadn't been updated in twenty years. His brother was listed as sole heir, but his brother had committed suicide eleven years ago. Chris went down the hall and into his messy office space. He sat in the leather chair that had been his father's, turned on the green shaded lamp, and began rooting around the drawers until he found his will. It hadn't moved or been altered. From the dust in the drawer, it hadn't even been seen in ages.

"Who should I leave it all to? There isn't really anyone. The art. The real estate. The jewels." He tossed the papers into the drawer and closed it. He sighed as he took in the stacks of banker's boxes filled with receipts from the bar. File cabinets filled with resumes and head shots, invoices and bills paid. He thought again of Mr. Folgate. He did want the land the bar stood on. Was it possible that he'd attempted murder? That was a little too Agatha Christie wasn't it?

Chris turned off the light. He thought more about his brother, Thom, as he wandered into the kitchen and drank another glass of water. He'd had no promise. Met new wives as easily as breathing. Divorced as easily as taking a shit. He was a nice guy, but could never settle down or settle for anything. No regular job. No regular home. He'd traveled around the world, mostly on Chris' dime. They were brothers. They didn't really understand each other, yet they supported one another. It was easy. They drank together. They laughed together. Chris gave him money and he left again for another jaunt or journey.

He got dressed—slacks, blouse, hat, and cape. He headed out to the club. The torn yellow police tape fluttered in the breeze from the river. Chris pulled at the tape, getting it all off the doorway, and then walked around to the alley and entered through the rear door. The kitchen seemed even cleaner, as if that were possible. He opened the large refrigerator and it was stocked with food. Not really stocked for dinner service, but more like an oversized, personal fridge.

The place felt cold, so he went down to the basement, turned on the lights, and made his way to the boiler. He made a few adjustments and got the steam heat turned on. Within moments, the radiators around the place banged and hissed to life. It would take a few days for the banging to stop, but the building would be comfortably warm all winter.

Upstairs, with flashlight in hand, he walked through the whole club, just as he did in the old days. He turned on every light switch, checked for dead bulbs. He shined his flashlight into the corners and those places in the ceiling where leaks had once been.

An hour passed before he was at the bar. He put on a pair of gloves and began hand washing every glass in the bar. Then, he ran them in batches through the dishwasher. He got two empty cardboard booze cases. He opened every bottle of liquor from the backlit, glass wall behind the bar, dumped the contents down the drain, and placed the empty bottles in the boxes. Bottles that hadn't been opened were washed in hot, soapy water before being replaced on the shelves.

By four o'clock the bar glass shined. He'd washed all the shelves and the mirrors and the bar top.

Chris unlocked the front door and flipped on the neon "Open" sign. He was alone in his club. No bartender. No patrons. Just him. He made a fresh pot of coffee. While it brewed, he drank a bottle of water.

Thirteen

Ingram rushed through the door into the empty club. "I got it! He hired me!" He jumped over the bar and hugged Chris tight.

"Congratulations. That's wonderful." Chris freed himself, went to one of the coolers behind the bar, and pulled out a bottle of champagne. He popped the cork without spilling a drop and poured two glasses.

They drank while Ingram prattled on and on about the final audition and the conversation and how glad he was that Chris had said everything he'd said earlier in the day. "Hey, what are you doing here? You're supposed to be home in bed." Ingram ushered him to a nearby stool, not his usual perch.

"I needed to get out of the house. And, I'm feeling fine. A little weak, I guess, but fine." He thought about telling the boy all he'd done, but decided he didn't want a lecture from the kid. "Benny hasn't come in tonight."

Ingram surveyed the barroom. "Well, I guess I can open a few beers if anyone wants something."

"You know how to bartend?" The kid made him laugh.

"Well, I know how to open beers. I can pour bourbon over ice."

"Boxcar? Old Fashioned? Long Island Iced Tea?"

"I can pour scotch over ice," Ingram said with a smile. "The people who come in here never...don't...we'll cross that bridge if..." He inspected Chris.

"I know you're trying to protect me, but I've been on the planet for a lot longer than you have. I've done okay. I've survived. Hell, even poison can't take me out."

"Poison. We should clean everything. This place was...the police made a mess with all their tests and checks. When...?"

"I took care of all that this afternoon."

"You're supposed to be resting," Ingram whined.

Chris hugged him from the side. "Yes, I know. I just needed...wait, I don't have to explain myself to you. I like you. You're a great guy. But,

I'm on my own with all this. I always have been." He shrugged Ingram off of him and stood up. "Were you going to make us dinner or something?"

"Sure. I shopped. The fridge is stocked. Is there something you want?"

"Whatever you make will be fine. I just need a few minutes alone. Go. Please?" Chris wouldn't make eye contact with Ingram.

"Sure. Sure."

The dining room floor creaked; the door into the kitchen swung open and closed. He took a deep breath, surprised at how he'd snapped at the kid. He didn't know where that emotion had come from, but what he did know was that he missed Jimmy. He missed knowing there was at least one person on the planet who loved and needed him.

Chris turned to hide his tear-stained face when Jericho burst into the bar with two women. They were laughing about something, joyful. He really wasn't in the mood.

"Christopher Marlowe, as I live and breathe!" Jericho rushed to him and hugged him.

"Hello. We're short staffed. I'll be back in a moment," Chris rushed into the hallway that led to the bathrooms. He went past them, through a door marked "Private." He fumbled with the doorknob in the soft red light; after an effort, he managed to give it the required combination lock turns. It was an ingenious lock, something thought up by one of those genius boys in the '70s Jimmy always dated—boys who went on to instigate the tech revolution. He entered and closed the door tight. The lights came on automatically. Everything seemed in place, though very dusty. He couldn't remember the last time he'd entered the office. A few days ago? A week? A year?

He ran a finger over the closed, roll-top desk. He could write his name in the dust if he chose. He opened the thing. Inside rested a bottle of bourbon, covered in dust, like the rest of the room. He unscrewed the cap and took a long swallow. The liquid burned his throat in a lovely, familiar way. He took another drink before the sensation subsided.

More tears came. He sat down in the desk chair. He drank and cried for a long time. The tapestry had begun to shred, not unravel, but deconstruct. Someone was trying to kill him. His club was dead. He was alone on the planet. No one loved him, and he loved no one.

Chris contemplated what it would take to force the letter opener through his veins.

He laughed at himself, glad there wasn't a mirror. The view in his head had to be worse.

"What is wrong with you, Miss Thing?" He drank more. "A little poison. A few threats. What kind of a queen are you? Sad. Pathetic. Well, it's time for your Big Girl Panties. It's time to kick some ass." Another drink and he screwed the cap on. He opened a few desk drawers, came up with a scarf, and wiped his face, glad he hadn't put on makeup. He rummaged through the drawer, found a pair of sunglasses and contemplated putting them on. He tossed them back.

"Never apologize. Never explain." He stood. Pushed the top down on the desk and left, brushing dust off his hands.

One of the girls, now behind the bar, poured drinks for everyone. Jericho ate a plate of food.

"This is delicious. I might have to fire you, just to keep you cooking," Jericho said through a mouth full of mashed potatoes.

"I can cook any time—"

"Don't worry, kid. The Great Jericho Taylor is yanking your chain," said the second woman.

"What's going on here?" Chris took a stool next to Jericho. "Bourbon, Miss."

"Yes, sir. The name's Nancy Ann." She winked and that brought a smile to Chris' face. "I've never been in a bar where none of the liquor bottles have been opened. Everything is clean and new."

"Well, after someone attempts to poison you, it's best to start from scratch." Chris raised his glass in a toast.

"Good thinking!" She raised her glass.

Something about this young woman rang Chris' memory bell. He studied her features, listened to her voice, watched her lanky frame move. Maybe a past-life experience.

"So, you've met my stage manager. She'll be working with me to mount a show or two here. She has directing dreams, too, so maybe we'll throw her a bone in a year or two, you know?" Jericho winked at Nancy Ann. "This other lovely lady is my personal assistant, Sarah. She's been with me for a bit and is more organized than Martha Stewart."

"Well, that's organized." Chris raised his glass to the heavy woman on her phone. "I didn't know we had a date tonight, Jerry."

"We got out of rehearsal and the girls wanted to check out the showroom."

"It's a nice space, Chris. Can I call you Chris?" Nancy Ann was on the patron's side of the bar now, standing near Jericho.

"Oh, this isn't the room." Chris stood up, picked up his drink, and started to lead the way. "Well, come on."

Like a caravan, the small group walked through the dining room and into the showroom from the main doors.

"Ingram, be a doll and run and turn the lights on," said Chris.

"Of course."

Any weirdness from earlier was gone, or at least buried. Chris and Ingram were once again a team, at least as far as performing and the Tamburlaine were concerned. The club and the opportunity to be on stage came before everything else.

Nancy Ann whistled with a catcall that filled the room.

Chris wished he could whistle like she did. "There's not much back stage, but we've got fly rails for at least five drops. We've double rigged the last two rails before. The lighting is limited. The board is ancient."

"Where's the booth?" Jericho asked.

"Oh, up there." He pointed to a window in the corner of the room. "There's a ladder and a catwalk to get there."

Chris sat down in an aisle seat while Jericho and the girls went exploring. Ingram hovered near the stage apron. Chris waved him over. "I'm sorry, Ingram."

"No need. You've been through a lot." Ingram reached for his arm, but withdrew his hand.

"Still, it's no excuse. You've been a doll through all of this. You've taken excellent care of me and I really am truly grateful."

"Hello?" someone called from outside the showroom.

Chris stood.

"No, I'll go," said Ingram.

"Stay here and get to know your boss a little better." He squeezed Ingram's hand for a moment and made his way out of the room. He felt old, probably for the first time. He went to take care of his patrons.

Jericho returned to the bar. He sat on a stool across from Chris who was butchering a lime on the cutting board. "Oh, hi, Jerry. I'm without a bartender tonight."

"Well, we have some ideas and would love to talk to you about them."

"Do you mind speaking here?" He returned his attention to the lime.

"Oh, that poor piece of fruit. No wonder you're always single."

"I don't see a ring on your finger, Mr. Director." He smiled. "And, at the moment, I've got the lad hanging out with me."

"I'm in search of another lad, too. I was with a guy, an old flame. Nice for a few months, and then I won the Tony Award and was unbearable to live with."

"I can see that. I remember you weren't all that humble before you were award winning." Chris winked. "Want a drink?"

"How about a beer."

He grabbed two beers from the cooler and opened them.

"You were amazing the other night. I had forgotten how talented you were, are. And, you're still doing all that Rusty Warren material. You'd think that would get old, but the kids all had a great time."

"Well, to the wee ones, it's all new."

The two men clinked beer bottles.

"So, what do you have in mind for my club?" He tossed the mutilated lime in the trash.

"Good for you. The first step is admitting you have a problem." Jericho laughed to himself. "Nancy Ann!" he called into the empty club.

The girl arrived in seconds.

"Please, act as bartender for a bit while I talk to Chris." Jericho pointed.

"Can I drink anything I want?" Nancy Ann headed over the top of the bar with a swing of her long legs.

"Of course," said Chris. "You, Ingram, and the other girl."

"Sarah," supplied Jericho.

"Yes, you, Ingram, and Sarah. And, if a guy named Benny shows up, tell him he's fired. Oh, and, you're out of lime."

"Yes, sir," said Nancy Ann, who went to work on a fresh fruit.

Chris and Jerry walked into the showroom where Sarah and Ingram sat on the edge of the stage talking and laughing.

"You two, go keep Nancy Ann company in the bar."

"You got it, Jericho." Sarah led Ingram out, their heads together conspiratorially by the time they reached the rear door.

"Why all the secrecy." Chris sat in the same aisle chair he'd been in earlier.

Jericho sat in the row ahead of him, two seats further in, angled toward Chris. "Okay, so my idea is to mount a small show with say a nine o'clock curtain and then a midnight review three or four nights a week. You still perform five or six nights a week out in the bar. I think you should line up a second and then a third piano player for the bar so we don't work you to death."

"What shows?"

"I'm thinking *Dames at Sea, Little Shop of Horrors, Pajama Game, They're Playing Our Song, Nunsense.* You know, six or eight cast members. Simple sets. A piano player, maybe bass and drums. And, then *Trunk Songs* or *Side By Side By Sondheim* or *Ain't Misbehavin'* at midnight."

"Is that really going to bring in the crowds? Old, tired shows and stuff no one's heard of? I mean, I love them, too, don't get me wrong, but still?" Chris was losing faith. This was a drag club. It had always been a drag club. He was about to remind Jericho of this important fact, when—

"Right, but, we're going to reverse all the roles. We're going to cast women as men, men as women, white as black, black as Latino. We're going to gender bend and racial blend everything. The audience is going to need a few minutes to catch up and then they're going to go nuts. We're going to be sold out for weeks. And..." Jericho was on a roll. "And, we're going to work as a company. A company of actors who are going to do it all. Cross dress, gender bend, sing, dance, act. We're going to mount a new show every four to six weeks. We're going to alternate that with a new review every few weeks. There's going to be music and dancing and costumes everywhere. The restaurant will be packed. The bar will be packed. The theater will be sold out."

"Well, that's ambitious. It sounds incredibly expensive. Union?"

"Well, of course. I'm thinking we should probably be a LORT D house, although, if we price above $20, we'll be into C. Yeah, we should plan on C."

"LORT?"

"Oh, what does it stand...League of Resident Theaters. You remember unions?"

Union contracts meant bonds and deposits and lawyers.

The two men were quiet for a moment. Chris' head whirled with all the information he'd received. "You're talking bonds with Equity. Salaries. Contracts. A lawyer. Stage Managers, designers." He quickly did some math and added 25% based on the numbers he remembered from his own performance days. "Two-hundred and fifty K to start."

"Or thereabouts." Jericho stretched his arms into the air and brought them behind his head. He interlocked his fingers and cradled his cranium.

"Well, you don't do things small, do you?" Chris took a deep breath. "I'm assuming there's more?"

"I'm glad you asked. I propose we start a new company, something like the Tamburlaine Players or Tamburlaine Playhouse. The company will lease the space from Tamburlaine to keep things above board. We can work out the details. But, that way, no matter what happens, Tamburlaine is isolated and safe."

"You said *we*?" Chris smiled at Jerry's Cheshire-esque grin.

"Yes, we. We talked about this years ago. A long time ago. I still have the..." Jericho took out faded, crumpled paper napkins from the pizza shop in the Village where the two of them, at four in the morning, drunk, makeup smeared, over drugged, recently sexed, hatched the plan for a theater. At Chris's suggestion, a gender-bending theater. They'd never followed through with it. Jerry, when sober, said it wouldn't work. And, here he was, with a plan to make it work.

"Well, well, well." Chris took the handful of napkin-notes and shook them toward Jericho. "Who knew we'd end up here?" Jericho laughed as Chris continued. "So, you knew it was a good idea. You said it would never... If you didn't believe, you never would have kept this trash." He handed the clump back to his friend.

"What I said then was that it wasn't time, that audiences weren't ready. I think they are now. And, I think you and I have enough money to give a go of it. If it works, which I think it will, we'll make some money and, more importantly, have some fun. If it doesn't go, we lose a hundred grand. Is that really a big deal? Honest. How much have you sunk into this place just to keep it open as a shell."

There were no smiles now—a moment for honesty, seriousness.

Chris nodded his head. "Too much to openly admit."

"So, sell another painting. But, not that Picasso I love so much. You still have that one, right?"

"It's hanging in the same spot it was twenty years ago." Chris studied Jericho's face. "We're really going to do this together? You're not going to get the thing started and then walk away and leave me holding the bag." That's what it had felt like the last time they'd parted company. Sure, they'd seen each other since then, even done favors for one another, but nothing serious, nothing like this.

"I'm in. You have my word." Jericho Taylor held out his hand. "What do you say, Mr. Marlowe?"

He left Jerry with his hand outstretched. He wanted to dive in. He wanted to profess his love for the handsome man acting as his savior. He wanted to take whatever The Great Jericho Taylor offered. Instead, he calmly raised his hand and the two shook on the agreement.

"We'll let the lawyers work out the details," said Chris as they continued to hold their clenched hands.

"Excellent. We should talk about a few details. How do you want to build the company? Do we start with drag queens and turn them into actors or start with actors?"

"Jerry, I think we need alcohol and a stack of paper napkins for this conversation." Chris laughed. His buzz was waning and he wanted another slug of bourbon.

"Singing drag queen waiters," said Jericho from behind Chris.

"Waitresses. If they're drag queens, they're waitresses. And, that's not a bad idea. That's how we audition them for the company." Chris' head was awash with possibilities. There were so many plans and thoughts he'd had over the years for the place that had never before come to fruition. Now was the time to trot them all out and see what might work. "What do you want? Beer, whiskey, scotch."

"A beer would be great." Jericho walked into the barroom and took up a table near the little barroom stage. He pulled out a notebook from his jacket pocket and screwed the top off a fountain pen.

Chris set beers and glasses on the table. He left again, returned with a bottle of bourbon. He poured shots for them and sat down. "Oh, notes. Maybe I'll take some notes."

"When was the last time you took notes on anything?" Jericho downed the shot. "Set me up again."

Chris drank off his own shot and poured two fingers into the glasses. They raised them to each other and downed the mellow liquor. He watched as Ingram wiped a table clean nearby. "What, boy? The men are working here." His tone was playful, but Chris felt annoyed that the kid hovered.

"Chris, you really haven't eaten anything." Ingram came nearer.

"I'm fine, boy." Chris waved him off. He softened his tone. "Thanks, but I'm fine."

Ingram backed away and went over to the bar. A moment later, he and one of the girls were cackling together over something. It was nice to hear some laughter in the place.

"Well, first off, I need to hire a new bartender, two."

"Yeah, my stage manager usually has a job to do for me. And, at the moment at least, I'm sure I'm paying better." Jericho raised his beer bottle toward Chris and drank. "So, I'm envisioning a company of eight that we occasionally expand if we do something bigger. We could go all men and allow them to play all the roles."

"Very Shakespearian," said Chris as he felt a bit lost in Jericho's eyes.

"But, I think we should have a group of boys and girls, with a little age range, and that will give us more options."

"And better vocals," said Chris.

"I think that takes us up to ten though. Of course, they won't all be in every performance, but it will also give us some crossover, some understudies. That would be good."

"It's a company, right, so they're all on salary?" Chris drank more bourbon.

"We'll have to work that out with Equity. It might be a salary and then performance pay. That would probably be cheaper…"

Jericho continued to talk about LORT contracts, showcases, union scale, stage crew. It all became a jumble in Chris's mind as he drank more deconstructed boilermakers. It didn't really matter. He wanted to perform. He wanted to write a check and have Jericho or someone else take care of the details.

Chris liked the idea of a company of actors. They all had friends, right? And, roommates and day jobs and families who would come to see them. He liked the idea of a restaurant filled with diners and a bar filled with folks before the show and having nightcaps after shows. He wondered if they'd get a cab stand going again. He wondered if they'd be returning to linen service for the restaurant. He wondered if drag queens would again flock to be singing waitresses and performers at Tamburlaine. That's how it had once been. But, for now, it was just a string of ideas in his head matched up with page after page of notes in Jericho's little notebook.

"So, how does that sound?" Jericho looked up at Chris for the first time in thirty minutes.

"Frankly, I stopped listening when you started talking about contracts. You know me, Jerry. I don't want to think about these details. I want a club filled with people having a great time. I want a staff who loves coming to work every day. And, I want patrons who come again and again."

"Well, that's what I want to build here, too." Jericho stood up. "But, I have an early morning tomorrow. We're going to finish casting, I think. And, there's lots to do."

Chris stood up, he was drunk and wobbly. "Well, thanks for everything. I couldn't do this all on my own. Hell, I can't do anything like this ever."

"You'll see. It's going to be fabulous." Jericho hugged Chris tight. He kissed his cheek. "So, me and the girls are off. Will you and Ingram be okay?"

"Yes." Chris followed Jericho to the door and made some pleasant conversation with the girls. He escorted them out to the street and closed and locked the gates. He then waved the others off on the street and reentered the bar from the alley.

There was a full meal put together in the pots on the stove in the kitchen. He took up a plate and dished up beef, mashed potatoes, and carrots. Everything was cold, but it tasted good all the same. He sat on a stool and ate alone. There were things he needed to clean up. There were unkept promises, even all these years later, and it was time to make it right; to finish what he'd promised he would do.

"Chris, let me heat that up for you." Ingram sounded like a tired mother speaking to a small, out of control child. He had a resolve in his voice that was both comfortable and uncomfortable at the same time.

"No, it's perfect just the way it is." He shoved another fork filled with food into his mouth. "This may be the best pot roast I've ever had."

"You're just being nice." Ingram perched on the stool next to Chris.

"So what if I am? But, no, this is very good and I really do appreciate that you made it for me. That's not lost on me."

Ingram bowed his head.

"Listen, I'm used to being alone. I'm used to having space. I'm used to processing my emotions with a thick helping of booze. I don't see that changing any time soon. I know I don't always appreciate people in the moment. It doesn't make it right just to say that, but it is true. I get caught up in my own crap and ignore others. I was a diva for a very long time before I strove to be a person and this is what you get."

"I'm starting to understand that." Ingram explored his feet.

"So, as long as you're interested in hanging out with me, I can't say I'll always treat you well. But, I can say there will always be room for you with me."

"I think I'll take what I can get." Ingram went to the other side of the counter. He began putting leftovers into containers.

Chris finished his meal and together they washed and dried the dishes, pots, pans, and utensils. They worked in silence, but found a rhythm in their tasks. He'd washed dishes at these sinks with a lot of men over the decades. Those men sought to push their memories into that moment, but Chris pushed back. He wanted this moment to be his and Ingram's. He owed the boy at least that.

Fourteen

Chris tossed his head back and released a throaty guffaw of laughter. "Frank, you're a riot."

"You don't need to be an asshole about it." Frank stopped drying the glass in his hands. "Do you want me to make you a martini or a Long Island iced tea?"

"No. The fact that you'd offer is plenty. You came highly recommended." Chris sipped coffee. "How about wearing a dress? Are you opposed to that?"

"Why the hell do you think I agreed to come work at Tamburlaine?" Frank made a quick flip of his wrist, as if he were working a fan.

"Excellent. Well, we're going to be making lots of changes over the next few months. New shows. Adding wait staff. Bringing in our own theater company. Reopening the restaurant. It's going to be a large staff. And, I'm hoping to find someone to run them."

"Well, let's see how you and I get along. Two middle-aged queens in one hen house."

"Frank, I like you, despite your mixed metaphor, or whatever that was. We both know I'm old enough...well, I'm much older than you. So, play nice, but not too nice."

"Yes, ma'am. And, the hours?"

"Tamburlaine is open from four to four six days; all but Monday. My plan is to hire a second bartender very soon and then create a swing. Four to midnight and eight to four, or something like that. And, if business goes the way we expect, we'll quickly add two more behind the bars."

"Bars?" Frank looked up from his prep work.

"There's a service bar for the dining room and showroom. That hasn't been opened in ages. But, it's there." Chris pushed his coffee cup toward the bar rail and Frank, without missing a beat, refilled it.

The two men passed some time in silence. Frank prepping, Chris reading the daily papers. Tamburlaine remained quiet for nearly two hours.

"Why do you open so early?" Frank gestured to the empty room. "It can't be for the crowds?"

"Watch yourself. We open at four because the club has always opened at four. We close at four, well, sometimes we close early." Chris slid off the stool, walked over to the small stage, flipped the switches, the lights came up, and the mirror ball started to spin. He sat at the piano and played a soft, romantic ballad, "They Say It's Wonderful," from *Annie Get Your Gun*.

He sang to himself: "They say that falling in love is wonderful, wonderful." He segued into "Moonshine Lullaby." "There's a little still..."

Frank came over to the stage, stepped up, and placed a bourbon, neat, and a bottle of water on the piano. "You play wonderfully."

"Thank you. I studied for many years. And, I've performed in this club nightly for decades." Chris continued to play, one tune blending seamlessly into another. "Rusty played piano in her mother's bordello. She did a great bit about that, playing tunes related to how fast the Johns fucked. I need to find that."

Frank returned to the bar and Chris traveled in a Rusty Warren time bubble until Ingram burst through the door.

"I'm in. I got it." He waved a roll of papers in the air. When he saw Frank, he stopped short. "Where's Chris?"

Frank pointed toward the stage.

Ingram rushed over. "He hired me. I have a Broadway contract."

"Oh, my boy, that's wonderful." Chris played "For He's a Jolly Good Fellow."

"Thank you. Thank you." Ingram bowed deep. "I'm so fucking excited."

"So, what now?"

"Well, the cast is meeting here, tonight, at eight to celebrate. I told them I'd whip up some snacks."

"Well, get to whipping," said Chris. He watched Ingram skip into the kitchen, pleased that the boy had his dream. Yet, when he turned to the piano, the tunes he played all sounded melancholy.

"That will never do for a party." Frank placed a fresh glass of bourbon within Chris' reach. "You'll need to pep it up for the happy little boys and girls."

"Make sure there's a case of champagne chilled. The young people will bring their energy and I shall feed off of them like the old vamp that I am."

"I hear's ya, boss." Frank patted Chris' shoulder and made his way to the bar.

Fifteen

"Chris, are you okay? What are you doing in here?" Ingram moved close to Chris who sat on the stool in the kitchen. "And, drinking water. You must be ill," he chided.

"Oh, it was a bit raucous. I guess I truly am getting old. But, your friend playing is very good."

Ingram sat on the other stool. "The Piano Player from the show? It's his first time as musical director for Jericho. He's very excited. Are you sure you're okay?"

"Yes, yes. I'm fine. Stop worrying about me and go enjoy the party."

The boy stood and grabbed a tray of rumaki. "Come join us."

Chris waved Ingram off. He sipped more water. Something inside him didn't feel right, felt soft or weak or...for a moment, he worried that he'd been poisoned again, but that had come on quickly. Perhaps a little flu, or simply old age. He finished the bottle and tossed it toward the garbage can. He missed, but left it for someone else to pick up. He slid off the stool and went out to the party. But, instead of joining in the jubilation, he took up his spot at the end of the bar. Frank provided him a bourbon before his ass adjusted to the Naugahyde.

"Mr. Marlowe."

Chris turned to his right to find one of the women from Jerry's entourage standing next to him. He couldn't remember her name, but she'd tended bar. "Sally Jo?"

"Close. Nancy Ann."

"Well, you're sweet. I wasn't anywhere in the neighborhood." Chris patted her hand.

"I just wanted to say that I truly love your club. When I walked in here the other night, it was like coming home." Nancy Ann placed her free hand atop of Chris'.

"Well, you're much too young to know Tamburlaine as home. But, it was built for people like us."

"Like us?"

"Smart. Sophisticated. Outside the every day. The trendsetters."

"Oh, I'm hardly a trendsetter."

"Can I get you something to drink?" Frank interrupted with perfect timing.

"Corona, no fruit."

"Careful, darlin'. If you talk like that, you'll offend some old queen." Frank indicated Chris with a wink.

"Just get the girl her beer and keep your commentary to yourself," said Chris. "He thinks he's funny."

"All you old guys do," she said, this time adding her own wink to the mix.

"I'm wounded." Chris held his hands over his heart. "Fatally wounded."

They laughed together.

"No, I mean it, Mr. Marlowe."

"Please, call me Chris. I mean, if you're going to suck up to me, you may as well do it in a familiar sort of way."

"Now, I'm embarrassed."

He touched her arm. "No need. No need."

"I can't explain it. The energy. The history. It does feel like I'm meant to be here. I feel like I know every inch of this place. I dreamt of an office with a secret lock and a dusty modern painting. I dreamt of running through a hidden, caged catwalk. I dreamt of shoveling coal in an old boiler in the basement."

Chris' breath caught. "Well, you've just described several of the Tamburlaine's secrets." He slid off the stool and picked up his drink. He placed his free hand into the crook of Nancy Ann's arm and led her down the hallway, past the restrooms, through the private door into the back hall, and to the office door with the secret lock. He opened that door, hit the light, and ushered her breathless into the space. "Picasso."

"I can't believe it." Nancy Ann moved as close as she could to the dusty painting. "It's just like the dream."

"The coal boiler has long been converted. First to oil and then to natural gas. No more stoking. And, I'm too old to show you up to the catwalk, but that exists, too."

"Do you believe in reincarnation, Mr. Mar...Chris?"

"I do, indeed. I believe it's why so many of us gay men enjoy wearing women's clothing. We've been women and enjoy the flounce and drama. But, I could be wrong."

For a long moment they took in the painting.

"How could you let it get so dusty? Oh, sorry."

"No, you're right to judge. I hadn't been in this room for ten years. Not until a few days ago. Forgotten. All of Tamburlaine was slipping away from me. But, now, it feels like there's a resurgence underway."

"Chris, may I ask you something?"

"Of course." He waited for her to continue.

"I've worked exclusively for Jericho for a long, long time. But, I feel it so strongly. I really would like to be your full-time gal here. I want to run your theater company. I know you're going into business with Jericho and it might not be possible, but I just know I'm supposed to be here for you, for Tamburlaine."

"Well, I'm open to that. We need a company manager and a stage manager. Jerry and I talked about having one person wear both hats for a while, until we start making some money. You know his style and you have some deep connection to Tamburlaine. I think it would be great. But, Jerry needs to not only agree, he must be okay with it, too. We can't begin a partnership with bad blood between us."

"So, you'd support it? Support me coming on full-time?"

"I will if it's okay with Jerry."

Nancy Ann hugged Chris tight. "I just know this is all going to work out perfectly."

Sixteen

Tamburlaine buzz built. Additional bartenders and wait staff were hired. Queens in heels slung drinks and sang songs while Chris or The Piano Player entertained from the barroom stage. Crowds filled the place, drinking heavily from ten to two.

Nancy Ann directed daily rehearsals of the new company, unknown, hungry boys and girls. Chris had difficulty believing they were all actually over twenty-one—a requirement to work there.

Money once again flowed into the club. Not a cascade. Not enough to cover all the expenses, but a comfortable trickle.

"Chris?" Frank asked.

He didn't stop reading the *Times*. "What?"

"They want you in the theater." Frank replaced the ancient black phone in its cradle.

"Damn. Take a look at seventeen down." Chris slid off his stool and headed for the showroom, his head a jumble of crossword answers and ideas about the restaurant. They'd all been talking about it. Should it be fancy and expensive or comfy and affordable? There weren't any high-end restaurants in what remained of the neighborhood—just the deli and Salvatore's—so Chris was leaning toward comfortable. He pulled open the door into the theater. The showroom had been steam cleaned—seats and carpet like new. The room had been painted, returned once more to its gaudy rococo style. The Chagall-esque mural along the right aisle restored and enhanced.

"Chris, I wanted you to hear this," said Nancy Ann, looking roughneck in khaki pants, combat boots, and tit-hugging white T-shirt. She gave an indication to The Piano Player, who rolled off a chord, and the ensemble sang a tight, a cappella rendition of the spiritual "Great Day."

Chris slunk into a front row chair, transported to his youth, to a high school in Ohio where a choir director there included at least one Negro

Spiritual in every concert. "Great Day" had been one of Chris' all-time favorite songs. As he listened to this group of talented people fill the theater with their strong voices, tears welled and spilled from his eyes.

"What is it, Chris? Are you okay?" Nancy Ann jumped from the stage. The company spilled to the edge of the wooden platform.

"Oh, just being overly sentimental. That song takes me to a special time in my life. I had a wonderful choir conductor who encouraged me to be myself, to follow my dreams." Chris felt the tears spill from his eyes. "Such a gift. Thank you for such a gift."

The company didn't move or speak for a long moment.

"So, you like the sound?" Nancy Ann breathed in, but didn't release it, swelling her breasts outward.

"Can I hear it again?" Chris asked, straightening himself in the chair. The velvet on the arm rests felt soft under his hands.

The group sang the song again. Chris listened intently, his eyes closed so as not to be distracted by the handsome men.

"Tenors, strengthen your line. Breathe deep, from the diaphragm. Don't be lazy. You're getting lost." As Chris spoke, a tenor voice came out stronger from the group. A second voice matched the first. Balance and strength by the end of the piece. "So, we're doing a spiritual review now? I think it's in poor taste to do spirituals when so many of you are white." He liked having a mix of races and sexes. Diversity brought strength to any group.

"Just a warm-up, boss. Just working on harmony and line." Nancy Ann used an unapologetic, teacherly tone.

"What else do you have for me?" Chris scanned the bright faces assembled before him.

"Well, we've begun working out numbers from three different shows: *Dames at Sea*, *Nunsense*, and *Side by Side*. It's Jericho's plan to alternate weeks. One week with a musical, one week with a straight play, and so on. The company is learning six shows."

"At one time?" His mouth dropped open. "Who learns six shows at once?"

"The Tamburlaine Players," said The Piano Player.

"Fine, what numbers can you do for me?" Chris reached toward a top pocket that he didn't have for a pack of cigarettes that weren't there.

With no warning or explanation, The Piano Player launched into "Nunsense is Habit Forming." Six kids, three boys and three girls, positioned themselves on stage and sang the song with a bit of unpolished choreography. The number ended, and he played "Here's to the Ladies Who Lunch," for a man he hadn't noticed before who did an amazing rendition that would put Elaine Stritch to shame. Next up, *"Dames at Sea."* Most of the kids sang.

"Want us to continue?" Nancy Ann asked.

"No, just keep working. You're doing an amazing job and the company is wonderful." Chris stood to leave; after a few steps up the aisle, he turned back. "If any of you want to try out your numbers this evening in front of an audience, let me know and I'll bring you up on stage." He turned again and began walking out of the theater, the company applauded and then chattered among themselves.

Chris stepped out into the dining room. He sat down at one of the tables and allowed the tears to flow. This was happening. Magic. Hearing a few numbers by this newly formed ensemble that already worked offered more hope to Chris than he'd felt in ages. Again the tears. He reached for a handkerchief, realizing he hadn't carried one for eons. He wiped at his face with the sleeve of his blouse. Magic had begun. Time to move forward. And, for the first time he could remember, he felt in the moment with the movement.

Seventeen

Tamburlaine unlocked its doors for the evening. The company scattered from all places visible to the public, Frank prepped, slicing lemons and limes into their respective plastic bins.

Chris worked his crossword puzzle. 27 down: Mixologist. No big guns tonight, just light makeup, his own hair, well-coiffured, and a comfortable, breezy blouse. Just an evening of piano, songs, and jokes for whomever might arrive. Chris wrote "bartender" in the space. He thought about Benny. What had happened to him? The thought surfaced again that Benny had to be the one who poisoned him caused shudders to run down Chris' spine.

The opened front door brought in a brilliant shaft of sunlight, the last of the afternoon before the sun dropped lower behind the empty buildings of the neighborhood. A slight frame silhouetted in the doorway, emerged from the light, and reintroduced darkness behind it.

"I'm Matilda," the small shadow announced to the room.

"Hello," said Frank. "What can I do for you?"

"Jericho Taylor sent me. Said I should talk to Chris Marlowe," she said, her voice strong, broad, bigger than the woman it came from.

"I'm Marlowe." Chris didn't move.

The figure approached. As Chris's eyes readjusted to the restored shadowy light of Tamburlaine, he enjoyed the person standing before him. Slightly deformed, perhaps malformed might be a better word, Matilda stood about five feet tall. She bent at an odd angle from the waist, one of her feet awkwardly turned out. Her arms, each a different length, dangled at her sides. In the hands at the end of those arms, she held canvas bags overflowing with greens and vegetables. Nothing about her appeared symmetrical, unless you looked square into her eyes. She had the most beautiful, silken brown eyes Chris had ever seen.

"Good evening. Jericho has sent me here to cook for you. He has told me you are considering reopening your kitchen to the public and you will soon embark on a search for the perfect chef to bring an affordable, but interesting menu to Tamburlaine. I have arrived here this evening to offer my services. I understand that you will want to give me a trial. You will, of course, want to sample my flavors. So, if you'll be so kind as to have a member of your staff point me toward your kitchen, I shall prepare your dinner."

Joyfully impressed by this strong woman in the distorted frame, Chris said, "Frank, show Matilda the way to the kitchen."

Frank came around the bar and led her toward the dining room. Her feet made a ker-swish-thump as she moved. Chris strained to hear if the two spoke, but heard no words.

"I don't like her one bit. Who will want to eat her food? After seeing her, no one will have an appetite." Frank verily hissed the words when he returned.

"Ah, Francis, my friend. We are all deformed. Some on the inside, some outside. But, everyone who finds their way to Tamburlaine is welcomed. They may not be invited to stay long, but all are at least welcomed when they arrive."

As the next hour passed, a few patrons came in, had a drink, and left—more early evening traffic than they'd been experiencing, so Chris was pleased that these commuters, or whoever they were, stopped in. Along with the arrival of drinking strangers, lovely aromas wafted out of the kitchen, intoxicating on so many levels. Chris' mouth watered in anticipation.

Matilda reappeared. "Your dinner is ready, Mr. Marlowe. Where shall I serve you? In the darkened dining room? Here at your place at the bar?"

"The kitchen, please." Chris slid off his stool and followed Matilda's ker-thumped movements to the kitchen. She held the door for him. He moved to the counter, taking up his stool there. She quickly, but expertly plated a beautiful chicken pot pie—pastry from scratch, perfectly cooked, tender veggies, and a perfect, thick gravy.

Chris dug into the food. No gourmet, still he loved good food, and she'd prepared a tasty, hearty meal.

Next up, a delicate apple cake, dusted with powdered sugar, and a strong cup of coffee. Both were excellent and Chris was pleased.

Finally, he spoke. "And, what would be our cost of this meal?"

"About four and a half."

"Markup?" Chris asked.

"Anywhere from twenty to thirty dollars, depending on your goals."

"My goals?"

"Well, if you want the place packed every night with a regular crowd, both nightly diners and those attending shows, then you'll want to come in around twenty dollars per person. It's an incredibly reasonable price. And, if you wanted, we could easily offer a three course, prix fixe that included house wine and coffee for twenty-five dollars."

"How many solid main courses do you have?"

"About eighty."

It pleased Chris that Matilda had not only a head for cooking, but understood the business end of the restaurant, too.

"How many staff would you require?"

"If we go prix fixe, initially, a sous chef, two cooks, plus an extra prep, a dishwasher, and three waiters. Once we hit a hundred covers, I'd want another waiter and an expediter, at least for the weekends."

"You're hired if you want the job, Matilda. I like you. I like what I've tasted. And, I know you can run the hell out of a kitchen. Write down your expected salary and perks and we'll see what we can do for you."

"Just like that, Mr. Marlowe?" She smiled crookedly.

"Just like that." He liked that she called him Mr. Marlowe. It felt right. "When can we begin opening for dinner?"

"Can I hire who I want?"

"For the kitchen staff, yes. I want approval for the waiters." Chris once again found himself drawn into Matilda's beautiful, doe-like eyes— less Bambi and more Bambi's mom; knowing of the world.

"Two or three days. There's food orders and a few other things."

"Take care of the staff. Make an initial list of what you require and we'll get it taken care of. There's an office for the executive chef, but it's downstairs. We can set up an office for you up here and you can begin dealing with all the details."

"You're very kind, Mr. Marlowe. But, I'll work from the office downstairs.

"Actually, I can be a raging bitch. But, I appreciate your kind words and sucking up."

Matilda tossed her head back like it was hinged, and laughed heartily, grotesquely.

Eighteen

Chris heard him, but didn't call back.

"Chris!" Ingram shouted again from the kitchen

He explored the racks and crates filled with paintings on the second floor. Lots of Pop Art from the '60s. A few Abstract Impressionists from earlier in the century. Two Impressionists. A small Dutch Master. He'd inherited most, added a few. Some gifts from friends. Some he'd purchased at auctions and estate sales. It was a way to dump cash into something that, while traceable, wasn't such a big deal in the 1970s. A Johns or Pollack back then went for a song. Now, investors, collectors, and museums were willing to sing arias for them.

"Chris? Your keys and wrap are here. Where are you?"

He followed Ingram's movement below by the creak of floorboards as the boy wandered the loft. He came to the stairs and called up: "Hello?"

"I'll be right down." The first step creaked. Chris bolted to the top of the stairs. "I've told you," he said with an overtly polite tone. "You're never to come up here."

"Yes. Yes." Ingram stepped to the floor. "How was your day?" he called.

"Fine." Chris came down the stairs, wiping his hands on his slacks. "And yours? Didn't you work your number today?"

"No, we worked 'On the Willows.' I'm gonna get a beer. Want something?"

"Beer is fine." Chris followed the boy, enjoying his peach of an ass as it shifted in the kid's tight jeans. "I love that number. That, and 'Day by Day.' Those are my favorites. I like 'All for the Best,' too, but I prefer the ballads."

"You took the night off?" Ingram handed Chris an opened beer.

"Well, we're still closed on Mondays and I had some things to do here. I wanted a night out of the club." He sat at the table. "Are you hungry? Should we order food?"

Ingram pointed to a pizza box on the counter.

"Clever boy," said Chris.

"Do you want some?" Ingram opened the box and took out a large pepperoni slice. It bent in half and grease began to drip off of it.

"No, I'll wait till it cools just a bit more."

"Okay." Ingram creased the slice, wrapped paper napkin around the crust end, and took a large bite of the pie.

Watching young men eat made Chris feel the way he knew Whitman must have felt watching the boys swim in the Hudson. Something about the style and finesse most of them put into eating a slice, everyone had their own way of dealing with the bend, of dealing with the grease, or not. Nothing screamed New York City like a big slice. And, nothing screamed guy like eating pizza.

"So, what do you have upstairs? Stray boys like me who have died and gone to bones, perhaps? Or some old wedding dress that you like to put on when you're alone and then play the piano? Or maybe your dead mother?"

"You watch too much late-night TV." Chris took a long sip of beer. He always reached this point. He wanted to share the collection, show it to someone. But, whenever he'd done that in the past, a piece or two would go missing and it was a pain in the ass dealing with the thefts. He just stopped showing it off. It was his collection and his alone. Every four to six weeks, he'd go up and dust. That was it. Occasionally, when he required an infusion of cash, he'd sell one. In the old days, when he had an influx of cash, he'd buy one. Sometimes, he'd buy back the ones he'd sold. Depended. There were still over a hundred paintings on the second floor of the building. Yes, it was the wrong place for them. It wasn't climate controlled and there was too much dust. But, they were his and there was no way he'd put them in some hermetically sealed vault never to see them again.

"Chris? Where did you go?"

"Sorry. I've been a little spacy today. There are so many changes and new people. Oh, what do you think of Matilda? Have you sampled her food?"

Ingram hesitated.

"I know you wanted the position, but with your show and your Broadway career, I thought it better to hire someone who wanted to be a chef."

"No, I really am okay with it. Well, mostly." He smiled, reached for another slice, and then closed the lid. "I love her food. Her flavor combinations are really nice. I like her comfort food twist. I think the prices are a bit low, but I understand that, too. I just…"

"What?" Chris finished his beer and tossed the bottle into the trash bin.

Ingram got two fresh beers. "You should recycle." He opened a bottle and handed it to Chris. "It's not the menu I would have planned."

"Well, we're not finished and there will be daily specials based on what's fresh that day." Chris caught himself. He would not defend his choice of Matilda for head chef. She was amazing and wonderfully strange. He liked everything about her.

"So, there's something I've been wanting to talk to you about." Ingram played with the pizza's crust.

"Okay." Again Chris drank, wondering if he'd be switching to bourbon early.

"Well, one of the guys in the show, he moved in with his boyfriend, so his roommate has an empty room; I can afford it on my new salary."

Chris breathed deeply, relieved. "Yes, take it. Take the room. You like the guy? You'll get along okay? It's in Manhattan and not Queens?"

"Yes, it's in the city. Way up. Inwood."

"Last stop on the A-train. But, you have a lovely park up there." Chris smiled at the kid.

"You know it?"

"Baby, I know everything there is to know about this city."

"Well, he wants me to move in right away. Wednesday is the first." Ingram cast his eyes down and away from Chris.

"How much do you need?" He felt as he had many times, more like a mother than a daddy.

"Two grand. Two months' rent and a security deposit. I've got fifteen hundred, so I only need another five and I could pay you back in a few weeks. A month tops. Or, I could work it off in your kitchen?"

"I like that idea, an advance on salary for you to work as a line cook. So long as it's okay with Matilda." Chris reached into his pocket and counted off ten hundred-dollar bills.

"You carry money like that around with you?"

Chris ignored Ingram's emotion. "You never know when you're going to want to buy something pretty for yourself." He held out the cash toward Ingram. "Take it."

The boy took the money and shoved it deep into his jeans' pocket.

"Are you sure it's enough?"

"Plenty. I can't begin to tell you how much I appreciate you and what you've done for me." Tears sprung into his eyes.

"Oh, my boy. You're lovely and handsome and I'm glad I could once again do my part for the theater community. Someday, maybe someday soon, when a kid needs a place to crash for a bit, you can repay me by offering him your futon."

Chris pointed at the pizza box and Ingram moved it over to the table. The two of them ate and talked more about *Godspell* and the changes at Tamburlaine. They'd have one more night together, but it was obvious that they'd never have sex. Chris let out a sigh, blamed it on memories of a guy he knew from the original Broadway cast. He pointed to the *Godspell* *Playbill* on the wall. He let tonight's boy go on talking.

Once again, he felt just a little too old for the everyday stuff of life.

Nineteen

Matilda tasted something and tossed the used spoon into a metal bin. "You're early."

"I know." Chris closed the door to the alley and took in the energy of the busy kitchen. "Who are all these people?"

"Your kitchen staff." Matilda smiled warmly at him from those wonderful brown eyes.

"It's nice that we're busy again." He stepped in a few feet, but remained on the edge of the bustle.

"We've got bookings for sixty covers tonight." She added salt to the pot and stirred the contents. "People are loving the prix fixe menu."

"I like that everything is fresh every night. That makes me happy." He turned and walked away.

The dining room tables were set with fresh white linen cloths and napkins, polished silver, and clear crystal glasses. The fixtures were clean. With lit candles, the room shimmered. The old hardwood floors shined.

Chris walked down the hallway. He turned the knob this way and that and his office door popped open. This room had received some much-needed attention, too. Even the women in the Picasso gave an impression of being joyous and happy. He sat at his desk and explored the stack of invoices. He turned on the computer, opened the bank account, and set up payments to be sent to the vendors. After all the years he'd avoided computers and electronics, in just a few weeks of harassment by his staff, he was an expert at the Internet, email, and online bill pay, not to mention, free porn videos.

The showroom was full every evening. They would officially launch the Tamburlaine Players in three nights. Even the dining room was breaking even. He bowed his head before the painting on the wall and prayed to Picasso that this new venture would be a success.

Chris logged off the computer and closed the roll-top desk. He checked his makeup in the mirror near the door and ran a finger along the lipstick line to clean it up a touch. He rubbed his hands together and then cracked his knuckles before heading out and locking the door.

Chris took up his usual spot and Frank placed a cup of coffee before him. A new bartender drew a draught beer from the restored taps.

"Here you go, boss."

"Thanks." He sipped coffee. There were patrons at the bar and seated at the tables near the stage. He wasn't due to go on for close to an hour. "What are they doing here so early?"

"Don't want to miss the show tonight. By seven or eight there's a line at the door. Last night, more than a hundred people were turned away."

"Well, keep pouring drinks down 'em." Chris rotated a ring on his finger, one of the many he wore that evening, bangles and bobbles that clinked and sparkled, some real, some glass.

"Should we turn the lights on for you?" Frank asked.

"No, I'm going to have another word with Matilda." He slid off the stool and headed to the kitchen. He had the girls there make him a plate of that evening's entrée, Yankee Pot Roast with potatoes and carrots. He ate half the food before him while sitting on his stool at the counter. He watched them work. Each of the kitchen crew displayed some physical malady. None seemed slowed by their awkwardly formed hand or strangely turned wrist. They communicated quietly, as if theirs were a private language. The waiters, some in drag, some in extreme makeup, came in and had dinner; the same food he ate; the meal they'd be serving. Chris liked that he was feeding them a hearty and wholesome meal.

Finished with his food, he returned to the barroom and had the boys turn on the lights. He stepped on stage to a smattering of applause. It felt good, even that half-hearted attempt at welcome.

"Good evening," he began, sitting at the piano and playing an arpeggio from the lowest keys to the highest. "I'm Christopher Marlowe. Not the dead poet, but the pickled drag queen." A few chuckles. He launched into a gaudy, Liberace-esque piano performance. While he played, one of the cute waiter boys brought up a lit candelabra to great applause from the audience.

His eyes adjusted to the lighting, Chris noticed a group of older faces watching him. These weren't the youngsters who had been filling the club the past week or so. No, these were his peers, the survivors. Chris knew in his heart that if those assembled shared names and stories that many of them had probably slept together, pissed each other off, gotten stoned together, and been in love with each other at some point in their journey. And, if it weren't those sitting there, it was with others, just like them, that they all remembered.

Was this how it was going to be? Chris wondered. He played "Life is Just a Bowl of Cherries," an old song from Rusty Warren's repertoire. The audience sang along and approved. He let his mind wander. It felt like he'd entered a time warp. Less drugs, more booze. Fewer sincere laughs from him, but the audience played along. Just like the old days, when he could enjoy an entire exploration of a series of rambling topics while still performing his act. Song after song, joke after joke, Rusty's material blended with his own gay twisted innuendo, just rolling out of him while his mind wandered somewhere else. Was this what dementia felt like, being in two places at once and not knowing reality from reality.

A waiter brought him more bourbon. Another waiter, in drag, sang "The Boy Next Door," an old Joyce Breach torch song. Great applause. Reminder to tip the wait staff, they were the entertainment. A reminder that dinner was available. A reminder that tickets were on sale for The Tamburlaine Players. Another song, another joke, another reminder.

And, so the evening passed. So the days passed. The numbers grew. The lines on the street brought press and media attention. The food received rave reviews. The Tamburlaine Players, directed by The Great Jericho Taylor, anticipated.

Twenty

"Thank you for walking me home, kind sir." Chris reached into his pocket for the key to the metal door.

"I'm not done talking yet. Want to invite me in for a nightcap?" Jericho Taylor held his hand politely at Chris' elbow.

"Sure, what the hell." Chris turned the key and pulled hard on the door. It creaked open.

"All these years and it's still the same door?"

"If it ain't broke—"

A scramble of sudden footsteps and a flash of light broke up the comfort of the familiar darkness.

Glass shattered nearby.

"Faggots!"

"Cock suckers!"

Chris and Jericho turned just as a bottle sailed toward them. Chris reacted first, pushed Jericho into the alley, but he got clocked in the head by the bottle. A second and then a third bottle accosted at him. The next one that arrived flamed. Chris raised an arm to cover his face. The bottle hit the wall and fire burst all around him—igniting liquid from the shattered bottles. He could feel the pain of the heat burning the skin on his feet and ankles, the smell of gasoline and smoke filled his nose.

In shock, Jericho dragged him into the alley, closed the door behind them, and then pushed Chris to the ground, covering him with a jacket, pounding out the flames.

"What in the world. Fuck, that hurts." Chris struggled to sit up, but Jericho was still punching his jacket over Chris' legs. "Breathe, Jerry. Breathe. I think I'm okay. A little burned, maybe. Stop trying to save me, you're killing me."

"A little burned?" Jericho laughed nervously. He tugged out his cell phone and dialed 9-1-1. While he gave the woman who answered details, he helped Chris sit up, both of them used the alley wall as support. Before he'd hung up with the operator, sirens could be heard.

"What on earth was that?" Chris made an effort to stand; his feet hurt terribly. He focused on them as best he could, but there wasn't enough light. "Damn. They'll want to take me to the hospital."

Sirens blared opposite the metal door. The revolving blue and white lights cast strange shadows above their heads.

"Where else?" Jericho stood up and felt the door. It was warm.

"Don't open it. The fire might not be out yet." He struggled to stand again, but decided to stay put and be rescued.

Jericho pounded on the metal door. A moment later, there was a pounding from the other side. He pushed hard and the door opened. Two firefighters attempted to rush in, but they stopped.

"His feet are burned," said Jericho.

"The ambulance is on the way," one of the firefighters said.

They went to the hospital. Second degree burns on his feet. For the next hour, they gave descriptions of what had happened while his feet were dressed and bandaged. They would keep him overnight, just to be safe. Chris got into a private room and called Frank and Matilda to let them know. He knew the club would be well taken care of. Frank would stop by the loft just to be sure doors were locked and everything was okay.

Jericho waited, his foot tapping rapidly and continuously.

"Jerry, what is it? Why don't you go home? It's late. You have rehearsals with the kids tomorrow. We open in two nights."

Jericho stared, his face in partial shadow, jaw set, small dimple deepened—a dramatic effect.

"What is it? Are you okay? Should I call a nurse?" Chris reached for the remote control with a nurse's picture on it.

"No need for that." Jericho moved close to him. "You saved my life tonight. You're a hero."

"You're being melodramatic. It was some drunken boys. I pushed you inside because you were in my way. I'm no hero; I'm a scaredy-cat." He breathed deep, euphoria filling him as the pain medication surged through his veins.

"No, you shoved me in and blocked me from being hit. And, those were no kids. They threw a Molotov cocktail. They were trying to kill us. Well, you."

"No....what? Do you think?" He looked out the window over the river. The poison. Now, fire. "You might be right."

"We should get you some protection." Jericho had Chris' hand firm in his own. "A body guard. Maybe a few undercover guys for the club. We don't want you, or anyone else to be harmed." He leaned in close and hugged Chris. "I can't imagine..."

Chris hugged Jerry for a long moment, enjoying the mingled scents of flop sweat and cologne that were Jericho Taylor to him. "Pull a chair over and sit with me for a bit."

Jericho did as told. He took one of Chris' hand in both of his own.

"We never did get to the nightcap." Chris squeezed Jericho's hand.

"Well, you did. Painkillers are about the best you can do. It's something when we can kill the pain; bury it forever." Jericho's eyes went somewhere distant.

"Who do you think might be trying to kill me?"

Twenty-one

The world moved in slow motion as Chris recovered. Luckily, the soles of his feet weren't burned, only the tops, along with the lower calves. Because of this, he could walk, or at least hobble around. And, with a handful of painkillers, he could do it without too much suffering.

The bell rang. He shuffled to the kitchen and turned on the surveillance camera. Frank waved up at the lens. He held up a stack of foil containers. Chris pressed the button and watched the screen as Frank, balancing the food containers in one hand, pulled with all his might on the door. It finally gave way and smeared his arm with soot.

Tired from the activity, Chris unlocked the kitchen door and sat down in a chair.

"There's the invalid." Frank was pleasant and cheerful.

"What have you brought me?"

Frank placed the container on the table, followed by a canvas bag that clanked and clattered. "Dinner."

Chris began opening the containers. Frank pulled out a bottle of bourbon and a six pack of beer from the bag. He got out plates and hunted the drawers for silverware.

"Forks are next to the fridge." Chris pointed. Frank found what he was searching for. "Wow, chicken parm. One of my favorites."

"It's really good. People are already asking when she's making it again so they can book in advance."

Chris eyed the cat clock. "People? It's only four thirty."

"Mommy, the place is packed."

"Look at you going Puerto Rican on me. Is that mascara you're wearing? We're going to turn you into a diva queen, yet."

"I watched *Wong Fu* last night. It rubbed off on me."

"So, I'm sorry I won't be in tonight. There are two piano players already lined up. They're going to come in, play standards, use the Black

Book, and the waiters' book. Be sure they don't take anything out with them. My Black Book is an original!"

"Yes. I know. So, eat."

"I will. There's plenty here, do you want to join me?"

"Chris, I can't. The place is already filling up and I'm sure Randy is having trouble keeping up. Oh, I wanted to make sure it was okay to bring in a bartender for the service bar. Randy sucks with people, but he's a helluva mixologist. I think the service bar is perfect for him."

"Fine by me. One complaint from Matilda or her team and he's gone. I don't really like his energy. Let the waiters in the dining room know they have to tip him out. I'll pay him an extra ten bucks an hour for being in there."

"Only ten, boss?" Frank dipped a finger into the red sauce and licked it clean.

"Get out of there." Chris slapped his hand away. "Only ten. Let's see what the tip-out looks like, and we'll make an adjustment in a few days if needed. I want to test him there."

"Okay, okay. I'm outta here. You call me if you need anything. Oh, the company is coming tomorrow to clean down the front of the building. It's covered by insurance. And, the cops found one of the guys from last night. They're sure he's not the one in charge, but they're hoping he'll leak them some leads."

"Anything else?"

"Rehearsal went great this afternoon. I came in early and watched the show. It was an invited dress. All the kids are really sorry about what happened to you. The show looks good. We're sold out through the weekend and at seventy percent for the next two weeks."

"That's great. See, you all don't need me there."

"You're so full of shit. Take it easy so you can be there tomorrow night."

"It's going to be weeks before I can play again." Chris wiped at his eye.

"Your hands are fine." Frank considered Chris.

"But, I can't use the pedals. And, none of my pumps will fit over these bandages. Go take care of my investment."

"You'll be there tomorrow if I have to come back here and carry you in. Got it?" Frank leaned down and kissed Chris on the cheek. "I'll make the bank drop tonight and make sure everyone does what they're supposed to do, okay?"

Chris patted Frank's hand. "It's in the freezer." He pointed. "Thank you." He felt more sincere about those words than he ever had before in his life. It was the first time anyone had displayed such concern in respecting and protecting his business, his interests.

Twenty-two

Chris finished his dinner, poured a tall glass of bourbon, and downed a few more painkillers before making his way into the living room. In the past, he'd found the space comfortable with its overstuffed antique sofas and chairs, grand piano in the corner, and paintings hanging heavily from long, ribbon-covered chords attached to faux picture rails at the top of the partitioned walls. From eye level, the space was perfect. Inspect the ceiling and it appeared to be a stage set. In fact, that's what it was. The stage set for a production of *Arsenic and Old Lace*, performed by drag queens in 1979. Now, the room felt overdone and cheap. Chris vowed that if all of the changes kept bringing in cash, he'd redecorate this room, and maybe his bedroom, too.

Nothing would change tonight.

He set his glass on an end table, plopped onto a sofa, and turned on the big television, strategically placed among the pieces of art. He trolled the channels, settling on an old Vincent Price black-and-white movie. When Chris was much younger, hating the family that had raised him, he'd imagined a variety of parental alternatives. Among those he'd visualized for his father: Vincent Price. His melodramatic style fit Chris' stage presence incredibly well. What a combination: a child created by Vincent Price and Rusty Warren. Rusty was, of course, always his first choice for mother. And, frankly, his second choice for father.

He rummaged around the coffee table and found Rusty's DVD. A poorly made documentary, it still had clips from several television interviews intermixed with voice over mingled with a live Las Vegas stage performance late in Rusty's career. After several attempts, Chris hoisted himself up, hobbled to the DVD player, and got the disc running. He settled on the couch, propped up his bandaged feet, and closed his eyes, listening to the foul-mouthed broad say her piece. Of course, by current standards, Rusty Warren wasn't only tame, she'd be rated G in most markets—even with "Knockers Up." But, in her day, she was the dirtiest woman around.

As Rusty spoke, he imagined himself in full drag doing the jokes, taping the interviews, singing the songs. Of all the role models, he chose a flat chested boy of a woman. But, she'd been fantastic. She'd changed the world. She'd written a new script, nurtured the sexual revolution, and did it with laughter, alcohol, and a unique style. And, that's what Chris admired.

The bell rang. He hit a button on the remote and the television picture changed to the surveillance camera. Jericho. Chris buzzed him in. He still couldn't find his balance. Too many pills. Too much bourbon.

"Hello!" Jericho called from the kitchen.

"Here," he said, his voice low and quiet.

Jericho, searching, entered the living room. "I can't remember the last time I was here, but it all looks exactly the same. Just like Jimmy...." He sat next to Chris, taking his hand. "How are you?"

"I think I've taken one too many pills."

"Overdose? Should I call someone?" Taking Chris's wrist, Jericho felt for a pulse.

"No, just sleepy. Will you sit with me? Keep me company? Talk to me?" Chris gained his senses for a moment and turned off the TV. He hit another button on the remote and Rusty Warren sang "Make Someone Happy." Chris turned the volume down.

"Some things don't ever change." Jericho took Chris' hand and pulled it to his chest. "I do love ya', Christopher. I always have. From the first time I ever saw you."

"You're a sweet man, Jerry. Tell me about your day."

"Well, we had a lovely rehearsal in the morning. These kids are incredibly talented. They sing and move well. The acting will hopefully come in time."

"That's it," said Chris, his eyes closed, his words a little slurred. "You have to give them time to come into their own. We all need to nurture our talent."

"For someone so fucked up, you speak a solid truth."

Chris pulled his hand away and curled it in with his other, under his chin.

Jericho grabbed a throw from the end of the couch and placed it over Chris. "So, we did a run through for the staff and a few friends. *Dames at*

Sea with gender-swapped roles is a hoot. There's so much strength in the real girls and so much style and softness in the boys. The early word is good."

"Frank said we're sold out for tomorrow."

"Yes, we are."

"What else, Jerry? Talk to me. I like having you here again. We're old men now, huh?"

"Speak for yourself. I'm not doing too bad."

"No, Jerry. You look good. Still fit. Still dancing. Still making boys drool."

"Maybe not quite as much or for the old reasons." He patted Chris' hand. "Your boy Ingram is doing well. You were right, of course. He has an incredibly versatile voice. *Godspell* is coming together, too."

"He's not my boy. Just a stray I helped out. Found him on the street, fed him a little milk in a saucer, sent him on his way. That's what you did for that kid from *42nd Street*, right?"

"Hm, Billy. Yeah. Hey, do you mind if I pour myself a drink?" Jericho stood up.

"Freshen me up, will ya?" Chris reached toward his half-filled glass, but withdrew his hand.

"Chris?" Jericho whispered.

"I'm here." He kept his eyes closed while Rusty sang on. He could see himself on stage. Was it him or was it Rusty? Was it '76? '96? Yesterday? Tomorrow? His playback blurred. Past performances. Chris in small titties, big titties. Bloomers, muumuus. Wigs everywhere. Stockings hanging over chairs. Naked men flowing in lines around him, doing the time step naked. Cocks and balls bouncing every which way while the audience applauded. Picasso's crazy women coming to life and doing Swan Lake with Degas' ballerinas. A nutcracker rode a two-headed llama as Dr. Doolittle sang "You're Nobody Till Somebody Loves You."

Jericho danced onto the stage with another handsome man. They flanked Chris as he sang a solo. "Life's a Bowl of Cherries." They tossed cherries out to the audience who clamored for them.

"Fuck me, Jerry. Harder. Harder," Chris whispered in a pant as Jericho Taylor pumped his cock into Chris' ass while the two gripped and held onto the dressing room hooks.

Another boy ran past in a jockstrap. "Come on, Jerry. We're on in a few seconds."

Jericho pushed hard and deep into Chris and came with an explosion.

He pulled out fast, bringing exquisite pain to Chris, and ran for the stage, while tucking his dripping dick into his jock strap.

"Jerry!" Chris called.

"I'm here." Jericho stroked Chris' sweating head. "I think we should call the doctor."

"I just had the craziest dream. We were at the old Tamburlaine. We were young and handsome. Remember?"

"I remember," Jericho breathed in a whisper. "You're burning up with fever. We should call the doctor."

Chris opened his eyes toward his friend. "No. The doctor said this would happen. There are drugs on the counter in the kitchen. I'm supposed to be taking these antibiotics and something else. Plus, the pain pills."

"Have you been taking them?" Jericho stood up.

"The pain pills. I can't remember about the others. Frank made me take something."

Jericho went to the kitchen and returned with two pills. "I'm going to get you a pill box so you can keep track of what you've taken. Got it?"

"Yes, Daddy."

"Please, you're older than me."

Chris swallowed the pills with bourbon.

"You should probably be taking those with water, not booze." Jericho took away the glass of bourbon, left the room, and returned with a tall glass of water.

Chris dutifully drank. "You should do a revival of *Hello, Dolly!* I've always loved that show. It's big. You could make all those boys dance and dance. I think I like that show because there are so many boys in it. All those waiters."

"Didn't you do a tour of that show?" Jericho asked, sitting down on the couch.

"No. I was offered a non-union bus and truck tour that stared Mimi Hines and Phil Ford. But, I got offered a lead at Tamburlaine at the same time. Jimmy was trying to keep me around. It worked out okay."

"I'll say. You ended up with the club and the loft." Jericho sounded perturbed.

"He offered them. I had the money and bought them. I made it happen. I kept the place open. You all took off. All of you. All the boys left and the queens were alone. Everyone died. Everyone left here and died. I lived. There wasn't anything else to be done."

They were at a familiar impasse. This had broken them up the first time.

"Chris, this was over twenty years ago. Nearly thirty," Jericho said.

Chris turned away. "Everyone died and you abandoned me."

"I didn't. I took a job. Jimmy was trying to screw all the boys. He wasn't paying us well. I got a better offer. I had to take the better job."

"Jerry, it was on a cruise ship in Hawaii. You just left. No goodbye. No letter. No fuck you. Nothing." Chris reached for his glass. Gone. He reached for the water, but withdrew his hand. "Oh, I'm tired. I really don't need to have my heart broken again and again by this same moment in my life."

"You're right. We can't keep having this argument. We've been fine all these years, so long as we don't spend more than an hour or two together. Times have changed. We're in business together. You have to let this go. Whatever it takes. You have to move on. Forgive me. Move into the present. Look toward the future."

"You make it all sound so easy. But, that's how it's always been for you, Jerry. You've always moved on easier than anyone else. You love them. Fuck them. Toss them aside."

Jericho said nothing. He looked hard into Chris' eyes.

"Nothing to say because it's true." Chris' feet hurt.

"It has been true. In the past. Yes. I've never been one for long-term commitments. There was a guy named Barry. Another blast from my past. It didn't work out."

"Oh, is that what I am, some twelve-step moment in your life?" Chris ached, but it wasn't his feet that hurt now.

"No. I just thought this would be fun to do. And, so far, it has been. I've always wanted to do something to revive Tamburlaine, to bring some of my past into the present. I got my start there like you did, like lots of guys did. It's an institution that should be saved from extinction. And, if we save you along the way, so much the better."

"Save me! Save me? Who the fuck do you think you are?" Chris wanted to throw something; to storm off; to stomp away. He couldn't. Instead, he sat with a sigh. "Wait. Don't say another word. I'm tired. I don't feel well. And, you're right. This is an ancient fight that we don't have to deal with today. Just go."

"I don't think you should be alone." Jerry reached for Chris' hand.

Chris tucked his hands under the afghan. "Despite this bad blood between us, I really do care for you. I like you, too. And, I'm not walking out on you. Not this time. We might not work as a couple and I think we've both found our ground with that. Let's see if we work as business partners. The personal shit, well, that's for moments like these, not moments at the club."

"I've never brought this up there. I won't. But, I still want you to leave."

"I'm going to the bathroom." Jericho stood up and left the room.

Chris hit the button, changed the CD, and Ella Fitzgerald sang "Someone to Watch Over Me." "The score of my life," he said to no one. He turned the machine off. A radiator banged.

Jericho returned. "Ingram will be here in a few minutes. He's going to spend the night with you. Keep an eye on you. Make sure you take your meds. Keep you off your feet."

"I really don't need a nursemaid."

"Tough shit. You've got one. Be nice to the boy. He loves you. And," Jericho came over to Chris, bent down, kissed the top of his head, "I do, too."

Twenty-three

With assistance, Chris took a seat at the rear of the house, just as the lights dimmed. The combo played a shortened version of the Dame's at Sea overture and the character Mona, played by a burly drag queen, stepped out and performed "Wall Street," including an extended tap break. His '30s dress split a side seam up to his left hip while he tap danced in size 13 heels. The audience went wild.

Number after number, genders swapped and switched; it was difficult at times keeping up with who played whom. Without the benefit of straight or gay couples, in a show where everything went, the nine characters gender bended their way into the hearts of the witnesses. By the end of Act II, folks were roaring their approval and stamping their feet because applause just wasn't loud enough.

The whole building reverberated. Which, mixed with a healthy dose of pain pills, had Chris in a jolly mood. At the end of the show, he waited for the others to exit. He didn't want to take a chance of being stepped on or falling on anyone.

He straightened his frock, checked his wig and makeup in his compact, and then simply watched the happy faces of the men and women streaming in slow motion out of the theater.

Chris sat until the stage lights came up. He watched Nancy Ann and two men in black clothing moving scenery and presetting for the midnight show.

Nancy Ann put her hands over her eyes and peered into the theater. "Mr. Marlowe, is that you?" She jumped off the stage and ran to his side where she knelt on the floor so they were eye to eye.

"Oh, Nancy Ann, it was a wonderful performance. A few cues seemed weird to me, but the show fits on our little stage perfectly. You young people did a very nice job."

"Thanks, Mr.—"

Chris held up a finger.

"...Chris. Has Jericho told you the plan?"

"Not sure. We've talked about so many things." He let her take his hand for a moment.

"We're going to be swapping roles every night. Everyone will have an opportunity to play every role."

"Well, I can't wait for that big old queen who played Mona to play the ingénue role of Ruby."

"Oh, Chris, it's a riot. You'll have to be sure to be here for that. And, I don't know if you noticed, but this chair you're in is yours. We've got a plaque on it and we've taken all the tickets out of the rack. This seat will be available at all performances just for you. No matter what is happening, you will always have a place to watch the show from. That was my idea."

"Well, Nancy Ann, you're very kind. I hope you'll let me buy you a drink tonight to thank you for your thoughtfulness."

"Of course."

"Nancy!" One of the crew boys called.

"I really do have to go back to work so we can get these boys out of here before we hit overtime." She patted Chris' hand a few more times and then bolted up to the stage.

Chris sat for a bit longer, watching them work on ladders, altering the lights. He knew, without a doubt, that so long as Nancy Ann was in charge, was The Tamburlaine Players' Stage Manager, that everything in this showroom would run like clockwork.

He couldn't help but remember his own performances in this space, but tonight's show altered that history. New memories filled his mind and that would take some of the burden off the older, dusty and threadbare memories.

Chris reached for his cane, used it and the chair in front of him to stand, regained a comfortable balance, and headed out into the edge of the dining room. He hated once again that the showroom let out in the dining room. They should be separated somehow, something for his Tamburlaine to-do list. That and renovating the restrooms. Once there was some money coming in, he'd get a contractor to offer some quotes.

He hobbled through the full dining room, out into the over-filled barroom. The Piano Player, while contemporary, played well. He was tinkling a modern melody, but somehow made it sound like something old-fashioned. Chris wound his way to his end of the bar. He couldn't bend his feet enough to gain the leverage to climb up and sit on his stool.

"What can I get for you, boss?" Frank asked.

"A bourbon. And a chair." While he waited for his drink, Ingram sidled up next to him.

"Hello, Chris." He held out a palm with several pills in it. "Don't give me any grief. Take your medicine like a good boy," he said good natured and a little silly about it.

Chris took the pills from Ingram; he downed them with the bourbon, pointed at the glass. Frank refilled it.

"Listen." Ingram's mouth was tight to Chris' ear, which sent a thrilling wave through Chris. "We've got a table for you right down front and to the side. You can sit there, enjoy cocktail service. And, when you're ready to play, it will be easy to get you up on stage." Ingram looked down at Chris' feet. "How are you...are you wearing bunny slippers? Actual bunny slippers?"

"What?" Chris turned his feet out, first one then the other. "Don't they go with my outfit?"

Ingram laughed.

"And, they'll help me remember without too much pain that I can't work the pedals. And, even better, they'll be funny. Go for the joke whenever possible. People haven't been overly morbid with me, and I don't want them to have too much of a chance."

"As you wish." Ingram took Chris by the elbow and gently led him to the table as one of the drag queen waiters mounted the stage and did a bold rendition of "Defying Gravity."

While Chris didn't usually enjoy the new music, he loved anything that empowered people and Steven Swartz did that with his music.

As Chris sat at his table, a parade of folks came and kept him company. Nancy Ann had her drink. Jericho arrived and spent a few minutes. Ingram checked in every twenty or thirty minutes, bringing drinks and food; at the proper intervals, he also brought medications. Finally, about midnight, with several men helping him up to the stage, Chris took his turn at the piano. As he began to play, people applauded. He made jokes. Worked the slippers. Sang Rusty Warren's sex songs and ballads. He kept the room riveted to him for over an hour, the audience following every word and musical note.

He congratulated the cast and crew as they continued to drink themselves silly. He thanked his partner Jericho. He mentioned Matilda and the restaurant. He reminded people to tip their waiters and bartenders. He closed with "Life is Just a Bowl of Cherries," and, with a little help, came down off the stage. He didn't sit, but instead, asked Ingram, who was on constant vigil, to call a cab to take him home. He was done for the night and others would have to see the evening through to the end. Chris hobbled to the door, not speaking to anyone, overcome with emotions.

Twenty-four

The cab dropped Chris at his door. He over-tipped the driver for the short trip before getting out. He stood on the street for a long time, the proud owner of a torched, scarred building. It was brick, so he knew the damage to be surface only. The flames had been extinguished quickly, so there wasn't much scorching.

He pushed hard to open the door, limped down the alley, and entered his kitchen. He downed a handful of pain killers before filling a bucket with hot, soapy water. After two trips, he managed to get the bucket and a scrub brush, along with the hose, out to the front and Chris started scrubbing. It wasn't long before his hands were red and raw; his clothes and slippers soaked. He felt no pain, felt nothing. So, he scrubbed.

Brick by brick Chris made his way from the highest blackened brick, barely at eye level. He scrubbed and scrubbed and rinsed. Brick by brick he rediscovered his sense of pride in his home. Brick by brick he found his anger at those who had thrown the bottles, at those who paid for them to do it, for those who poisoned him. Brick by fucking brick he released that anger as he scrubbed and rinsed until the building and door were cleaned. He left the mess on the sidewalk for others to take care of.

Chris stepped backward and contemplated his work under the bright light that cast a large, round shadow about him and then dumped the bucket of soot-stained water into the street. He got the hose inside the door and the pain crept up his legs, into his torso, until it exploded in his head. With effort, he navigated the alley, got into his home, and swallowed another group of pills.

Stripped, in the shower, he let the hot water rush over him, warm him. He wanted a joint, so that this over-drugged sensation might mellow. Chris couldn't remember if there was any pot in his home. It had been so long since he, or any of the boys he'd dated, had been open about smoking the drug.

"Chris? Chris!"

Chris didn't recognize the feminine voice calling him. For the second time that day, he couldn't find words.

"Chris?"

The voice came closer.

"Here," he squeaked out.

"Can I come in there?"

"Who?"

"Nancy Ann."

Chris leaned against the wall. "Yes, if you can take an old queen in the shower."

Nancy Ann came into the room. "How are you? The boys were worried about you, and I was the only one dispensable."

"So, the evening is going well?" Chris continued to let the water rush over him. "Any chance you have a joint on you?"

"In fact, I do. Want me to spark it?" She reached for her ever-present fanny pack.

"Well, first, I think I need to figure all of this out." Chris turned his head toward her.

"What is 'All of this'?"

"Well, I've taken a few painkillers. I've over done it from an energy standpoint. I've made a mess of my dressings. And, I'm naked."

"Okay. Let's get to work." Her voice low and calm, Nancy Ann reached into the shower and turned off the water; she began to hum something familiar, but Chris couldn't remember the song. Within an instant, she'd ushered Chris out of the shower, onto a soft rug and toweled him off, while encouraging him to help.

From the towels, she had him easily into a plush robe and ushered him toward the bed.

"No, living room."

She guided him down the hall until he stopped. Once inside, he turned on a light and sank onto a couch.

Nancy Ann got his feet up atop a pillow covered by a towel. She disappeared for a few moments, all the while humming. Was it "Unforgettable"? Chris felt his consciousness sink into the yielding sofa. She returned and masterly removed the sopping bandages, gently dried his feet, applied medication, and rewrapped his feet and legs like a medic. All the while, humming that song—that song the drag queen had been singing about flying... "Limited. Together we're unlimited..."

Once finished, the tea kettle whistled, as if she were calling the cue as easily as a travel spot or entrance on stage.

Chris, propped up with pillows around him and his afghan over him, sipped tea while Nancy Ann lit a joint and returned to humming her song. He took several long tokes, feeling the drug quickly enter his system. He melted deeper and deeper into the couch, first handing back the joint, then the tea cup.

Blackness and silence filled not only his head, but his whole being. Chris felt consciousness drift away.

Twenty-five

Chris woke on the couch with no immediate memory of how he'd gotten there or why he'd spent the night there. He generally abhorred sleeping on the sofa, and hated when others wanted to. His feet were elevated and felt better than they had since the attack. He contemplated the moment and instead of rushing into his day, he chose to lay there and enjoy the experience of feeling stronger.

His mind cleared and memories of Nancy Ann and a joint surfaced. Gently, he rolled into a sitting posture. He put a little weight on his feet, hardly any discomfort. He worked himself to the edge of the couch and stood. No wobble. Into the bathroom, peed. Into the kitchen, coffee on. The place was spotless, the day's papers on the table.

"Hello?" he called into the loft; no response.

Chris sat, drank coffee, and read the papers, his feet propped up on a kitchen chair. Without any motivations, he made his way through the thin, Saturday papers. There, on page twenty-seven of the Daily Post was a review of *Dames at Sea* and Tamburlaine. He couldn't believe his eyes. Next to Jericho's, his name was spelled correctly. "MARLOWE" Most folks left off the final "E." The show was a hit. The restaurant was a hit. The club was a hit. The concept was a success—Tamburlaine was now in the legitimate press. Jimmy always wanted that.

He wanted to call someone. He wanted to brag or gloat or something. But, Chris refrained. Now, there would be more people to hire. He remembered back to Tamburlaine's successful days, when he'd become a star. There would be nonstop phones ringing at the club and lines around the block and police escorts to make large cash deposits at the bank.

The black phone book on the table was open; Nancy Ann's number was penned in black Sharpie. He called her. Second ring she answered. "Thank you," he said.

"You're welcome, Mr. Marlowe."

Chris wanted to chastise her once more for the use of his last name, but she'd dried and dressed him like a child; he just couldn't. He liked the way she said his name, the deference and respect she offered. "I need to hire some people to help at the club. Is that something you can take care of?"

"Tell me what you need and you can consider it done."

They talked about a receptionist and security, a few additional drag waiters. He knew, when they hung up, that it would be taken care of. He called Matilda and told her to bring on whoever she needed in the kitchen and dining room. He called Frank about extra bartenders.

Tamburlaine had returned to the top of the heap. Chris knew from experience how fleeting this time might be. He also knew it could last for years, depending on the buzz and desire the company and the staff might generate.

The bell rang and he buzzed in whoever might be there without thought or concern. Jericho arrived in his kitchen and poured himself coffee and freshened Chris' cup.

"You're well? I was worried when you left so early last night."

In a playful tone, he said, "I watched the show, which was wonderful, and I played my set. What more do you want from me?"

"You've seen the reviews?" Jericho asked.

"Reviews? I've only seen the *Post*."

"New York One loved it. The other channels loved it, too. All the reviewers want comps to love it again."

"The *Times*?" Chris asked.

"Nothing yet." Jericho added milk to his cup before he sat. "So, the front looks good; the sidewalk needs attention. Did they come early this morning?"

"I did it." Chris turned the page of the newspaper without looking up.

"What? Are you insane?"

"Don't be melodramatic."

"What do you call cleaning a building at midnight in bandages?"

"And, bunny slippers. Don't forget the bunny slippers," Chris snapped. "It didn't feel melodramatic. It was drug induced. And, it's done. I feel great. Nancy Ann is a wonderful nurse."

"Nancy Ann? I'm confused."

"She came by, rescued me, got me settled, got me stoned..."

"Nancy Ann?" Jericho set his cup down.

"Yes, she's been a God send. She's been taking care of the show and me and Tamburlaine."

Jericho glared at Chris, who refused to blink first.

"What's the problem?" Chris asked.

Jericho looked away and then back at him.

"Why are you making that face?" Chris watched the subtle movements of Jericho's eyes and brow.

"I've just never known Nancy Ann to be nurturing. She's great with the shows. Anything you need there. But, she's never really been great with people. It took me years to get her to open up about anything, her personal life, or anything outside of the theater."

"Well, she's been very committed to me. And, devoted to Tamburlaine. I can't remember how she worded it, but she said that she felt a kinship with the club, like coming in there she'd come home. Her words and attitude reminded me of Jimmy's lover. You know, that guy who died really early during the AIDS crises, before it was even called AIDS."

"Oh, shit, yeah. What was his name. No, it was two names, like Jimmy Bob or Chester Jason or...shit. I can't remember. He was that really tall, incredibly skinny boy. Very seventies. Always with the roller skates on."

"Yeah, that's him."

Both focused, trying to remember the guy's name, but neither of them could find it.

"God, we're getting old. Can't remember some fool's name." Chris closed the paper and pushed it away. "Anyway, that's what her tone reminded me of. He was always there at Tamburlaine. Always involved. Very protective. Like there was gold under the floors or something."

"Whatever that means." Jericho got up and refilled his cup. He held the pot toward Chris, who shook his head. "So, you seem to be doing better today."

"Gold dust sifted between the floorboards. Never seen *Paint Your Wagon*? Anyway, Nancy Ann gave me tea and got me way stoned. I slept solid through the night and into the late morning. Woke up feeling good."

"So, you'll be there today?"

"Not for the show, but I'll be there for my set. We're going to be swamped after these reviews. I've added phone support and more staff. And, there will be security tonight, too. The line should be around the block."

Jericho sat at the table. "Just take it easy. No heels, okay?"

"Yeah. And, I ruined my slippers last night, so I might come barefooted."

"I'm sure you've got something else festive to wear. It's Saturday night, will you pull out the big guns?" Jericho laughed as he cupped his hands around imaginary breasts on his chest.

"No, not until I can balance them with heels."

The two passed the next hour kibitzing and talking about renovating restrooms. Chris wanted to spit and release the possibility of the Evil Eye, but just kept going with the conversation. Tamburlaine was once again a sensation. Life was good and there was no tempting fate about that.

Twenty-six

"Chris, what opens tonight?"

"Hm?" Chris, engrossed in an article about the terrorists' return to activity in New Jersey, about the use of Molotov cocktails to set off the series of explosives. He wondered if it could be possible that he was being targeted by terrorists? The reality of that, the chance of that, seemed impossible.

"The show," Frank began, phone held to his chest. "What show opens tonight?"

"Oh…*Ain't Misbehavin'* at midnight."

"Still doing *Dames at Sea* before that, right?"

"Yep." Chris closed the paper, slid off his stool, and headed to the kitchen. Matilda prepared chicken parm again tonight, his favorite, and he wouldn't take a chance of not getting a portion. 150 covers a night, selling out, night after night. The kitchen was making money. The bar was making money. The theater was on the verge of repaying the initial investment. Tamburlaine was awash in cash and success. The reviews continued to pour in. Bloggers loved the place. #Tamburlaine was all over Twitter, or so Ingram said—Chris didn't understand all of this internet stuff, but the young people got excited about it.

"Are you wearing actual shoes?" Matilda asked as Chris hoisted himself up on the stool.

"I am. They're not heels, but they are shoes."

"I'll miss the array of slippers you've been wearing. It was becoming something of a signature for you." She heaped extra sauce atop the plate.

"Oh, I can't eat all that," said Chris. He knew she knew it wasn't true, but he appreciated her not contradicting him. "Anyway, slippers are not the statement I ever want to make my own." He cut up the cutlet and ate a bite. "By far, the best ever."

"Thanks, boss." Matilda gave instructions to two girls who went about cutting veggies.

"Is there anything you want or need that we haven't given you?" Chris wiped sauce from his chin.

"No, it's all good. I'm thinking about two more busboys and another dishwasher, but no real rush there." She stayed busy.

"Well, whatever you need. It's your kitchen, run it. Hear me?" Chris and Matilda nodded, acknowledging each other. He finished his meal while watching the collection of line cooks and prep chefs prepare the meal for the night. They were all women and all of them seemed slightly not "normal." Not in an offensive way, but they all seemed a bit battered or put together wrong. Yet, each of them worked nonstop, taking their marching orders from Matilda and executing as requested. They were selling out of food night after night. He wasn't complaining or judgmental about anything. He cleaned up the remaining sauce with a piece of bread.

Chris slid off his stool, thanked Matilda, and headed into the dining room. Every expertly set table glistened in the soft lighting. He walked toward the office and changed his mind. The bills could wait. Instead, he headed into the theater. The small crew was setting the stage, working the backdrops and scrims, shouting numbers and instructions to each other. He took his seat in the corner and watched them work. He liked observing. They all seemed so talented and so open and comfortable. Each of them was playful and fun. Everyone was respectful of everyone else.

As they worked, a brick shithouse of a man came out in a women's "Star Tar" costume, with all the sequins and American bravado a dress can hold. He sat on the ground, stretched out a bit, and then worked his splits, both legs, shifted right front, then left. He stood and began singing softly to himself, tap dancing, hand movements with feet. He dropped into the splits, still singing, rolled, and was up.

"Perfect, Jacob. You're going to be wonderful tonight as Ruby." Nancy Ann came out onto the stage. "Just remember to hit this mark." She tapped a spot on the floor. "This is your light. It's always your light. Whenever you're on stage, in general, if you don't know where to go, hit this mark and you'll be lit. If you need anything, look easily to me, and I'll feed you the line. Got it?"

"Nancy Ann, you're the best," Jacob said before turning to the stage and beginning the number again. Then, he stopped. "Nancy?" he whispered.

"Sorry, can't do the dance for you. Haven't been able to do a split in years."

"Nancy Ann, is that Mr. Marlowe?"

She looked out into the house with a hand above her eyes. "Yes, it is. Hello, Mr. Marlowe," she called.

"Hello young people. Jacob is it?" The guy nodded. "You look good from here. Hit those splits and the audience will forgive and forget everything else that happens."

"Splits? Oh, you mean the dead fall. Yes, sir. Thank you, Mr. Marlowe."

Chris could remember a time when he, too, could drop into a split. They'd done a cancan number and he learned to drop on a beat. If he hit the floor now, he'd never get up again. "Remember, after the show, to come down to my reserved table and I'll buy you a drink. Everyone who plays Ruby gets a free drink."

"Doesn't everyone working here drink for free, Mr. Marlowe?" Nancy Ann said, playfully.

Chris played along. "That doesn't mean I don't enjoy a handsome drag queen sitting at my table while I perform." The drugs helped him feel like his youthful self.

"You're a tramp, Mr. Marlowe," Nancy Ann continued.

"Bet your ass I am." Chris stood up. "Keep up the good work."

"Yes, sir," they said together as Chris left the room.

The bar lighting was set for the evening. The mirror ball already spun. There were a few people sitting at the tables. Chris made his way to the stage and one of the men waiting nearby applauded. It was the developer, Norton Folgate.

Chris said: "What are you doing here? I didn't think we were your type of people, Mr. Folgate?"

"It's a free country, and I came in to see what all the hubbub was about." He drank off his glass of booze.

"Well, it may be a free country, but I own this little corner and have the right to refuse service to anyone. I want you out of here. I don't like you. I don't trust you. And, I don't want you in Tamburlaine ever again. Consider yourself banned."

"That's no way to talk to your neighbor."

"Rocko!" Chris called toward the bar. A linebacker of a man with muscles for days appeared. Why were guys like this always named Rocko or Slugo? But, they were. Chris had never met a bouncer named Elliot or Roger. "Please show Mr. Folgate and his friend the door. They are no longer welcome here, ever."

"As you wish." The big man turned. "Please come with me. The house will pick up whatever tab you might have at the bar."

Folgate and his companion didn't move. Rocko stepped closer to the table.

"You don't scare me. There's nothing you can do to me." Folgate still hadn't stood up.

Rocko took another step toward them. Folgate's companion stood and headed for the door. Folgate didn't move. Rocko reached for his arm.

"I'm warning you, if you don't want to be sued, you'll not touch me."

"Sir, I'll ask you one more time to stand up and leave the premises."

Police sirens could be heard outside. Folgate looked at Chris, then at Rocko, but still he didn't move.

Rocko wrapped a meaty paw around Folgate's arm, and with a quick, well-practiced move, Folgate was on his feet. Rocko's hand grasped Folgate's wrist, pinning his arm behind his back, and he steered the man expertly toward the door. One solid thrust and the door popped open, released Folgate to the street, and Rocko, also on the street, closed the door behind him. The sirens stopped, but the red and blue lights still flashed.

The others who sat quietly at the tables applauded. Chris made his way to the stage, sat behind the piano, and played "Get Happy." On the third chorus, Chris sang the lyrics. He felt good and enjoyed getting to once again manipulate the pedals of the piano. It was going to be a good night.

More folks filled the room: Some waiting for dinner, others early for the first show, and still others happy to have an opportunity to sit in the barroom. Chris launched into a Rusty Warren routine about kids, a divine trucker on the highway, and sex. Always sex. The audience ate it up.

Twenty-seven

Chris, in his office at Tamburlaine, pecked with his index fingers at the little buttons on the keypad.

Two in the afternoon on a Monday. The club closed on Mondays, but Matilda and a few of her team were busy in the kitchen, cleaning, restocking, and accepting deliveries. He could hear them laughing.

The computer beeped at Chris.

"Now what, you stupid machine?" Chris said aloud while entering figures in an accounting program on the new laptop computer.

"Did you say something?" asked Nancy Ann

Startled, Chris turned to the doorway. "Just talking to myself. I do that. Hold on." He turned to the computer, hit the send button, and the confirm button, and logged off the program. "Hello, dear. What are you doing here, it's your day off. Don't any of you people take a day off?"

"When you work for Jericho Taylor, you rarely get an actual day off. There's always something to do or something to check. And, as always, he was right. Two of the lights have frayed cords. We need to replace those lights, and he said to see you about getting a check. We don't have credit established with the supply company."

"Here, sit."

Nancy Ann came further into the office and sat in the solid chair next to Chris' desk. "I just love that Picasso. You know, I spent time in France and Spain. I've been to his museums and read all the books there are on the man. I've never seen this one before."

"Well, if you know so much about Picasso, then you probably know that he created thousands and thousands of works. Paintings, sculptures, drawings."

"Of course."

"Not all of them have been photographed or featured somewhere. Only pieces that are part of large museum collections or part of museum shows have fully been documented. This work has been on this wall since just after he painted it in the late '60s. Someone gave it to the man who opened Tamburlaine; when he died, he left it to me, along with a few others."

"You have others?" Nancy Ann turned, shocked, toward Chris.

"Come on, let's get out of here. We'll go view some art and then we'll buy your lights." Chris took up his cane and used it to stand.

"You're getting around better." Nancy Ann stood, too. "Do you mind if we buy the lights first?"

"Wow, Jerry has you trained."

"You call him." She lowered her voice. "You call him *Jerry*?" She laughed.

"I knew your Mr. Taylor before he became The Great. I knew him as a beautiful, usually shirtless dancer who backed up drag queens here at Tamburlaine."

"That's not on his Wikipedia page."

"His wikiwhat?"

"Wikipedia. It's a giant, endless online encyclopedia."

Chris pointed to the computer. "Show me."

Nancy Ann deftly hit buttons and arrived at a screen that said in big, bold letters: "No Connection." "You need an internet connection for us to get there." She pulled out her cell phone and tapped at the little screen. She turned the results toward Chris.

"Look, there's his name." He read through the information. "Nope, no mention of Tamburlaine. Do you think I'm on there?"

"Let's see." Nancy Ann searched for Christopher Marlowe. "Sorry, only the poet comes up."

"Oh, him. He's been haunting me my whole life." Chris was disappointed not to be listed, even though he'd only this moment heard of this wiki place.

"Hmm. He wrote a play called Tamburlaine...but it's not about a drag bar in New York City."

"And, I certainly don't want to talk about that stupid play."

"May I ask you a question?"

"Of course," said Chris. He hit the power button and closed the laptop.

"Your name and the play's name, it's an odd thing that a..."

"Very few drag queens use their own names."

"But, your name isn't something campy or silly, like Hedda Lettuce or

Marsha Dimes or Sharon Needles. I'd think you'd have become Rusty Nail or Game Warden or some other clever take on Rusty Warren."

A sense of nostalgia rose in Chris. "My name, and the bar's name, were birthed the same, stoned night. A handsome, kind man christened us both. Being hopelessly in love with someone can change your life, even if he's not...and.... I don't..."

"But, wasn't it Tamburlaine when you arrived here?"

"I don't want to talk about this anymore."

"I didn't mean to upset you." There were tears in Nancy Ann's eyes.

"Oh, dear. I'm fine." He patted her arm. "Come, let's take care of your lights."

The two stopped in the kitchen.

"Matilda!" Chris called. She thumped to the bottom of the stairs. "I'm stepping out. You and your team are the only ones here, so be sure to lock the door when you leave, okay?"

"Of course, Mr. Marlowe." She smiled sweetly at her boss.

"Okay, let's go shopping," said Chris.

Nancy Ann held the door and then pushed it closed tightly. The two headed to the street. The sun warm, the sky a romantic fall blue. Nancy Ann blew her taxi whistle and a yellow cab appeared, as if by magic.

"Well, that was wonderful," said Chris. "Maybe I should carry a rape whistle, too."

She laughed. "I'll get you one." She held the door for him and he climbed in. "No skooching. Just sit." She went around the cab and got in on the street side. Once settled, Nancy Ann gave the driver the address, and they rode in silence for a while.

"So, are you doing what you love?" Chris asked.

"Stage managing? I guess. I do like it a lot. I love working with Jericho. We've been doing shows together for years. He treats me well. Pays me bonuses under the table. It's a pretty good life."

"You didn't really answer my question."

"Well, love seems so strong when it comes to describing work. Do you love what you do?"

"I love to perform. I cope with the details, paying bills, hiring people, all of that. But, because I have my own club, I have Tamburlaine, I always have a place to play the piano for a crowd. Granted the past few years, the crowd has been a bit small, but still..."

They were silent as the cab pulled up in front of the address, a building covered with graffiti.

"Where have you brought me?" Chris asked. "Can you wait for us?"

"Yes, sir," said the cab driver.

Nancy Ann jumped out and opened Chris' door. The two went into the store, purchased the new lights, and Chris put a credit card on file so Nancy Ann could get whatever she needed for Tamburlaine.

Their cab driver, now on the street, smoked a cigarette, talked to another cabbie. He opened the trunk and the store staff loaded lights into it. He held doors open for his passengers, tossed his cigarette into the street, and got in smelling of smoke.

Chris took a deep breath. "So, let's take these lights to the club, then we'll walk to my place. Are you ever going to answer my question?"

"What question?" Nancy Ann peered out the windows.

"About doing what you love." Chris maintained his pleasant, easy tone.

"What about food? Do you need groceries?"

"Avoidance?" Chris let it drop. "Oh, my pantry is stocked or we can stop for something, have food delivered, or get Matilda to..."

They pulled up to the club and there were two fire trucks, one on the street and one in the alley. Matilda stood on the street, along with two others dressed in chef's jackets. Their faces were smudged with soot.

"What on earth?" Chris was out of the cab before it had fully stopped. He left his cane behind. "Matilda, what the hell happened?"

"I don't know. We had just finished loading a meat delivery into the big cooler downstairs. Came up and the kitchen was ablaze. We got it before the sprinklers came on, so that was good. And, Tilly pulled the fire alarm. The men were here in minutes. They're checking the place out to see if it's safe to go back inside."

Chris wanted to hug Matilda, but didn't know where to put his hands and arms to get them around the woman. "Were any of you hurt?"

"No, not really. I burned my hand a little." She held up a hand bandaged as big as a baseball mitt. "I think the other girls are fine. Just shaken up."

A tall, handsome man in his forties came up to them. "Miss, we're sure everything is fine. The damage limited to the kitchen. Someone cut a gas line, but we think it ignited faster than they expected."

"A gas line?" Chris asked. "What the hell is going on?"

"Who are you, sir?" asked the fireman.

"I'm Christopher Marlowe, the owner of Tamburlaine." He spoke with defiance. He felt proud of that statement for the first time in ages. "So, you think someone started—"

"Someone did start this," the fireman said. "No question there. I don't think you're dealing with an expert."

"Well, there's something to be said for that." Chris thought of Folgate and resolved never to give in to his tactics.

The fireman asked Chris and Matilda questions. Small crowds gathered and dispersed. The police arrived. They spread yellow Caution tape. Asked questions. A report filed. The all clear determined, they removed the tape.

Once they were given permission to enter the club, Matilda and Nancy Ann both made calls. Within an hour there was a full crew cleaning not only the kitchen, but every square foot of the club. By the end of the evening, the smell of smoke was barely noticeable and the crew were all enjoying dinner and beers in the dining room.

Another close call, thought Chris as he sat in his office, alone, drinking bourbon. All this fire and destruction. Impossible not to think of Norton Folgate as the perpetrator of these threats and crimes, but, also difficult to think of him being so inept.

Chris filled his glass and said to the *Streetwalkers*: "Does Folgate believe that if Tamburlaine burned down I'd sell? Would I sell?" He drank off the bourbon. "I don't know." That response caused a sadness deep within. He'd kept Tamburlaine going for decades over a promise, but if it were physically gone, would there be any reason to rebuild. That wasn't part of the pact. He looked deep into the Picasso. If the place was truly being attacked, actually under threat, the painting should be removed. Its loss would be devastating.

Twenty-eight

Chris, in his kitchen, alone, eating Chinese food, jumped when his bell rang. The monitor showed Nancy Ann smiling into the camera. He buzzed her in. He continued to watch the screen as she shoved the door closed with a bang and then kicked it. He turned on the patio twinkle lights and walked outside to meet her.

"Come toward the light," he whispered.

Nancy Ann laughed nervously. "Hello?"

"Walk down the alley and you'll be in the light." Chris smiled. No one ever came to visit anymore, unless they were on health watch. It had been ages since he'd had company that didn't involve a stray.

"Hello!" said Nancy Ann. Her eyes sparkled as she did a small twirl around the patio, now lit with colored twinkle lights. "What a great space."

"Thank you. Sadly, it's a bit too cold to sit outside. Come in."

"No, I just wanted to bring this to you." Nancy Ann held out Chris' cane. With all that happened today, you must have forgotten it."

He took the cane. "Thanks. That's incredibly kind of you. Please, come in? It's very cold here." He shuddered involuntarily.

"Of course." She stepped inside and turned. "Oh, I'm interrupting your dinner. I should go."

"Oh, nonsense. It's just take-out Chinese. There's General Tso's chicken, beef and broccoli, sesame noodles, fried rice. Plenty of food. I insist you join me?"."

"No, I won't eat your dinner."

Chris thought he heard her stomach grumble. "Nonsense. There's plenty of food. Sit." She did as told and he got out a plate and cutlery. "Beer?" He held up the bottle.

"Tsingtao? Really? I would love some. I did a tour of the Far East, years and years ago. We drank a lot of this in Singapore one night. These big bottles. A concrete table in a Satay Club. A very humid summer night.

So many bottles the perspiration from them ran like a river off our table."

While she told the story, he poured her a glass of beer and added more to his own. She ignored the fork and spoon and picked up the chopsticks instead. She pulled them out of their wrapper, separated them, rubbed the ends together to remove any splinters, and dug into the noodles. Chris relished her energy and style. And, for a few moments, they sat and ate together.

"Oh, sorry. I guess I should use a plate, too." Nancy blushed crimson.

"No, it's fine by me. One less dish to wash." He continued to eat and drink and watch the beautiful woman. There was something about her cheekbones that seemed familiar, but he couldn't place it. "So is everything okay at Tamburlaine?"

"Everything there is fine. I just felt like our time together today wasn't finished. I was worried about you, Chris. I wanted to make sure you were okay."

"Oh, I'm fine. I just keep hobbling through. It was nice spending time with you today, too. I like that I've made your life a little easier."

"How's that?" She stopped eating, chopstick's poised, noodles dripping into the carton.

"By leaving my credit card at the light store."

"Of course, yes. Thank you for that. I did want to talk to you about upgrading the system. The lights and the sound are a bit, well, old."

"Oh, is that what you—"

"No, that wasn't why I came. I've spoken to Jericho about the systems. He said once we were making a little money, he...you...that the investment would make more sense." She shoved noodles in her mouth.

"He's very practical. You should write up an estimate and a plan. That way we can put it in the budget."

Chris wished he'd ordered the dumplings, even though there was plenty of food still on the table. He enjoyed the chicken, pushing red peppers off to the side, waiting for Nancy Ann to broach whatever subject she was here to discuss.

"Chris, I was hoping we could continue our talk about art. You were going to show me something earlier today and I didn't want you to think that I wasn't interested."

"Oh, you're very kind to remember. It has been a long day."

Nancy Ann dropped her chopsticks on the table. "Stuffed."

"Good. I like when young people are full." He began cleaning up the cartons and debris. Nancy Ann helped by quickly washing the dishes and silverware and placing them in the drying rack. Chris filled both their glasses with more beer. "Well, I would be happy to show you what I had in mind if you'll answer the unanswered question." He examined the girl's eyes.

"What question?"

"You've been running scared from telling me what you would love to be doing. It's clearly not being a stage manager, even though you like that job and it's been good to you." Chris sipped his beer; foam tickled his nose.

"Oh, Chris, I never talk about this anymore. I avoid it, actually. There isn't room for what ifs. I'm a very good stage manager. I meet interesting people. I make good money doing it. And, I like it. Some would say that's a lot."

"I would agree with them. That is a lot. But, what is it you would love to be doing?"

She stalled, avoiding eye contact. Chris reached over and with a single finger, raised her head until they were eye-to-eye. Nancy Ann's were wet and red with tears.

"Oh, my dear, it was not my intention to upset you." It felt awkward to be standing in the middle of the clean kitchen. "Come with me." He led her to the living room and they sat down. He opened a stone box on the coffee table and produced a joint. "Shall we?"

Nancy Ann nodded and together the two shared it, enjoying the smoke's effects almost from the first puff. While she hit the joint again, Chris turned on music. Rusty Warren sang "Does He Love Me?"

"Who's this?" Nancy Ann asked as she exhaled smoke toward the ceiling. "God, this is really good pot."

"It's Rusty Warren. One of the greatest comediennes of all time. She won entertainer of the year several times in Las Vegas in the '70s."

"Another great performer I've never heard of." Nancy Ann passed the joint to Chris.

"Well, we can't be expected to know everyone. Personally, I don't think I know a single popular singer of today. Well, there's that gaga girl. When I was a girl, we were gaga over boys."

"Stop." Nancy Ann laughed at the joke.

"And, there's that bouncy girl. I think I've heard the company talk about her."

"Beyoncé," Nancy Ann corrected through laughter.

"Well, in my youth, we were listening to Sinatra and Sammy, the Rat Pack. Brenda Lee and Ethel Merman." Chris leaned back, enjoying the wave of ease the drug brought over him.

"Did you know her?"

"Who?" Chris turned his head. "Ethel Merman?"

His guest had laid her head against the back of the couch, too. "Merman" Nancy Ann burst into a rendition of "There's No Business Like Show Business" in a gruff, mimic of Ethel Merman.

Chris laughed. "Not bad. No. I met her a few times, but we queens, well, we were seriously underground in those days. All the queers were. Sure, there was Stonewall in the '60s, those drag queens fighting back against the police raids; a whole weekend of a neighborhood fighting the police right in the middle of Greenwich Village. They get credit for the modern gay rights movement, but there were fags all over the country pushing back in their own way: San Francisco, New Orleans, LA, Chicago. Even with the flower power and all that, we kept ourselves fairly well hidden on a general basis. I never did meet Rusty Warren, either. I saw her shows many times here in New York, in Boston, even in Las Vegas. But, some of her jokes were anti-hippie, anti-counter culture, anti-gay. Of course, that was her audience, straight, working-class, broads and their husbands. Listen to me ramble."

"It's all fascinating."

"Well, that must mean you're stoned. Me caterwauling about the past is not fascinating. Come with me." Chris stood up and offered Nancy Ann a hand.

"Where are you taking me, kind sir?" She giggled.

"I have something to show you." He led her toward the stairs. "Wait." Chris stopped at the first step. "You never answered my question before. What is it you'd love to do?"

She only hesitated a moment. "Paint. I've always wanted to study painting. I've always wanted to travel Italy and visit Paris. I want to see the work of the great masters. I've always wanted to learn from extraordinary, talented people. But, it hasn't worked out. I've painted some. I set up a studio for myself. Bought canvas, paints. I watched videos on YouTube. I just don't seem to have the talent. And, so, I visit the Met and MoMa. I look at the works of others and wish and dream." Nancy Ann stopped speaking; tears dripped down her cheeks.

Chris stepped toward her and handed the girl a hanky from his pocket. She wiped her eyes and blew her nose.

"Thank you," she said, eyes cast down to the floor, her face red.

"I'm sorry. I just kept getting the feeling that you had something else to do with your life. I feel like there's a step or two you've gone off your path. Or something like that."

"So, what do you want to show me?" Nancy Ann sounded a little angry.

"Well, here goes. It's been a long time since I've invited anyone up here, but I feel like you're someone who will appreciate it." Chris led the way up the wooden stairs. They were well-polished and creaked under their steps. All along the wall, like a gallery, were paintings. Monet. Renoir. Picasso. Brueghel. Pollack. Rothko. Warhol. Degas. On and on the list went. Master after master. Periods merged and divided. As they walked the gallery, Chris flipped light switches. Each work had its own spotlights. The colors brilliantly illuminated. The brush strokes visible.

"Are these all…" Nancy Ann moved from painting to painting.

"Yes. Friends left them to me. I've added some, too."

"Chris, you've got millions, maybe hundreds of millions of dollars in art here."

"Yes." All the lights were lit. Chris sat in a leather, high-back chair. He watched as Nancy Ann moved from picture to picture. She reached up to touch an O'Keeffe, but pulled her hand back. "Go ahead," Chris encouraged, but she didn't reach up again.

"Why have you showed me these?" Nancy dropped down to her knees in the middle of the room.

"I wanted to share them with someone who would appreciate them. I've seen the way you admire the Picasso in the office every time you come in there. It seems like sometimes you come in with a made up excuse just to look at the picture."

"Guilty. I do. It's brilliant. All of this is brilliant. How does a normal person end up with all of these?"

Chris didn't respond.

He wanted to joke about "normal," but didn't want to laugh at the moment.

Nancy Ann rubbed her eyes, as if this might be a dream, and then took in the room more fully, scooting across the floor like a small child. Rusty sang below them, "You're Never too Old to be Young," contributing to the surreal scene.

Chris broke the moment, pulled a joint from behind his ear, and lit it. He breathed deep the pungent, fragrant smoke. After a few moments, Nancy Ann took the reefer from his hand and hit it hard, holding the smoke for a long time.

"You're welcome to visit them any time you want. You just can't tell anyone they're here. That's all I ask." Chris took the joint and drew several more short drags of smoke deep into his lungs. He'd been quite stoned the first time he'd seen this art collection, too. Stoned, and naked, and having his cock sucked.

Stoned was the best he could do for Nancy Ann. It was her turn to be silent.

Twenty-nine

From his chair in the back of the house, Chris watched the *Little Shop of Horrors* rehearsal, taking his own set of notes for later.

"Cut!" Jericho shouted. The house was so small, his voice traveled throughout the whole building. "Urchins, what the fuck is taking so long? You have forever for this costume change. On stage now!"

Two of the boys playing two of the urchins came on stage, neither fully dressed. The dresses were simply too small for their manly frames. The third urchin, a black dyke with a boy's haircut, swam in her dress.

Jericho fell out laughing. It was, of course, obvious that the three of them had ended up with each other's dresses. "Take ten. Nancy Ann, get this fixed." He heard the ripping of tape; those dresses were about to have names taped in them. He turned to leave and saw Chris sitting in his spot in the back row.

"I think it's going well," said Chris as Jericho walked up to him.

"I do, too. This might be the most difficult show we ever do here."

"I do like the Plexiglas walls and flower shop counters. It certainly opens up the stage."

"Saw something like that in a summer stock production years and years ago." Jericho stepped over Chris and sat down next to him. "You're happy?"

"How could I not be happy? Sold out, two shows a night. Full barroom. People drinking, tipping well. Full restaurant every night. Matilda said they're up to a hundred fifty covers a night, plus the cast and crew. Amazing. It's like we've turned back the clock."

"Except the shows are good." Jericho poked Chris in the side and laughed.

"Our shows had their own charm then."

The trio—piano, bass, and drums—started playing "Somewhere That's Green."

"The band sounds good." Chris was pleased to be giving musicians jobs.

"It's pretty tight up there, but they're managing. At least we have high ceilings."

"Building that platform, perfect. Somewhere to put the band, and somewhere to hide the plant," said Chris. "You're very good at this."

"Just now figuring that out."

The two men were holding hands in a friendly way. "Are you hungry? We're going to have to end this rehearsal soon. *Ain't* starts in an hour." Chris leaned in toward Jericho.

"Okay. Let's get this one cue and we'll end the evening." Jericho stood up, climbed over Chris, and walked up to the front of the house.

"Let's go. From where we stopped. "Ya Never Know.""

Together, Jericho, Nancy Ann, and Chris watched the four actors get through the song. It required more work, better choreography. But, they made it through. Obviously, they'd reached that point, the moment where a company goes into overload. Too many shows in their heads.

"Okay." Jericho clapped his hands when the number ended. Everyone on stage." The company assembled. "We'll get through this. Tomorrow at noon. And, tonight, have a bite to eat and I want each of you to run your numbers in front of the bar audience. The band, no The Piano Player and bass player will play for you."

"What about me?" the drummer asked.

"If you want to move your kit or your snare, go for it," said Jericho. "That's it. See you tomorrow. No notes. Just learn your songs and your lines between now and tomorrow." He turned and walked out of the theater without another word. Chris could tell, Jericho was not happy.

Chris slipped out the rear of the theater, skirted the dining room, and walked quietly through the kitchen to the alley. There, he discovered several of the actors passing a joint around. Chris endeavored to slip past them unnoticed, but they acknowledged their producer. The smallest of the boys, the one currently holding the joint, cupped the smoking length in his hand.

"No need to attempt subterfuge, dear boy," said Chris with a smile. "It was a rough one tonight."

"You got that right."

"Well, difficult techs mean good performances." He turned to go. "No more smoking in your costumes, got it?"

"Yes, sir."

Chris walked down the alley to the street. He contemplated a cab, but decided to walk. It was the first time since the attack. He'd walked a block when he heard footsteps racing up behind him. He contemplated his options, thought about his cane, realized he didn't have it, and remembered once again that he was a slow, old man. So, he turned.

"Chris!" Jericho raced up behind him. "I was waiting for you in the bar, but you didn't come out. I finally went searching for you and the kids said you'd left."

"Well, you pushed The Piano Player onto my stage, so I thought I'd call it a night."

It did seem to Chris, because of Jericho's awkward stance, that Jerry wanted to say something, or talk about something, but he wasn't forthcoming.

Chris said: "Jerry, it's chilly. Do you want me to come back to the club?"

"No." Still, he said no more.

"Shall we go somewhere else? Do you want to talk?" Chris pulled his shawl tighter around his shoulders.

"No. I don't want to go to a club. How about your place?"

"Fine."

Silence.

They hadn't been alone together on the street since the bomb. Chris busied his mind: he wondered about the backdrops and scrims for *Little Shop*. He thought about the nightly transition to *Ain't Misbehavin'*. He was curious where the giant Audrey II would live during the off weeks when other shows were being performed. He held his tongue and walked, hoping that the two of them wouldn't once again be attacked.

Chris turned the key and pushed hard to open the door. Since the fire and the cleaning and the colder weather, the door was even more difficult. Once inside, he waited and slammed the metal door behind them and then led the way up the alley. It was dark and cold. But, within a moment more, they were inside the warm loft.

"Cocktail? Beer?" he asked, tossing his wrap aside on the chair.

"Beer." Jericho scrutinized the cat clock. "I can't believe you still have this after all these years."

He handed a beer to Jerry and poured himself a glass of bourbon. It all felt so easy and repetitive. "I've had to have him fixed twice."

"You mean neutered?"

Chris chuckled at the joke. "Come on in the other room. It's warmer there. Since I've gotten older, the cold bothers me more and more. The past few winters I've thought about retiring to Florida or Arizona."

Chris sat in his spot, Jericho chose one across from him. Chris waited, sipping his drink. Jericho nervously set his beer down, picked it up, didn't drink, set it down again. Chris said nothing; he'd decided this conversation was on Jericho. He didn't like the way this great director was treating the cast. He didn't like the way he burst in and out of rooms. It was as if he'd forgotten where he'd come from, his past and how poorly they'd all been treated when they first started working together at Tamburlaine. Now, Jericho was just like one of those asshole choreographers from back then.

"What did you say to Nancy Ann," Jericho finally said.

"What?"

"The stage manager. She said she's spent some time with you." Jericho again picked up his beer and set it down without drinking.

"We did spend some time together. I went with her to pick up the new lights. I set up credit for her at that shop. We were together when the gas line.... That's what we returned to that afternoon."

"But, there was more?" Veins bulged on Jericho's forehead and in his neck, his face red.

"We've spent some time together. She's very nice. She helped me when I needed it. She's running our shows. We've spent time together." Chris sipped more bourbon. "What has you all worked up?"

"Nancy Ann is mine. She works for me. She's worked for me for years. She's opened all my hit shows. You need to step away from her."

"Jerry, I don't understand. You brought her in to work at Tamburlaine. I didn't even know her before she served me that first drink." Chris' glass was empty and he stood up.

"Where the fuck are you going?" Jericho stood up, too.

"Another drink." Chris turned and left the room. He filled his glass and returned to the living room with the bottle and sat down.

Jericho was still standing where he'd been left.

"Jerry, I don't understand what has you so upset."

"She's resigned."

"From Tamburlaine?" Chris was truly disheartened at the thought of losing her.

"No, from me, from my production company. She said she'll only be working at Tamburlaine."

"Well, that's good. You'll still be near her. And, when she's ready to step into your Broadway shows—"

"It's all so easy for you, Chris, isn't it?" Jericho slammed his bottle down, causing foam and beer to pour over the mouth. Jericho ignored the spill. "You just go with the flow. Your shows are up and running. Your club is making money. You have an audience once again for your ridiculous act." Jericho began pacing.

"My what? Who the—"

"You heard me."

Chris backed down. He wanted to wipe up the spilled beer, but instead, he kept his focus on Jericho. "It's our shows, Jerry. We're both making money from this company. We're sold out for weeks and booked ahead for months. It's going exactly as we planned."

Jericho paced and then stopped. "You can't have her. I can't replace her."

"Jerry, I really don't understand."

"I don't understand. I don't understand. I don't understand. You sound like a fucking broken record."

Chris sat silent; sipped his bourbon. He'd been here before: An angry man desiring a punching bag. He'd been beaten before, by thugs on the street and street trash in his home. He'd been beaten and bullied; he'd survived a Molotov cocktail. He wasn't going to take this shit any longer, especially from someone who was a business partner and a friend.

"Well!" Jericho shouted.

Chris sipped more liquor.

"You can't have her." He broke. Tears welled into and out of Jericho's eyes. He crumpled onto a chair. "Chris, I won't tolerate it. You can't have her. Nancy Ann is mine." He took a deep breath and began to sob.

"She's a grown woman and can do as she pleases. I had nothing to do with her decision. This is the first I'm hearing of it." Should he get the man a hanky? Chris sat, sipped his drink, allowed Jericho a moment to wallow in his emotional breakdown.

Just as suddenly as this odd mood came on, Jericho was again on his feet. "Sorry, sorry." He repeated over and over. He headed to the door and was out of the loft before Chris could stop him. He followed Jericho out to the metal door. He watched him cross the empty street and walk toward the river.

Thirty

The bell startled Chris out of his lost thoughts. He paused *The Pirates of Penzance* and checked the monitor. Nancy Ann and another woman stood at his door. He buzzed them in and went into the kitchen. He liked living his life with full mobility again, although his ankles still hurt too much to wear heels.

"Hello!" Chris sang out as the women came into his home. "To what do I owe the honor?"

"Have you seen Jericho?"

Chris couldn't remember the woman's name. She worked for Jerry.

"Sarah and I haven't seen him in hours. He's not returning calls or texts." Nancy Ann's face tightened with concern.

Sarah, that was it. Chris felt better knowing her name without having to ask. "Nancy Ann, what did you say to him? He was crazy. Almost like he was fucked up on something, some drug or something."

Nancy Ann sat down at the table. Sarah patted her shoulder.

"Oh, Chris. After our talk, our time together, I realized that I really want to be doing some other things. I want to go to school. See if I really do have what it takes to become an artist."

Chris sat at the table facing Nancy Ann.

"Really? You want to paint and stuff?" Sarah asked. "That's so cool." She remained standing. "Oh, I like your kitty clock."

"What did you tell Jerry?" Chris pushed.

"I told him that I would stay on at Tamburlaine and continue to manage the company and the shows there, but that I wouldn't be his stage manager on his next Broadway show. Fury filled his eyes. I've never seen him like that before. But, I want to go to school. I told him that, too. I got a bachelor's degree a long time ago. But, it was in theater arts. I want to do something else. I've got the money. I've got the time."

"You don't have to convince me of anything." Chris patted the girl's hand.

"So, he was here? Jericho was here?" Sarah asked.

"Yes. He found me after the rehearsal and came here. We had a drink and he started ranting about how I couldn't have you, Nancy Ann. It was like he was crazy. Not drunk, but actually acting insane. He raved, paced around, and then left. I watched him walk away."

"Where? Which way did he go?" Sarah asked, already buttoning her cheap overcoat.

"Toward the river," said Chris.

"The pier, of course." Sarah practically pulled Nancy Ann out of her chair. "He's sitting on the pier. That's where he goes when there's trouble."

"No, he goes to that bench in Central Park, outside the Children's Zoo." Nancy Ann said, dismissively.

"What sort of trouble?" Chris asked.

"Not at night," said Sarah. "He goes to the river and sits on the pier because that's where *he* used to jog." Sarah barely whispered the "he."

"Oh. Would he compare this to that?" Nancy Ann asked as she stood.

"What are you two talking about? It's like you've begun speaking a secret language or something." Used to not understanding young people, Chris thought this different. They avoided telling the story, avoided using names.

Nancy Ann spoke quickly as she buttoned her coat. "Jericho had this thing for Billy Lake. The kid lived with him for months. We all thought they were sleeping together, but it turns out they weren't. Jericho was crazy in love with the kid. Billy is in amazing shape and jogs every day. He used to jog down here along the river."

"Billy Lake? He's with that other handsome performer. Hank something?"

"Hank Miller. They sang at Tamburlaine a few weeks ago," Sarah said.

"That was a few months ago," corrected Nancy Ann. "Okay, we'll go seek him out there."

"Wait. Is there something I'm missing? It's only been an hour. He's a grown man. Maybe he's working something out. Give him some space." Chris stood with the women, held the cuff of Nancy's Ann's coat.

"No, I think this is a time I need to find him and talk to him," said Nancy Ann. She took Chris' hand. "I've worked with him a long time. It's like a break up to him. That's what Sarah thinks. So, we should find him and comfort him and assure him."

The girls were out the door with a wave. He watched on the monitor as they slammed the door shut and headed toward the river.

Chris sat on the couch, but he didn't start the movie. He thought about how Jericho was acting. Was it possible he'd popped some pills or smoked something? He didn't remember Jerry ever doing drugs like that. Sure, a little grass, too much whiskey. But, drugs?

He replayed the scene that had happened here a few hours earlier. It didn't seem like the Jerry he knew at all. Stealing a woman from him. That's what he'd accused Chris of, stealing Nancy Ann. Like she was property.

Chris gave up the thought and turned the movie back on, getting lost in Kevin Kline's chest hair and a young Rex Smith's tight ass.

Thirty-one

Again the doorbell pulled Chris from his movie. He paused the film. Now who? Ingram waved his hand and smiled toward the camera. Chris buzzed the boy in. He got up and met Ingram as he came through the kitchen door. The boy kissed both of Chris' cheeks.

"What are you doing out in this weather without a coat?" Chris shut the door and then picked up his shawl and threw it around Ingram's shoulders.

"We need you at the club and you're not answering your phone."

"It never rang. The house phone didn't ring and the cell didn't either." Chris went to the princess phone on the counter and picked it up. He listened to the receiver. "Dead."

"Really? That's strange?" Ingram watched as Chris tapped the cradle and listened to the phone again.

"Nothing. No one usually calls, so I didn't think about it. It might have been dead for days. Weeks. Months, even." Chris went into the living room. Ingram followed him. "My cell is..." Chris stopped and turned. "I thought it was here. Oh, I might have left it in the office or dropped it in the theater. I don't remember the last time I had it. No matter. You said you needed me at the club?"

"Yes. The Piano Player and the cast have run through all their songs. You're supposed to be on stage. When you weren't there and not picking up, Frank worried there might be something wrong, so he asked if I'd come over and check."

"Well, aren't you all such sweet boys. Let me put shoes on and touch up my face." Chris headed to the bathroom and the boy followed. They sat on the stools while Chris put on eyeliner and mascara, a touch of lipstick and some soft rouge. He powdered his face. "We pretend it covers lines and blotches. Like everyone doesn't know I'm an old queen." He rooted through a heap of shoes in the bedroom, choosing flat, golden slippers; he still couldn't enjoy heels.

"We love you because of that." Ingram smiled into the mirror at Chris.

It bothered Chris to have his tool used to view him. "How are rehearsals? You'll be going into previews soon, right?" Chris asked.

"Everything was going really well until today. It was like Jericho was a different person. He was angry with everyone about everything. The costumes were all wrong. The set needs to be repainted. The lighting is all wrong. Everyone said their lines incorrectly. It was three of the longest hours I've ever spent in my life. And, from what they were saying at Tamburlaine, he was like that with the *Little Shop* cast tonight, too."

"Well, we all go through shit. Maybe Jerry is going through something personal. It's sad he's taking it out on all of you, but perhaps you should be supportive." Chris stood up, checked his face and makeup from different angles, and, satisfied, led the way out of the bath. He picked up a flowing duster and threw it on as they left the house and headed the short walk to Tamburlaine.

Neither of them spoke as the cold hit them. And, instead of going around to the alley, Chris led the way, past the line, and through the main entrance. He couldn't believe that there were dozens of people standing out in the cold waiting to get inside.

Chris made his way to the bar and got Frank's attention. "Thank you, dear, for worrying about me. Can you send some hot coffee outside to those poor people standing on the street?"

"Of course," said Frank. He tapped Chris's hand. "We all love you."

Chris walked toward the stage. A drag queen waitress was finishing up an amazing rendition of "Somewhere That's Green." It surprised Chris that she'd be doing one of the show numbers, but all performers have their specialties.

With the applause for the singer, Chris stepped up on stage, whispered to the boy playing the piano, someone he'd never seen before, and the guy got up and left. Chris launched into his routine to the delight of the crowd. As he pattered and bantered and tinkled at the piano for emphasis, he regarded his wristwatch. It was one fifteen. It felt good to be performing to a full room. He launched into Rusty Warren's most famous song: "Ladies, it's time for the march of the knockers. Ladies, get your knockers up, up, up. Doesn't that make your navel tingle..."

Women and drag queens alike were out of their chairs parading around the room to the cheers and delight of all the men there.

Thirty-two

"You're Nobody Until Somebody Loves You" closed Chris' set, just as Rusty closed many of hers. At three thirty there were still twenty or so people at the showroom tables and another dozen at the bar. "That's it, ladies and gentlemen. If you had a good time tonight, tell all your friends. If you had a lousy time, well, go fuck yourselves."

Those who remained, the diehards, were fans. They applauded and catcall-whistled as Chris stood and politely curtsied. This, as always, brought more applause. He stepped behind the curtains and turned off the stage lights, leaving only the mirror ball spinning and sparkling over the ceiling and walls.

Chris wandered among the tables, thanking the patrons with a touch of his hand or even a kiss on the cheek. When he had a clear shot at the bar, and the glass of bourbon waiting there for him, a man stepped in front of Chris and pressed his hand, said nice words, and didn't let go.

"I'm sorry, dear, I can't really hear you." Chris tried to tug his hand away, but the man kept hold. "Frank!" Chris called.

The bartender was over the top of the bar, baseball bat in hand. Still, the man held Chris' hand. Frank pulled him away and escorted him to the door. Chris went to his stool at the bar and a bartender, whose name he couldn't remember, poured him a double bourbon.

As the minutes ticked by and the latest drink went to work, Chris breathed a little easier. He slid off the stool and walked into the dining room. The soft light illuminated the tables stacked with chairs, ready for the morning cleaning crew. He went into the kitchen. Two women in dirty whites were wiping walls, metal shelves, and counters.

"Is there something we can get for you, Mr. Marlowe? There are leftovers from dinner service in the cooler. Or, a sandwich perhaps?"

He recognized the girl speaking, but like the bartender, he didn't know her name. He remembered meeting her, but couldn't recall her name. He walked out of the kitchen without responding, and entered the theater. A single ghost light blared on stage; the theater quiet and cool. He sat in his back-row seat. Something felt wrong. He'd lost his ability to speak. His ability to move left him. He felt himself slumping over in the chair, sliding down to the floor. He willed his hands, feet, legs, and voice to respond to his desire, but they didn't. He was falling, with his eyes open, his mind working.

"Chris!? Chris? Stay with me." The bartender he didn't know was next to him. The girl from the kitchen was over his shoulder. "Call nine-one-one!" the bartender shouted. The girl raced off. "Chris, can you speak?"

Chris wanted to shake his head. He willed himself to say something, anything. He didn't know the guy's name.

The bartender picked him up and moved him to the aisle. He straightened Chris' blouse and trousers. He brushed hair from Chris' forehead. "Why do all these things keep happening to you?"

He wanted to say he didn't know. It didn't make sense to him. This was different than the last time he'd been drugged. And, clearly he'd been drugged again. His hand burned. Could it be from a handshake? The handshaker guy. He prayed the new security cameras they'd installed on the street had captured his picture. He wanted to look at his palm, see if it was reacting; tell someone to check it. But, he couldn't move his limbs.

Sirens could be heard. Paramedics entered the theater with a gurney.

"Sir, what's your name? What have you taken? Tell me what you're feeling."

Chris kept his eyes open. He watched the men. He forced a blink. It happened. He tried again, and again. Linked three together. The action exhausted him.

"Wait, he's blinking. One, two, three, four, five, six, seven, eight, nine."

Chris stopped. He willed his eyelids to move again. He blinked three slow times and then willed himself to flutter his eyelids three fast times before he finished.

"Morse code. That's S-O-S in Morse. Chris, just blink once if I'm right."

He blinked once more, holding his eyes closed for a moment longer.

"Damn, I don't remember much of that from my navy days." The paramedic pulled out a walkie-talkie. "I need someone who knows Morse code. Tamburlaine headed to St. Vincent's."

There was a crackling response.

"You stay with me, sir. We've got you. Stay alert; a translator is on their way."

"His name is Chris. Chris Marlowe," said the bartender.

"Like the playwright? Mr. Marlowe, you stay with me. You keep blinking. Two blinks if you understand me."

Chris blinked two times in quick succession.

"Excellent." The paramedic began asking him yes and no questions. Two blinks for yes, one long blink for no. And, as they moved him to the gurney, they'd determined all his vital signs were good.

Chris desperately wanted to tell them about the handshake; there was nothing he could do with this two blink, one blink routine unless they asked the correct question, which they hadn't.

When they arrived on the street, a cop pushed through the crowd. "You wanted someone with Morse code experience?" It was a woman, short with huge tits.

"Here," said the paramedic. He quickly explained the eye blinks.

They jostled Chris into the ambulance and the cop got in with them. She focused on Chris' eyes. "Talk to me, Baby," said the woman cop.

"Nice tits," Chris blinked.

"Thank you, doll. And, they're all mine. The real deal."

"What did he say?" asked the paramedic.

"Never you mind. What's his name?"

"Chris Marlowe," said the paramedic.

"What happened, Chris?" asked the cop.

Chris blinked: hand.

"Check his hands," said the cop. She slid to the side a bit to allow the paramedic more room.

"The right one, it's red, inflamed."

"Chris thinks he was poisoned."

Thirty-three

Chris opened his eyes to a giant spider stain on the ceiling tiles. His whole body ached, the pain worse in his joints than anywhere else. His arm bent tightly. But, he appreciated that it moved.

A machine near his head beeped. Ah, another hospital scene. Chris faced the sound. His neck felt like it might snap. But, he could move.

"You're awake!" The voice that spoke feminine and strong.

"I..." his throat felt like he'd swallowed sandpaper.

"Here." That voice again. Huge breasts accosted him. She held a cup with a bendy straw.

With some effort, he sipped. Water in his mouth. Some dribbled out; some down his throat. Cool and good.

"Code Breaker," he whispered.

The woman's wholehearted laugh, soft at first, grew bigger and overtook her whole body. Those big tits shook and bounced. "That's me. I've been called lots of things, but Code Breaker is a new one. I like it. Gonna have business cards printed up."

"You saved me."

"You saved yourself. Turns out that little guy who held your hand pressed a patch to your palm...instead of it being nicotine or estrogen, it was a poison called tetrodotoxin. It's related somehow to blowfish or snakes or something. Some odd combination of toxins. They're trying to trace the maker. It's really unique. Poisoning by patch. No one has ever heard of it. But, you survived because of the Morse code blinks. Where'd you learn that?"

"I *dated* a boy when I was in the Navy." Chris winked. "He taught me. We'd send messages to each other."

"You were in the Navy?"

"Enlisted in the Navy instead of being drafted."

"Me, too. Maybe we met over there."

A nurse came in. "Mr. Marlowe, you're awake." She nodded to Chris' visitor. "It's nice to see you." She poked and prodded, took vital signs and temperature. She left the room.

"You've sat here all this time? How long has it been?" Chris gave up the effort to sit up. "What's your name?"

"Detective Nashe, Elizabeth Nashe. If I had friends, I'd ask them to call me Liz."

"Well, Liz, a friend you are. I can't believe it. With your humor and fashion sense, they must swarm around you."

"Well, I'm not like the rest of the gals."

"To me, you're a perfect lady, Liz. There's now a bottomless tab at Tamburlaine for you." Chris reached up with some effort and rested his hand on Liz's.

"You're a perfect gentleman. Or, is it lady?"

"I tend to be somewhere in between these days." He again did his best to adjust himself; it was too much effort. "I wish I could see you better."

"Oh, here." She stepped aside, pushed a button, and the head of the bed rose. "Better?"

"Much."

The machines beeped again and then stopped.

"Please, sit. How long have I been out?"

"Almost three days." Liz pulled a plastic chair closer to the bed. The feet scraped the floor. She sat and took Chris' hand in her meaty paw.

"Three days. Have you been sitting here for three days?" Chris couldn't believe that anyone would do that.

"No, I've had to leave to work my shifts. I'm a dispatcher for the force. And, I slept some, too. You've had a string of folks coming in, spending time. You've got lots of people who care for you." She took her hand away and searched her pockets. She pressed a crumpled, stiff tissue to the corner of her eye.

"Who the hell is doing these things to me?" Tears formed and began to spill from his eyes. "I don't know who I've pissed off so much that they'd want me dead."

"Don't upset yourself. The important thing is that you've survived. A tall, young woman with two names told me about the other poisoning, the fire, the gas line. I find it strange that they'd attempt fire twice and poison twice. You'd think if they failed they'd move on to something new, something different. Or, you might have two different people trying to kill you. A firebug and a poisoner."

"Are you trying to make me feel better? 'Cause I don't think it's helping."

"Sorry. I worked cases for a long time."

Interested, but tired, Chris asked "You don't anymore?" Anything to turn the attention away from him at the moment, to get his mind off recent events.

"Twenty years. I solved lots of crimes in our fair Gotham. I was about to retire and I got shot. Survived. That's good. Didn't really have anything to do during my retirement. I've always been something of a loner. So, I weaseled my way back into the force. I like being a dispatcher. It gives me something to do. Sometimes gets a little hairy. But, I do miss solving cases." Her face brightened. "So, tell me the details of your recent experiences and we'll see what we can figure out."

Chris relayed everything that had happened: the developer, the new partnership, the hiring and firing of employees, and the revival of Tamburlaine.

While he talked, Liz took out a journal from her shoulder bag and made notes with a marker. She wrote things inside boxes and flourished lines connecting them.

He liked Liz, not just because she'd saved his life. It was rare to meet someone near his age without an agenda or too much baggage. "What are you doing over there? An art project?" Chris asked. His joints still ached horribly.

The last nurse he told that to returned with a syringe. "This will help with the pain," she said, pushing the drug into his IV.

Within moments, a warm sensation creeped through his body. Sleep came quick and heavy.

Thirty-four

"Home again." Chris led the small band who brought him from the hospital to Tamburlaine. They'd filled three cabs. "Matilda, hello. Frank." He hugged them both in turns. "Food and drinks for my caretakers. How wonderful to have all of you watching over me at all hours." He walked to his end of the bar and sat down.

His friends, a rag-tag bunch, ordered drinks and took bites from the trays of food set out on the tables.

"What shall I pour for you, boss?"

"Bottled water, Frank. We've got to clean out my system. Very strict diet the next two weeks." Frank set the bottle in front of Chris. "Thank you. Your quick action probably saved my life. If he'd held on to my hand any longer, well, they don't think I would have survived. If he'd have actually gotten the patch to adhere to me, well, that would have been the end of it for me."

"Happy to be of service." Frank blinked back tears. "Do you want me to turn on the lights? The music?"

"No. It's nice like this." Chris sipped from the bottle. He longed for bourbon or coffee. But, he'd followed orders. At least for a day or two.

"You're sure you're okay?" Ingram asked. "If there's anything you want or need me to do, just let me know." He popped a meatball into his mouth.

"I see you've come to enjoy Matilda's food." Chris poked Ingram playfully in the side.

"Very good," he mumbled through a full mouth.

"Why are you here and not resting at home?" Nancy Ann asked, placing an arm over his shoulder.

"I've had plenty of rest. I wanted to see the place. Make sure you all hadn't given away the fixtures." Chris laughed at his own joke. "I do plan on getting home before the festivities begin here tonight. I'm going to take a few nights off from performing. Get my stage legs back."

Chris didn't want to admit it to anyone: he was afraid to get up on stage. The thought of being around people he didn't know frightened him. He'd have to get over that. For now, he'd trust his gut. Chris contemplated checking into a hotel, a room with a great view and room service, but he decided to simply go home.

"Well, we want you back here on stage as soon as you can muster it." Nancy Ann hugged him close and kissed his cheek.

"Has anyone seen Jerry? I thought he'd be along today." Chris took in the group drinking at his bar. A few waiters, the kitchen and bar staff. A few performers.

"No. Haven't heard from him. I can call Jericho if you'd like?" Nancy Ann tugged her phone out of her pocket.

"No. That's not necessary. Just curious." Chris drank more water. He was ready to go home, but didn't want to appear inconsiderate to those who had been taking care of him and his club. He finally decided it was time when a patron walked into Tamburlaine.

Without saying a word, he slid off his stool and headed toward the front door. Just as his hand touched the knob, Ingram cupped Chris' elbow. Chris jerked his arm away.

"Can I walk you home?"

"No. I'll be fine." Chris raised his hand toward the door again.

"We've made a promise to Jericho. You are to be accompanied." Frank approached.

"Fine. Frank, please walk me home." He knew his words would sting Ingram, but went with his gut. He didn't fully trust the boy. He didn't know why.

"Of course, boss." Frank escorted Chris to the loft. He waited while Chris opened the creaky, metal door and walked him down the alley and into the kitchen. "You call me, any time. I've got your back, okay?"

"Thank you, Frank. I like knowing you're in my corner." Chris kissed Frank's cheek and engaged the locks after he exited. "Afraid of my shadow." Chris tossed his wrap on the chair. There were several throws there. He picked them up and carried them to the dressing room. The house was clean, but chilly. He hung the wraps before altering the thermostat.

He stripped naked. In the bathroom, he turned on the hot water in the shower, his figure gaunt in the mirrors; he discovered tape and tabs and debris stuck on various parts of his body.

Chris took a moment to pick the stuff off and then focused on his hair. It was going to be a nightmare to get his curls in shape. He sat and slowly untangled his ringlets until a brush ran smoothly through his hair.

The shower was perfect and he stood under the flow of water so long his fingers and toes pruned. It felt good to be warm and clean. He toweled off, pulled on a thick robe, and spent a few moments brushing and flossing his teeth. Wrapping a towel around his mop like a turban, feet in slippers, he padded to the kitchen.

He contemplated a drink and decided to stick with the water diet; the doctor told him that he needed to drink at least two gallons of water every day before he had anything else. The liver and kidneys had to be flushed of all toxins, like a broken record.

He took a bottle of water from the refrigerator. He picked up the pink princess phone. It again had a dial tone. He replaced the receiver in its cradle.

Chris got comfy on the couch. He didn't want music. He didn't want a movie or television. He breathed deeply and listened. The only sound was his own breathing and the wag of the cat clock's tail. It was nice to have a moment to himself.

The tears came on like a surprise attack. Chris went with the flow. All the water he'd been drinking seemed to flush from his eyes. He cried. Huge, physical convulsions washed over him.

As he cried, he thought of the pain he'd been through recently. Was it worth it? Maybe he should just sell the club and the land. Get out of New York City. Move to Miami or San Diego or Hawaii. That's what Rusty Warren did, retired to Hawaii. They could be neighbors, perhaps. Play bridge together. Share a kugel on the holidays.

Silly. Such silly thoughts. He'd lived in the city his whole life. At least, his whole adult life. He'd been connected to Tamburlaine all that time, too. He'd promised Jimmy to keep it going. He'd promised Franz that he'd keep the place open forever. He thought of Jimmy's art collection. Most of it gifted by old Franz. A wonderful man. Jimmy, Franz, the promise, thinking of them brought on great sobs. He could barely catch his breath from one convulsive sob to the next.

All the queens from the past sashayed before him. Each with their own style, like an o' so odd collection of Radio City Rockettes. So many of the girls now dead. Most of them dead. All of them from those early days dead. So many lost during the eighties, AIDS. So many of the queens and boys didn't survive. He and Jerry were among the only ones left. Sure, there must be a few more, in nursing homes, tucked away by their families. They never returned to Tamburlaine in person, but they were there, still. Their energy kept life in the place.

The tears subsided. His breathing calmed. He drank water.

Detective Liz was right. It didn't make sense that the same person orchestrated all the attacks. He wasn't safe. Even with all those people at the bar interested in his wellbeing. All the attacks had happened at Tamburlaine, except for the Molotov cocktail.

The bell rang. Chris got up from his wallowing and went into the kitchen. He viewed the monitor. Jerry. He picked up the phone and pushed the number to speak. "Jerry. I'm sleeping."

"Just for a minute."

"No. Come see me tomorrow." Chris held no desire to go another round with The Great Jericho Taylor. He hung up the phone, got a fresh bottle of water from the fridge, and walked down the hallway to his bedroom. He dropped his robe and climbed under the covers. He turned the electric blanket up to seven and cuddled with one of the pillows in the warm cocoon wondering when he'd see Liz Nashe again.

Thirty-five

Alone at Tamburlaine. Chris went in early, after the cleaning crew, but before the kitchen staff. He made sure the alley door closed and locked behind him. He walked through the kitchen with only the Exit sign lights to guide him. He went down into the basement, took the big flashlight from the shelf, and turned it on. He walked down the narrow stairs, vowing for the hundred-thousandth time to replace them. The kitchen prep area, with its stainless steel tables and shelves and steel door coolers, reminded him of an operating room.

He walked through the hallway into the old basement. The large space, divided into a dozen rooms, each separated by elaborately patterned brick walls and smooth-worn brick floors, had been a speakeasy in the '20s and '30s. Jimmy told him the place was a whorehouse before that. Rooms below the stage had been cleared and cleaned and housed the *Dames at Sea* and *Little Shop* stage sets. A trap door allowed the set pieces to be raised and lowered with ropes and pulleys.

Chris passed through to the deeper basement. Here, the floors were still dirt. After entering a code, he opened an old door. The tale: this was an original door from the first building, erected in 1807. It still had leather joints and massive brass nails. He closed the door behind him and shined the flashlight toward the walls. A rat scurried out of the light.

When he'd remembered and thought about Franz a week ago, it stuck in his head that there had been a newspaper article. That there was some odd connection between Jimmy, Franz, and the Picasso. That's why all the cloak and dagger in the dungeon.

The cabinet Chris sought was against the furthest wall. He tripped on the uneven dirt floor. The lights hadn't worked down here for a long time. He balanced the flashlight while searching through the ring of keys, sorry he hadn't found the correct one before he came downstairs. But, he found the skeleton key and opened the wooden cabinet. With some effort,

Chris dropped to his knees and searched through the brittle, yellowed newspapers. There it was, well, not it, but rather he. His stomach turned and Chris thought he might puke, but he held back, taking deep breaths.

"Jimmy said he'd show up again." Chris folded the paper, used the cabinet to regain his footing. He locked the cabinet and then the door with the rusty keys.

Just as Chris came up into the kitchen, Matilda arrived through the alley door and flipped on the bright overhead lights. She shrieked. "Chris! You scared the hell out of me. What are you doing here in the dark?"

"Everyone knows I'm a tightwad, hate turning on the lights." He smiled at the woman.

"That's not true and you know it."

"I've been prowling Tamburlaine in the dark longer than you've been on the planet."

"Now, that I believe. Can I make you some coffee? Maybe eggs and toast?"

"Coffee would be great. I'll be in my office." Chris turned to go. He caught sight of himself in the mirror the wait staff used. Covered in dust, dirt, and cobwebs, he was a fright. No wonder Matilda screamed.

Chris went into his office and shut the door. He rolled open his desk and set the newspaper down on the blotter. He quickly disrobed, changed into a fresh pair of trousers and a clean blouse from the armoire, and ran a brush through his hair; the cobwebs in his curls caused him to shudder.

He thought again kindly of Franz. Jimmy introduced Chris to Franz here at Tamburlaine. Handsome, beyond compare. Great manners. He thought of him as an aged Nicky Arnstein, and himself as a youthful Fanny Brice. They played out the off-stage scenes. Chris sucked him off in the dressing room more than once, let the old man fuck him in the men's room. Who knew, a few years later, the crazy guy would leave his paintings to Jimmy and then Jimmy would leave them to him?

A knock at the door. "Chris, I've got coffee."

"Come in." He closed the cabinet.

Matilda entered with her heavy walk carrying a tray with coffee pot, cup and saucer, and a plate with scrambled eggs, bacon, and toast that all rattled as she kerthumped into the room. "You should eat."

He didn't protest. "Thank you."

Matilda, with odd maneuvers, set down the tray on his desk and left, closing the door behind her.

Chris wondered if she'd seen the paper or what she might think of his antics. He was sure he'd be the talk of the staff, the crazy old queen with spiders in her hair prowling around the dark club with ancient news clippings; not as bad as Mrs. Haversham in her wedding dress.

He sat at the table and poured coffee in a cup. The bacon smelled good. He ate it and wondered how she'd cooked perfect bacon in just ten minutes. He opened the paper and explored the picture. It was unmistakable. Nigel Folgate stood next to Jimmy, with Franz behind, his arms around them, the Picasso—the *Streetwalkers*—that hung on the wall of Chris' office—originally Jimmy's office—there in the photograph, propped in front of the men. Folgate was there when Franz gave the pictures to Jimmy. It didn't make any sense. Chris had no memory of the three of them ever being together. He looked. The paper's date wasn't part of the clipping.

The young Nigel Folgate in the photograph looked nothing like Norton Folgate—who had been harassing Chris over selling the property. How were those two related? And, why was Nigel, with their shared history, allowing Norton to come after Chris like this?

Chris scanned the article for Folgate's name, but it didn't appear anywhere. He started at the headline: "Eccentric Millionaire gives Priceless Collection to Westside Businessmen." Graf by graf he read. There was Jimmy's name over and over. Franz's name and background. Not one single mention of Folgate, not even in the caption. What on earth could it mean? Chris, of course, knew about Nigel's history with Jimmy; that was a shared history. What he didn't know: Who was Nigel Folgate to Franz?

Chris folded his dirty clothes and tucked them, along with the old newspaper, into a tote bag. He left the office, making sure the door locked behind him. Without a word to Matilda or her crew, he left Tamburlaine and headed toward home.

When he arrived at his metal door, someone he didn't know stood there, pushing the buzzer.

"Hello? May I help you?"

An older gentleman, in a long trench coat, turned and smiled with crinkled blue eyes, eyes Chris knew. It took a few moments for this out of context experience to register.

"Detective Nashe? Liz?"

Liz, out of drag, was rather average, a bit drab. "None other." He twirled; his coat bottom fluffed out.

Chris took Liz's hand with his free one. A handshake wasn't enough, so he pulled the detective into him and they embraced. "Thank you. You saved my life." Chris whispered into Liz's ear through his tears.

When they separated, Detective Nashe wiped away his tears. "May I come in? I'd like to talk to you."

"Of course, where are my manners?" Chris finagled the key into the lock and with some effort pushed the door open. As the air grew colder, the door became even more difficult to manipulate. He led the way down the alley and into the rear entrance of his home. "How about coffee? I can have some made in a few minutes."

"That would be lovely."

Chris tossed his wrap over the chair; Detective Nashe took off his coat and did the same.

"So, as you see, I'm a queen, a queer. I've always liked that word, queer. It has defined me, in more ways than one, for a long lifetime."

"I like the word queer, too. I'm glad we've taken it over, us, the community. Using it for fun takes away all the power of if." Chris busied himself with water and grinding beans and filters.

"Oh, it's too much effort. Just water from the tap for me."

"Nonsense. Do you really have anywhere else to be?"

"No, actually, I don't. I broke some protocol and have been relieved of my dispatch duties. It was just a part-time job to keep me busy. They can't take away my pension, although they looked into it."

"Why? For what?"

"Well, helping you."

"You saved my life." Chris turned in melodramatic disbelief—his hand raised to his throat.

"Well, it's not the assistance I gave, but instead, the impersonating an officer. You see, I'm retired. And, I'm a man. I was at Tamburlaine that night. I was waiting in line on the street to get in. When I heard them clambering for someone who knew Morse Code, well, I stepped forward.

I never thought about how I was dressed. As a policewoman."

"And they fired you for that? Even though you—"

"Rules are rules."

Chris sat down at the table. Liz continued to inspect the items hung on the walls, old copper molds and pans, the blue cat clock with its vigilant eyes and swinging tail, yellowed newspaper clippings clinging to the sides of the refrigerator, and hundreds of *Playbill* covers that papered the kitchen walls.

The room filled with the aroma of fresh brewed coffee.

"Sorry, I don't have any cake or Danish. Chris stood, filled their cups. "Cream? Sugar?"

"Black is fine." Liz let out a sigh.

"So, why are you here?" Chris asked. "Don't get me wrong, it's wonderful to see you. And, even more wonderful to know."

Liz reached out and took Chris' hand. "I'm so glad you feel that way, too. I felt like we'd found some bond at the hospital. I like you a lot. It's obvious you don't remember me from before."

"Before?" He liked the feeling of Liz's hand around his. It felt comforting, familiar somehow.

"Oh, we were just boys. We had sex in an alley. Barely sex. Just a quick blowjob and wank together."

He whistled. "Pretty sure I was drunk or stoned or both."

"We both were. You'd gotten out of your show at Tamburlaine—I was third from the right in the second row. I waited on the street for you. We talked about nothing, walked for a bit, to I don't know where, and we dipped into an alley. We kissed. I pulled out your dick, dropped to my knees, and gave you a blow job while I jacked off. All so fast. I ran off before you'd even zipped up." Liz drank some coffee, watching Chris.

"Ah, the good old days." Chris winked her a big, signature wink

"Stop, you almost made hot coffee come out my nose."

They laughed.

"So, when was the last time you were on your knees in an alley?" Chris watched Liz's face as his eyes sparkled mischievously.

"So long ago, I can't remember. I like that you dress and act as you want. I had to keep everything quiet for so long. I got used to being a man by day and a lady by night."

"There are worse scenarios." Chris got up, brought the coffee pot to the table, filled the cups, and set the pot on a cork trivet. "So, was this what you wanted to talk to me about? Or, is there something else?"

"Well, I actually was using the something else as the excuse. But, we launched right into it."

"Liz, at our ages, whatever those might be, we don't really have time to fuck around."

"I'm Elmer when I'm a man."

"Which do you prefer?"

He moved the tote bag to a farther point on the table. "Liz."

"So, Liz it shall be. What was the other thing?" The movement of the tote reminded Chris of the puzzle he was trying to solve.

"Well, the drug they poisoned you with, I followed up with the hospital. It was an odd combination of poisons from a blowfish, a snail, and some South American frog. They'd never seen anything like it before. But, there have been two other victims since your encounter."

"Victims?"

"Both men died. Both of them actually had the patches attached to them. Yours didn't stick to you, and that probably saved your life."

"You saved my life. You understood what I was blinking."

Tears again welled into Liz's eyes.

"Do the names Henri Dietrich or Herman Junker mean anything to you?" Liz reached into his shirt pocket and pulled out two small photographs. He faced them toward Chris on the table, pushed them closer.

"This man I don't know. The cops showed a similar photo after the fire. Chris pointed from the first to the second photograph. "And, this one was my bartender at Tamburlaine. Benny Bushnell. He disappeared right after I was poisoned the first time. He's dead?"

"Yes. He was the second victim. You were poisoned before? When?"

"A few weeks ago. I've been attacked several times recently." Chris relayed the events to Liz. "Here, hand me that bag." Chris pulled the old newspaper out. "A memory reminded me of this picture in the paper. That man there, I thought it was Nigel Folgate, but now, I don't know. There's no name given in the article or the caption."

Liz read the article and looked at the picture.

"So, my bartender Benny was actually Herman..."

"Junker. And, I'd guess this guy in the old paper piece is a relative of Dietrich and the guy you call Folgate. You're right, they're spitting images, although they're decades apart in age."

"Liz, what the hell is going on? Is there a picture in a closet that's aging somewhere so these guys remain young looking? Are they vampires?"

Liz laughed. "Oh, I love Oscar Wilde and Anne Rice. Nothing like a sexy vampire or an old British poof." She tapped the news photograph. "I have a lot of time on my hands and a lot of connections in this city. Do you mind if I take this paper?"

Chris hesitated.

"I'll get it back to you if I can."

"Take it." Chris refilled their cups. "Well, isn't that a kick in the head? All these people not seeming to be who they are. What the hell is it that they want from me?" He scrutinized Liz. "How do I know you're not one of them or in on this somehow?" It dawned on Chris, even though he'd started out joking, that he didn't know anyone anymore. How could he know who to trust? Or, who was out to get him?

Liz pulled out his wallet and handed over an ID. He also sifted through some papers and receipts and produced a rather worn business card for Detective Elmer Nashe.

Chris didn't know what to do, but he knew he had to trust someone. And, if Liz saved him to kill him, there was some level of comfort knowing it was a drag queen queer who might do it.

Thirty-six

Chris, mid-set, saw Liz enter Tamburlaine.

"Come on, booze it up, I don't make any money if there are empty ashtrays." Chris stopped playing the piano. "Those were the days, huh? Smoke and drink right inside a club."

He kept his eyes on Liz as she got a drink from the bar and found a spot in the dark corner of the showroom.

He loved the idea of the Knockers Up March with Liz and her huge bazooms leading the line. But, Liz told him that she never took part, not wanting to be seen. Tonight would be no exception.

"Now, you have to go outside to light up; if you haven't tipped the doorman, you end up waiting in line for an hour to get back in." The audience laughed. He played another song, kibitzed with those sitting at the tables down front, and continued to steal as much of Rusty Warren's material as he could.

The audience, fairly young tonight, hadn't ever heard the old jokes before and laughed along. The older folks, especially the older men, didn't always laugh. They were often lost in the memories of seeing and hearing Rusty in person, or at least remembering listening to the LP albums.

While he talked and sang, he kept track of Liz. She didn't move from her spot. She nursed her drink. She watched the crowd. Detective Nashe was incredibly alert.

Ain't Misbehavin' let out. The room filled with voices. Chris changed to underscore music for a few moments.

"Well, folks, that's my last set. He's been playing piano for *Nunsense* all week You know it's habit forming? There are still tickets for next weekend's performances, so stop by the bar or the box office before you leave. Please welcome Jason to the keyboard." Chris stood, stretched a little, and patted the handsome, mustachioed, too thin Jason.

The audience applauded as Chris left the stage.

Jason took the bench, cracked the knuckles of his spindly fingers, and rocketed into a Fats Waller style stride piano. "Yowsa, Yowsa. Thank you all for visitin' Tamburlaine tonight. So pleased to play all the ancient hits for you. Yesiree, Bob!" Jason had a whole black, '20s shtick he did on stage in the showroom. He called it his "Negro Drag." And, even though he was white, folks on the street would talk about that black piano player. Chris loved the guy and paid him well to take the last set several evenings a week.

Chris walked over to the bar, checked in with Frank, then went into the dining room. All the tables were empty, yet the candles glistened invitingly, just the way he liked it for the last crowd out of the showroom.

The lady's room still had a line. He went into the kitchen. It was still warm and the floor a mess, but the chrome and steel shined like it was new.

"Is there something you'd like, Chris?" Matilda had finally taken to calling him Chris and he was pleased about that.

"No, just checking in on everyone, seeing how your night went." Chris thought about asking if there was any leftover chicken fried steak. He didn't want to keep her there any longer than required.

As if she'd read his mind, Matilda said: "Chris, I put together some leftovers for you to take home." She opened the service fridge and pointed to a big, brown paper bag with Chris' name written neatly on it. Like an overgrown lunch bag.

"Thanks, that's very kind."

"I know it's your favorite!" She smiled brightly.

Chris didn't know how she did it, working fourteen-hour days, six and sometimes seven days a week. It's what chefs did, he'd been told. He walked out of the room with a good-night to Matilda, and down the hall. The *Ain't* cast headed out with nods, pats on his back, and a chorus of "Good-nights."

The man playing the Andre Shields role, Jesse Roma, thin-waisted, flat-stomached dancer's body, dressed sharply in a torso hugging shirt, that showed every muscle and nipple, and skinny jeans, that showed just about everything else, held out his hand and shook Chris'. "Headed in to sing a bit, boss. I was hoping you'd be playing." His eyes were big and bright, his body compact and tight.

Chris's heart skipped a beat. He felt the actual heat coming from the dancer. "Nope, it's Jason tonight." He wished it were him. This man excited Chris.

"Maybe we'll do our Amos and Andy routine. Make all 'em libral queers uncomfortable."

Chris laughed. "It's our job to entertain so be sure to take the sand up on stage so you can dance for the folks." He liked that he made Jesse laugh. Twenty years ago he'd have this man shoved up against a wall somewhere, with something of his shoved into one of Jesse's orifices; not caring who saw them together. Coffee and cream.

"Yassuh, massuh boss, sir." Jesse released Chris' hand and headed into the barroom.

Chris continued backstage. The theater, dark except for the Exit signs and the single work light on the stage, smelled of humanity and grease paint. He walked out to center stage and stood, peering into the darkness. Chris felt the wind just before the crash. Less than a foot from him a rolled up backdrop crashed to the floor. One step this way or that and it would have clocked him. He stood, in shock, as a flock of people ran into the theater.

"Chris? What the hell happ—" Nancy Ann was on stage, next to him. She seemed to appear from nowhere. "Are you okay?"

"Fine. It didn't hit me, just scared the shit out of me."

Liz Nashe pushed through the crowd. She got up on stage and hugged Chris. "Are you okay? What happened?"

"I'm okay. I don't know what happened. The thing just crashed behind me."

"What were you doing here on stage?" Nancy Ann asked.

"I do this every night. I walk the whole club several times a night, actually. But, I always come in here after the last show...after I visit Matilda and she tells me what leftovers I'm taking home...after I say good-night to the last cast. I come out here in the dark, look to the back of the house, and for a moment, I'm seventeen again. It's just a moment. My moment." Chris felt his knees go soft. He didn't know who, but a flock of hands helped him off the stage and into a chair. "I'm getting too old for this shit."

The stage lights flashed on. Nancy Ann and someone Chris didn't know hauled an extension ladder on stage and got it open. The stage manager was up the ladder examining the ropes and bars that the backdrops and scrims hung from.

"This rope is frayed. I'd swear it's been cut with..."

"Don't touch anything. Call the police," Liz shouted into the room.

"More police. They're going to have to open a precinct here at Tamburlaine." Chris leaned his head against Liz's shoulder.

"Maybe that would keep you safer." Liz patted Chris' hand.

"Maybe it would." Chris sighed. It was going to be another long night of questions and answers with the New York Metropolitan Police Department. He wished he hadn't had so much bourbon while singing at the piano. He wondered if the accident would make the news. Any press is good press, as the saying goes.

Thirty-seven

The early assessment: the lines holding the backdrop were cut, not worn. The inspector conjectured a line attached to the backdrop was connected to a small device below the stage. It wasn't on a timer, but remote activated and that the time registered on the dial synced with the moment of the accident. The perpetrator had to be in Tamburlaine at the time of the occurrence because the infrared eye wasn't very strong.

Liz and Nancy Ann helped Chris home after the hours of police questioning.

"Who would have access?" Liz closed the kitchen door and got a pot of coffee brewing.

Nancy Ann held out a chair for Chris who did not sit.

"I would like some bourbon," he said.

"I thought you were still on water." Nancy Ann said in a mothering voice.

"I would like some bourbon."

"Fine." Nancy Ann rooted around the cupboards. Chris gave directions.

Liz took charge. "Take him into the living room and get him settled on the couch. I'll bring coffee *and* bourbon for all of us."

It might have been her tone, but more than likely it was Liz's age that motivated Nancy Ann to follow directions and guide Chris into the living room.

"I'm not a fucking invalid!" he yelled. "Sorry. My nerves are about shot. Maybe it's time to dump the club and move to Florida. Someone is trying to kill me. It's time for this to end, but the police don't seem any closer today about knowing who is doing all of this."

Liz entered the room with a tray and set it down on the coffee table. She served shots of bourbon and cups of coffee to Chris and Nancy Ann.

"Where are your tits?" Nancy Ann blurted out.

"Never something to ask a lady." Chris chuckled.

"Fuck, they were heavy and annoying and I slipped out of them. That's certainly one advantage of being a drag queen. You can just slip out of the padding and bumps and curves when you're done with them."

Everyone laughed.

"Let's work through a few things. Who has access to the basement?" Liz opened a small, black notebook and, like a '40s reporter licked the end of a pencil.

"Me," Nancy Ann began. "And, all the tech crew. We open the trap door twice a night and swap the sets."

"How many on the crew?"

"Four of us."

"Matilda and her staff," Chris said, finishing his bourbon and holding out his glass for a refill.

"How many?" Liz asked as Nancy Ann poured more bourbon for Chris.

"Don't know really. Nine or ten, plus Matilda." Chris touched Nancy Ann's arm.

"Yeah, but those girls aren't going back into the dust and dirt of the basement." Nancy Ann took a sip of bourbon, made a face, and set the glass down.

"The four bartenders and the bar-backs. They use the dumbwaiter all night to hoist beer and booze upstairs." Chris felt a mix of emotions. There were a lot of people working in the club. It felt good to employ so many people again. But, any one of them could be the person, or the point person, who'd tried to kill him.

"Well, you should include the waiters. I've never seen them down there, but they could, right? Early or after hours." Nancy Ann sipped coffee. "Mmmm. This is good. Better than he ever makes."

"Hey now. Don't kick a guy when he's down." Chris laughed.

"And, if we're including the waiters, five of them, right?" Nancy asked.

"Right. Then we should include the cast. Ten for the first show and six for the second. Three musicians both shows. All the drag queen waiters." Chris finished another glass of bourbon.

"Slow down there, cowboy." Liz turned the page of her book. "And, who might be pissed at you?"

"Obvious choice is Folgate. He's been after my piece of property for a while. It's difficult to imagine that he'd kill me. Scare me maybe, sure, but kill me? He has no idea what would happen to the property with me gone." Chis pulled a chenille throw off of the couch. Nancy Ann helped him tuck it around his shoulders.

"Anyone else? You've lived a long life. What about that photo? What connection did that bring back for you?"

"What photo?" Nancy Ann asked.

Chris began: "I was thinking about it when we went upstairs. When Jimmy owned the club, he introduced me to Franz. Franz gave Jimmy the first paintings."

"The Picasso at the bar, right?" Nancy Ann asked.

"First. Right. There was a story in the paper about Franz and Jimmy and the *Streetwalkers*. I went into the basement this morning and dug it out."

Liz produced a photocopy of the article from her bag. "Upstairs? Upstairs where? The club doesn't have a second floor, does it?"

"Just the catwalk and light booth." Nancy Ann took the printout. "Here. Chris has an art gallery upstairs here." She pointed toward the staircase.

"An art gallery?"

Chris ignored the question. "So, there in the picture is a very young Folgate; that's Nigel. Liz came up with some head shots of guys who recently died. One could have been a young Folgate and the other was my old bartender. I knew him as Benny, but he had a German name. They both did."

"Henri Dietrich or Herman Junker," Liz supplied.

"Before we go any further—" Nancy Ann began.

"That's all we have right now," said Liz, thumbing through the notes in her book.

"Still, it didn't seem like a big deal before, but now it does. And, since I waited to tell you, Chris, well, it feels like it's getting bigger and bigger." Nancy Ann looked away and then back at Chris.

Chris took her hand and stroked it. "You can tell me anything."

She blurted out: "I'm Jimmy's niece."

"Who is Jimmy?" asked Liz?

"The guy who built Tamburlaine. The..." Chris watched Nancy Ann, her hand shook in his. He patted it, not speaking for a long moment, but never straying his eyes from hers. Finally, he said, "That explains so much. When I'm with you, I feel this sense of calm. I always feel like I know you better than I do. I think you've got so much of his energy in you." He touched her cheekbone. "You haven't been trying to kill me to take over the club, have you?" Chris only half joked when he asked.

"No! I would never! I can't believe you would think that. I didn't even know until a few weeks ago. I walked into Tamburlaine and it felt like coming home. The energy, the way it was laid out. The people, especially you, Chris. I called my mom and she didn't want to talk about it. I pressed her and she came up to the city to visit me. She brought a big photo album. It was filled with pictures of her and an uncle I'd never met. No one in the family had ever mentioned him before. No one. It was strange and a little creepy."

"Well, Jimmy was pretty out there; he embraced the freedom of the times. He never talked about his family and I never asked. We all had secrets about that stuff. Most of our families didn't want us. We became each other's families often because we lost the real ones."

"It's just so sad." Nancy Ann wiped at her nose. No one spoke for a bit. "So, I wanted to tell you, but I was afraid. And, then I decided not to do Jericho's next Broadway show, but instead to focus on Tamburlaine, and I lost him. I became scared that when I told you who I discovered I was that you'd think I wanted something from you and I'd lose you and Tamburlaine, too."

Chris didn't know what to think. A wave of nausea came over him. He leaned forward, quickly refilled his glass, and swallowed a mouth of bourbon to wash away the taste. Again he wondered who he could truly trust; who might actually be in his corner. Without answers, he patted Nancy Ann's hand. "Well, we'll work this one out, too."

"See, I was afraid if I told you…"

"Don't get your panties in a twist. I just have to process this a little." Chris turned to Liz for guidance.

Not one to miss a sign or cue, she said: "Well, it's time for me to do a little more digging. Chris, I really think you should stay home for a few days."

"I'm not going to let some anonymous asshole keep me from my life or Tamburlaine. And, if I'm going to die, it's going to be there. So, fuck them!" He tossed back more liquor.

"I'll stay with him," said Nancy Ann.

"Yeah, but what if you're the killer?" Chris asked.

"What if Liz is?" Nancy Ann asked.

"Yeah, what if…this isn't some elaborate suicide thing is it?" Liz asked.

They all paused, and then laughed. Chris thought about Nancy Ann. She'd been working with Jericho for years and years. That would be a pretty long setup for a random meeting with him. Chris decided there and then that he'd trust Nancy Ann. The duo was a trio. In his best Ethel Merman impersonation, he sang: "Together, wherever we go."

Liz set her glass on the table. "I feel like I've had too much. I've missed something."

"I love fighting crime. Jericho told you that we took down a terrorist ring last spring, after the flash mob at the train station, right?" Nancy Ann knocked back her shot of bourbon, made a face, and let out a sigh. "It's time to do it again."

"There should be dramatic music or something," said Liz.

"Ba, Ba, Baaaah," Chris sang.

Thirty-eight

The city building inspector shut down the theater while they checked all the pulleys, ropes, cables, and apparatus involved in the theater backdrops and lights. Chris had already given Nancy Ann permission to immediately fix anything that was now or might soon become a problem.

Liz forced Chris to take the day off, so the two of them lounged in Chris' living room, eating. Chris took a messy bite from a corned beef on rye, dropping crumbs all over himself. Mustard smeared his cheek; he was happy. Liz wiped the mustard away with her napkin.

A whole day had passed without someone trying to kill him. He'd made a point, at Liz's suggestion, to take different routes on errands and to Tamburlaine. She suggested he shop at different stores and eat at different restaurants. Anything so he wasn't in his usual routine. That's how they'd ended up with deli sandwiches from the Jewish place instead of eating in Tamburlaine's kitchen today.

Liz had figured out quickly everything that had happened to Chris was connected to how he lived his life. Not the actual how, but the patterns involved in the how. "You always show up at the theater at the same time. You always walk the place at the same times. You eat at the same restaurants, even order the same dishes, over and over. That is why it's been easy for your tormentors to make their attempts."

Chris nodded, but ate instead of talked. He couldn't remember the last time he'd had a good corned beef sandwich. No one cooked corned beef like the Jewish deli around the corner. All these years, they were still there. Another generation of sons cutting and slicing and pulling pickles from the big barrel. Chris thought of the sons' grandfather who was the one pulling pickles from the barrel when Chris first moved into the neighborhood. There were still sides of beef being hauled through the streets back then. The old man had done a double take when Chris walked in in drag, but then took the order and made a wonderful sandwich.

Never flinched, never said a bad word. For weeks, months after, he had all the drag queens ordering in their sandwiches from the Jews around the corner. Their business, even in the dead neighborhood, had survived. There weren't cow carcasses being carried around now. The gutter didn't run red in the afternoons when they hosed off the sidewalks. But, you could still get a great corned beef sandwich.

"You know, if Jericho hadn't been with you the night of the fire, that you probably wouldn't have been so quick to react and protect him. You might…"

Chris dragged himself back into the moment. He swallowed. "What are you saying?"

"If Jerry hadn't been with you the night of the fire, you might have fought back or egged on the guys on the street. But, because there was someone else there, you went into mother hen mode. It probably saved your life."

"Maybe." Chris ate a chip. He wanted to turn up Rusty Warren singing "Somewhere I'll be Looking for You," but he didn't want to be rude. He liked Liz, liked being around her. Having someone your own age to commiserate with is a blessing, especially if you're a queen of a certain age.

"It was the same thing with the other almost fire, the gas leak," he continued. "You broke your pattern by taking Nancy Ann to the light store. That was clearly something you'd never done before. If you hadn't been with her, you probably would have been eating lunch in your corner in the kitchen—that's where the fire damage was the worst. And, we know that the first poisoning by a bartender who knew you, was by a guy who is now dead. Killed by the second poison. It had to be connected."

"You're very good at this." Chris patted Liz's hand. "How's the roast beef?"

Liz offered her sandwich toward Chris who took a small bite.

"Hmm, good." He ate another bite of corned beef, then offered the sandwich toward Liz. She shook her head.

"Benny worked for me for years. Why try to kill me now?"

"My guess? Someone paid him."

Chris asked: "So, what about the second poison and the backdrop?"

"Well, I'm not sure about the second poison. The why of it. But, you always come off stage through the audience and shake hands. They knew that. I didn't think at first that the fire and the poisonings were connected. But, since we know Benny probably poisoned you the first time, and we know he died by the second poison, he had probably talked to whoever is in charge of all this about your penchant for patterns."

"Penchant for patterns. I like that phrase. It would make a good line in a play. Or maybe I'll use it for the title of my memoir." Chris finished his sandwich and balled up the wrapper.

"Thanks. And, since there were two fires and two druggings, I can't begin to explain a timed drop. If it had been a bomb, that might connect, but this thing was too precise. They had access to a part of your bar no one really goes into. Someone would have needed a key to get into the club the morning the gas line was cut, right? And, to get out the night of the backdrop falling. The fact you had just been down in the basement where the trigger was is strange. And, that you didn't see or notice anything is stranger still. That tightens the timeline. And, no one saw anyone that struck them as out of place."

"I wasn't looking for anything like that. I saw a rat," he whispered. "That freaked me out a little. I only had the small flashlight. The doors that were supposed to be locked were locked. I unlocked them and got what I needed."

Liz balled up her wrapper and took Chris', tossing both of them in the greasy paper bag. "Who might have keys to the club? Or better yet, is there any way into the club other than those two doors off the street?"

"Gosh, over the years, lots of people have had keys to Tamburlaine. Before it was our bar, it had been vacant for a number of years. For some time it had been a speakeasy, then a blue collar bar, then it closed for a number of years before Jimmy bought it."

"Okay, but these events are all recent. Who might have a key now?"

"Well, Benny had a set; Frank, Nancy Ann, and Matilda all have keys. There's an extra set in the register, for the alley door anyway." Chris wracked his brain. "There hasn't been a need in years to have keys made if that's any indication. If Benny was working with them—and we're pretty certain about that, he'd have keys, and know my penchant."

"So you didn't have to make keys for Frank or Nancy Ann or Matilda?" Liz leaned closer.

Chris inhaled, enjoying the subtle perfume Liz wore. Chris never liked wearing perfume or using scented soaps. Early in his performing days, he'd gotten away from them for the sake of the performers with him on stage. There's nothing worse than a snoot full of cheap cologne when you're trying to hit a high A. "No. I have several sets of keys in the office. I can't even remember when it was, but I had a bartender who kept losing keys so I had a dozen of them made for the alley door. The extras are in the safe at the club. No one has that combination. And, as far as I know, no one knows how to open the office door except me."

"Right, that strange doorknob lock thing."

Rusty Warren sang a soft ballad in the background.

"No one has the basement keys, those are skeletons, you know, old-fashioned things: big and heavy." He took Liz's hand into his own. "I like that you're gnawing on all of this. I've just sort of been taking it, but not doing anything. I don't know why. I'd about given up on things."

Liz squeezed Chris' hand. "You didn't answer my other question. There's the front door and the alley door. Is there any other way into the club? A coal scuttle maybe?"

"A scuttle is like a bucket. I know that because of the *Times* crossword. No, the coal door, Jimmy had that sealed shut before I took over the club." The song ended. "Shit, I hadn't thought of this until now, it's been so long..." He stood up. "Come with me." He led them under the gallery staircase. "That's a way in." He pointed to a metal door with a crank handle.

"Through there? Your club is a block away."

"The speakeasy days. This place was a machine shop then and its owner created that bar and the tunnel to it. So, men came into the shop here, walked the tunnel, and ended up in the basement of Tamburlaine. I can't remember what it was called back then."

"You have your own tunnel under a New York City street? That's incomprehensible."

"Being a detective, you should know that there are tunnels all over the city." Chris turned and walked into his office space. He dug around in a cupboard and came up with two flashlights and returned to Liz. "I haven't used this in years and years. I get a little claustrophobic in the tunnel." He cranked on the handle, expecting it to be difficult, but it was as if someone had recently sprayed a bit of WD-40 on it, it easily spun with very little effort. He pulled the door open and handed Liz a flashlight.

"Oh, I should have brought a broom instead of a flashlight," Chris said as he led the way down a wooden staircase. The corners at top and bottom were filled with cobwebs.

"I'm glad I'm wearing a wig. I can just throw it away when we're finished." Liz coughed. "Do you want me to lead?"

"No, no, I'm fine. Here we are." Chris reached the bottom step and then the dirt floor. A cool draft blew over his feet. "I don't remember there being another outlet for this tunnel under the stairs. Chris tried to slide between them and the brick wall, but he couldn't. Liz tried as well, but couldn't get through.

Liz shined the flashlight back under the stairs. It was a solid brick wall. She shined it toward the ceiling, about twenty feet up. Nothing seemed out of the ordinary. It would be a long drop from the street. "I think we should press ahead."

They walked for a bit and then came to a door. Chris sorted through the keys on a rusty ring, chose one of the skeleton keys, and with a little effort, opened the door with an ear-splitting creak. "I don't think anyone has used this in a very long time."

"Look." Liz shined her light into the top corners. "The cobwebs have been pushed away. I don't know if they got through this door, but they've been here recently."

"Now they're a they?" Chris shined his light at Liz who shrugged.

"Maybe a they."

Chris and Liz continued forward, until they arrived at a dead-end, a brick wall.

"Now what?" Liz asked. "Do we need a code word?"

Chris pushed on the wall which opened up and forward. He stepped in and held the wall up for Liz. "Hurry, this fucking thing is heavy."

"Sorry, hon." Liz stepped into the room. "Okay, let it go."

Together, they closed the brick door, which became a box that looked like a filing cabinet. It stood next to another filing cabinet, the one Chris had found the newspaper clipping in.

"Here, look." Liz shined her flashlight on the ground. "There are a set of footprints that go from here to the other wall. And, there are a shuffle of footprints at this cabinet that go to the door and back."

"I was just in here a few days ago, getting out that newspaper clipping."

"Right, and you came through the door, right?"

"Yes, Liz."

"So, someone else went through the wall." Again, she shined her light. "I can't believe the building inspector didn't find this or question it."

"Come with me." Chris opened the door into Tamburlaine's basement. They walked a few feet. He directed his flashlight. "That's where they discovered the line that pulled down the scrim. They went further. These are the old whore's rooms; we're storing costumes and scenery in them. Careful of Audrey II." Chris patted the oversized foam plant, taller than him in heels.

"Oh, I saw *Little Shop* the other night. It was really fucking good." She stopped at the plant and opened its mouth, sticking her head inside like a lion tamer. "You know how it works; you know there's a trap door or something, but for a moment, you believe that she's being eaten by this thing."

"I know. If it weren't for suspension of disbelief, well, I wouldn't have a career." He pulled her out of the plant. "You're right, though, my kids are doing a swell job." Chris opened another door.

"What's that?" Liz shined her light upward.

"The trap door to the stage." Chris was on the move again. He opened another door and they went from stark darkness and dirt floors to a shiny, state of the art food prep area with a huge walk-in refrigerator and a walk-in freezer. As they came out, one of the prep girls screamed and dropped her knife. "Sorry, dear. No need to be alarmed. We may be old enough to be ghosts, but we're not."

Matilda thudded down the stairs. Chris waved at her.

"Chris! What are you doing here? How did you get in here? I've been in the kitchen all afternoon and never saw you come through."

"Never you mind," said Chris.

"Can we go back for a moment?" Liz asked.

"Of course." They turned and left with no explanation and Liz led them back to the furthest room. She found a spot in the middle of the wall and pressed. It took a few tries, but then a section of the brick wall lifted, just like the entrance. "Anyone who knew this was here would have easy access to the club."

"Sure, if they knew about it and had all the right keys. You saw, the doors were all locked." Chris set his flashlight on top of the filing cabinet, the real one, and then brushed dust from his blouse.

"Yes, but they could have access. We need to see if we can find out who has these keys other than you. Or, is it possible they used your keys? You don't carry anything but the alley key and your house key, right?"

"Right. I have to go back and change. I'm on in about an hour."

"Okay," Liz said.

Chris envisioned the hamster on the wheel inside Liz's head.

Thirty-nine

Chris gazed out at the full house as he played "Roll me over, lay me down, and do it again." The audience did its part by singing the prescribed choruses: men, women, virgins, etc. The number, one of Chris' favorites, raised raucous great laughter from the audiences. Years had passed without him hearing this tuned-in joy from an audience. Years. He thought about those years; he wondered what had kept him going all that time? That long ago promise. "Yes," he'd said as Jimmy lay dying. "Yes, he'd keep Tamburlaine open, no matter what." And here he'd arrived, nearly full circle: Tamburlaine's popularity was growing; there were articles and reviews and tweets, whatever those were. Ingram created a website and Facebook page for Tamburlaine and people were clicking on links and liking things, that's what he'd said.

The number ended and Chris, still tinkling lightly on the keys, started into the long story of the housewife, a station wagon full of boy scouts, the divine trucker on the highway, the Tupperware...it remained his favorite of Rusty Warren's routines. As he talked, the audience laughed at all the right parts and held their breath at the right time. And as he talked, he found himself taking the time to look deep into each person's eyes. That had been one of his things when he'd headlined at Tamburlaine all those decades ago. He'd sing, because in those days, drag queens actually sang; while he sang, he'd look at the audience members he could see—the stage lighting in the big room often hindered his sight, leaving him only the first few tables. But, he looked deep into the dark house, imagining the eyes of those patrons in the back. Sometimes, a guy with eyeglasses that reflected the stage caught him, held him for a moment. No one ever said it, but Chris knew, without doubt or question, that that's what truly made him the headliner. In those few moments, one here, another there, looking deep into a patron's eyes, he made a connection. In that moment, he changed, no longer just the entertainment, but a person. That was the point for him, that in drag he remained a person, someone important on the planet, someone who made a difference, who existed, dammit. Despite what society or others might think.

Chris stumbled for a moment. His fingers continued, but he went up. He'd been so deep into his own thoughts that he'd forgotten where he was in the story he told. Chris looked to Liz, sitting her post in the corner, watching the comings and goings of everyone who entered and left the bar.

Liz mouthed, "Boy Scouts."

"So, I picked up the Boy Scouts and barrel assed down to the church to set up..." Chris was back on track. He continued telling the story, his favorite of Rusty Warren's...he'd already thought of that tonight. This used to be so easy for him, performing and thinking of other things. Maybe it was the booze, too much or too little, that was the question. "Two of them fighting, three of them have to pee, are you ready for this?" Yes, those were the words, they continued and his thoughts wandered. Where had he been? Oh, yes, Jimmy dying. The desperation in his eyes as Chris held him in his arms. Wanting to be done, but not wanting to be done.

They'd never been lovers. That's not to say they'd never had sex. That happened in the theater. You drank too much, you slept with everyone, at one point or another. Most of the boys simply moved on over time. They got their big break or they found themselves in a day job or working as a dresser for a show. It didn't matter where they went, just that they went. And, as they moved on, there were other nubile men to take their places; there were new drag queens looking for a home, a place to be and perform.

For so many, like Chris, like Liz, performance didn't define their choice of living their lives dressed in women's clothing. For so many, there was no alternative. They were them, they felt right as women. They didn't want to be women; those, like Chris, relished being a man, sleeping with men, being gay. No, this life expressed an inner self stronger and more important than just being a gay man or a straight man or any other type of man. Chris was a drag queen. A queen.

"Mommy!" Chris yelled. The audience laughed heartily and applauded raucously at the punchline of the story. He brought up one of the waitresses, a very tall, very thin, very funny queen. Chris played "Adelaide's Lament" from *Guys and Dolls*; the queen sang.

Midnight, the peak of everything: Four hours to go. Chris brought up The Piano Player from the big room, who played for anyone who wanted to sing show tunes. Despite being decades younger, The Piano Player knew almost as many songs as Chris.

"Here, boss," said Frank, as he poured Chris a double bourbon. Chris downed the glass and set it on the bar. Frank refilled it.

People came up to him, wanted to meet him, shake his hand, tell him about some other experience they'd had at Tamburlaine and how glad to know it had reopened. All the while, Liz sat in her corner, watching.

Chris finished his second or was it his third double bourbon before heading into the kitchen. The evening's seatings were finished. The stainless steel kitchen sparkled like a jewel. Matilda, propped against the counter, wrote in her notebook.

"Hello, Mr. Marlowe. Would you like something to eat? I can make you a plate lickity split! Wonderful, fall off the bone chicken tonight."

"Are there a few drumsticks? Maybe some coleslaw, too?"

"No coleslaw left, but I can cut up fresh cucumbers and tomatoes?"

"Perfect." Chris pulled himself up on a stool and watched as Matilda put together a plate of humble foods in a five-star manner. "Thank you," he said as she placed the plate and utensils in front of him.

"If you don't mind my saying, you're not looking great tonight, Mr. Marlowe."

Chris swallowed a piece of cucumber. "I don't mind." He wanted to tell her that he'd had a few too many bourbons, that he was drunk. But, he didn't. Instead, he ate heartily, allowing Matilda to add two more drumsticks to his plate. The skin was salty and crisp, the meat fell off the bone. His fingers, with red lacquered nails, were sticky with chicken grease. Pieces of paper napkin stuck to them.

When he'd finished eating, Matilda came around the expediter's counter, stood next to Chris, and, with a warm, wet, dish towel; she cleaned and then, with another towel, dried his hands.

Tears came to Chris' eyes. "Thank you," he whispered.

Matilda simply smiled; she picked up the remains of Chris' dinner and thumped back to her own side of the shelves. No more words were exchanged. Chris sat for a while longer, enjoying his full stomach and the kindness that had just occurred.

Forty

"Chris, we've got to talk about this."

"Oh, Liz, can't we just sit and listen to some music, rub each other's feet, pet the cat." Chris pushed open the metal door, allowed Liz to pass him, and pulled it shut with a bang.

"Chris, you don't have a cat, do you?"

"A what? A cat, no, just the clock with its ever wagging tail." Chris held the door open for Liz. He tossed his wrap on the chair and kicked off his heels. "Beer?"

"Sure."

"Oh, Lizzy, don't sound all verklempt." Chis handed her a beer before pouring bourbon over ice in a crystal glass.

"Ice cubes?"

"My doctor said I should continue to drink more water." Chris offered a hand to Liz, who pulled herself up. "Come on."

"I don't think ice in whiskey counts."

"You get your water your way and I'll get mine in my way, right? Of course, right."

"I can see you as Dolly! Wouldn't that be wonderful, you walking down all those stairs and all those handsome men singing and dancing just for you?" Liz plopped on the long couch, pulled off her sweater, removed her big guns, and dropped them on the table before putting the sweater back on."

"Elmer, that's disgusting, letting your tits just sit there like that." Chris laughed.

"Listen, you treat your tits your way and I'll treat my tits mine."

"Now who's auditioning for Dolly?" Chris had turned on the CD of Streisand's *Hello, Dolly!*

"Hallelujah, something other than Rusty. Here, give me your feet."

"Rusty Warren paved a great career for me." Chris nudged Liz with his foot and she started rubbing again. "Oh, that feels good. You give the best foot." He laid his head back. "So, what do you want to talk about? Like I don't know."

"How have you remained so calm? There have been five attempts on your life in a very short time period."

"No one tried to kill me today. And, for that I am truly grateful."

"Most people would be scared shitless." Elmer rubbed lotion into Chris' dry heel.

"Back in the early days, people were arrested for being us; there used to be beatings and worse on these streets of New York."

"I know, I know, you were born a poor black girl—"

"Someone said I should stop with that, that it's not politically correct." Chris shifted feet so Liz could reach the other one. "Fine. Fine. Well, we know Benny's dead and that he had something to do with the second poisoning attempt and we guess the first one, right? Not sure about the Molotov cocktail at my door. Not sure about the gas line being cut. And, not sure about the backdrop falling from the fly space. We know very little. The cops seem to know even less. We haven't seen a cop in days, maybe that's good." Chris finished off his bourbon and enjoyed the sound of the ice cubes in the glass.

"Do you want more?"

"Oh, yes please."

He maneuvered out of the couch. With no tits or heels, Elmer barely stood five feet tall. He took the glass and went into the kitchen. "More ice?" he called.

"Yes, please, and just bring the bottle."

"Yes, your majesty!" Liz handed the glass to Chris. He pointed at the speaker. "See, all those men singing. That's why that show was a huge hit. People love to hear men singing."

"That and watching their tight dancer asses."

"I'll drink to that." Elmer clinked his bottle against Chris's glass and took a long swallow of beer. "I want to blame all of this on Folgate, but it doesn't make sense."

"What, Honey? What doesn't make sense?" Chris sipped.

"That is the first time you've ever called me Honey."

"Is that okay?"

"Yes. So long as you don't start making honeydew lists." Elmer laughed at his own joke. "Get it? Honeydew like the melon? Honey like the boyfriend? To-do, like the errands?" He waited a beat; Chris rolled his eyes dramatically. "Anyway, it can't all be Folgate. Why would he want to blow your kitchen up? If he got caught, that would be the end of his career. It doesn't make sense to set fire to this building, does it? It's brick, anyway, so that wouldn't burn. Has to be an attempt on your life."

"All these things are attempts. Thankfully, not successful ones." Chris thought for a long moment. "You know, a few months ago, I don't think I would have cared if someone had killed me. But, now..."

"Now, you have all of us. Me. Frank. Nancy Ann. Matilda...Jericho?" Liz was back to rubbing Chris' feet and calves with lotion.

"Yes, all of you. I'm the richest drag queen in Manhattan. Ring a bell so Clarence will get her wings."

Your skin is healing very well. Liz lightly tickled Chris' soles.

"Stop! Stop. I'll spill my drink. I don't know about Jericho. He hasn't been around in awhile."

"He'll find his way back. His name is on the marquee. Okay, so we know that Benny is, was somehow connected to Folgate and Jimmy. His look alike was in that photo in the paper. But, Benny is dead. Wait, have you heard from Folgate in a while?"

"Not since the health inspectors came. That was months ago. Oh, don't stop rubbing."

Liz, with more lotion, went back to the task. "We should contact him, see if he's okay, ask a few questions."

"We can't just stop in his office and ask questions, we can't change our whole way."

"That line doesn't work in the show either. No, I think I can. I have my badge. Sure, it says retired, but it looks pretty damn official; it is official."

"What would you ask?" Chris poured more bourbon.

"We'll have to make up a list of questions. Tomorrow is going to be a great day. I haven't been out on the beat, working a case for a long time." Liz finished off her beer.

"Now who's running old lines?" Chris laughed, enjoying the heavy buzz of a night of liquor, knowing he'd sleep hard and solid. "So, get your pad. If I'm going to talk to Folgate tomorrow, I want to be prepared."

Forty-one

Chris and Elmer walked up the small street, arm-in-arm. Chris stopped; Elmer stumbled.

"I just don't think this is a good idea," said Chris. He looked at himself in the dusty glass of a closed shop. With the skilled pinky of an artist, he corrected his lipstick. "It doesn't feel right; you dressed like a man, me as a woman."

"But, you never really dress as a man." Elmer freed his hand from the crook of Chris' elbow. "I do it all the time. I had to for my day job. Thirty years. Forty, fifty, sixty hours a week. Don't try and do the math, I've done it. Poor Liz had to be kept shut away and quiet for more than sixty-thousand hours. Just imagine."

"Well, I can't imagine that. I've been lucky to have lived my life the way I wanted." Chris reached for Elmer's hand, but Elmer held it to himself. Chris dropped his untaken hand to his side and shifted his attention further up the empty street.

"You have been lucky and you've done well. Yet, over the past few weeks, it seems someone, or everyone, is trying to eighty-six you and you don't know why and aren't you lucky to have met Liz who introduced you to me?" Elmer's tone had grown dark and serious.

"I don't like you talking about yourself in the third person. You're here; you're both Liz and Elmer; and, now, you're free to be either of them any time you want." He took a step, then another; he waited for Elmer who finally took the two steps to catch up. Chris led the way up the street to the corner. The Folgate building stood tall. Built of red brick in 1901, that's what the cornerstone proclaimed. Those red bricks, now chipped, pitted, and sandblasted, were nearly pink. Despite the obvious effort to keep the building neat and tidy, the wall nearest them had been tagged with blue spray paint letters in an intricate pattern. Chris decided they spelled "BITCH" but there were certainly many other combinations.

Of all of them, he liked the outcome of bitch the most. "I still say this is a bad idea."

"Well, I'll drive this train. You can stay out here if you want. Or, sit in the lobby." Elmer opened the elaborately, rococo designed metal door with its stained-glass inserts that spelled out F-O-L-G-A-T-E in a high arch. "Has his family owned this building for over a hundred years?"

"Their name is carved into the frieze around the top." Along with the frieze were gargoyles with varied, hideous faces randomly placed among the Folgate Building's five stories who kept watch over New York City. "This is one of the tallest buildings in this area. Most are one or two stories because there's no reachable bedrock to support taller structures. So, either there's bedrock underneath us or they jammed pilings deep into the earth."

Elmer again opened the door. Reluctantly, Chris walked inside. The lobby was circled with impressive, highly polished wood panels.

"What do they call this pattern?" Elmer asked.

"Something like fire or...flame, maybe?" Chris ran his hand along the wood where the seam showed the two panels reflecting each other.

"How may I help you?"

Chris turned toward the woman. She couldn't be more than twenty-two or twenty-five. He whispered, "We don't have an appointment."

"We'd like to see Mr. Folgate if he's in." Elmer took over, his voice stern, authoritative.

"Which Mr. Folgate?" She held herself with poise. Her skirt was flat and straight in black wool. Her top, a butter yellow, softer, perhaps cashmere.

Elmer turned and looked deep into Chris' eyes.

"Senior," said Chris, unsure what result this might bring.

"Oh, yes, well, please follow me." The woman led the way toward a small elevator in the corner. It was exposed on three sides; all its cables and works visible to riders and watchers. The three got into the brass cage, metal frame doors closed, and they ascended slowly, smoothly to the fifth floor. The woman then allowed Chris and Elmer to step out.

The floor, covered in deep, plush carpet, Chris imaged a shade of blue the same as in Nixon's oval office. The windows were covered with heavy, damask curtains—even without a ruler, it was clear: each window's paired fabric panels opened exactly the same number of inches.

An older version of the man in the newspaper photograph walked up to Chris and Elmer. "Christopher Marlowe, how wonderful to see you again. It has been a long, long time, now hasn't it?"

Chris brushed his lips near Folgate's check. "It has been a very long time. The club is hopping again, you should come out some evening and see what we've got going on."

"Are you...Marcie, please bring us," he turned to Elmer, "coffee? Tea? Soft drink? Bourbon?"

"Coffee," said Elmer. "With cream."

Folgate turned back to Chris. "Bourbon's still your drink, isn't it?"

"How kind of you to remember." Chris took Folgate's arm; the old man, in a custom fitted suit, silk paisley tie, and highly-shined Italian leather shoes led Chris and Elmer into a big office, a room that took up nearly the entire fifth floor.

Folgate offered Chris a wingback leather chair. Chris slipped down into the soft leather; a small sigh escaped unwittingly from his lips as the chair seemed to mold perfectly to his body. Folgate took up the matching chair, leaving the leather couch for Elmer, who looked uncomfortable. Chris felt bad for a moment, knowing that it was now impossible to explain his relationship with this Mr. Folgate.

Marcie returned with refreshments on a silver tray: one coffee, a small silver cream pitcher, two cut crystal glasses, a silver bucket of ice, and a bottle of A.H. Hearst bourbon.

Folgate picked up the bottle and broke the wax seal.

"I'm very impressed," said Chris. He turned toward Elmer and reached out with his well-manicured hand. "This is one of the all-time best bourbons no one has ever tasted, or very few have tasted." Elmer didn't look impressed. Chris turned back to his host who was pouring the amber liquor over two cubes of ice. He handed the glass to Chris and then poured one for himself. He'd left Elmer to fend for himself on the coffee side of the table-sized tray.

"What shall we drink to?" Folgate raised his glass toward Chris.

"The future of Tamburlaine," said Chris.

"Of course," said Folgate.

Chris sipped the bourbon, enjoying the soft, cool play of it on his tongue. "Damn that's good." He sipped again.

"So, what brings you all the way up here to see me?" Folgate added a splash more bourbon to each glass before sitting back in his chair.

Chris surveyed the room with its big, carved desk, the map table with its flat drawers. A wardrobe he guessed housed a television. The pool table and old-fashioned racks of cues. They probably weren't old-fashioned when they'd been installed.

"Are you stalling? And, who is your friend?"

"Oh, where are my manners? This is my great good friend, Elmer."

Mr. Folgate gave a big wink to Chris.

"You know, in the old days, well, you remember? 'Great Good Friend' was the code."

Chris sipped again, wanting the taste never to leave his mouth.

"I know and remember better than you." Folgate smiled a broad, toothy smile. Chris could tell they were new choppers.

"Well, there have been some strange events happening lately. They may be related or they may be random," said Chris.

"And, you two are the Hardy Boys?" Again, that kind, broad smile.

"Yes." Chris leaned forward and, as much as it pained him, he set his glass on the tray.

"This is no bedtime story, Folgate. Chris' life is at risk," said Elmer, sounding hardboiled, like a Chandler character.

Nigel Folgate added more bourbon to Chris' glass, giving him his full attention. "Tell me what is wrong and I will move heaven and earth, will do all I can to help you."

Elmer wiped his mouth with a handkerchief.

Chris said: "Well, your nephew. I'm assuming he's your nephew? He's bought up all the buildings in Tamburlaine's block."

"But not Tamburlaine, right?" Nigel picked up Chris' glass and handed it to him.

"Thank you. You're correct. I can't..." Tears well up in his eyes.

"Of course not," whispered Folgate.

A silence enveloped them as Chris took another drink.

"Tell him," encouraged Elmer.

Folgate never took his gaze off of Chris' face.

"Okay. I was poisoned. Everyone is pretty sure it was in my bourbon." He again set his glass down. "After that, Benny, my bartender, disappeared. Later, I was poisoned again, this time with some odd patch, you know, like people wear when they're trying to quit smoking? The one they tried to stick to me had an odd combination of poisons from South America. A bit later, Benny was discovered dead and so was the guy who stuck the patch on me. The police say it was from the second poison that they both died." He pointed a finger toward Elmer. "That's when I met Liz...Elmer by day."

Folgate turned toward Elmer, smiled broadly, and winked.

"There's more. Tell him the rest," said Elmer.

"Some boys, young men, threw Molotov cocktails at me—not very tasty."

"His burns were pretty bad," said Elmer.

Folgate nodded, but remained silent.

"Someone cut the gas line at Tamburlaine. The kitchen staff discovered it before any damage occurred. And, most recently, someone dropped a drape pipe, nearly fell on me, on my head. Booby trapped or something from the basement." Fear rose into him as he finished. Someone really did want him dead.

"This has all happened in the past few weeks?" Folgate poured more bourbon into Chris' glass.

"Well, the first poisoning must have been three or four months ago." Chris didn't drink, but settled once again deeper into the chair.

"And, why have you come to see me?"

Chris didn't respond; instead, he looked deep as he could into Nigel's eyes. They'd known each other, quite intensely, for a very brief time.

"Is the painting still there?" Nigel asked.

"The *Streetwalkers* remains." Chris smiled. "I thought this would be easier. Seeing you."

Nigel set down his drink and took Chris' hands into his own. "Oh, my dear, you mustn't get upset. The memories should by now all be good ones, no?"

Yes, he was an old man; Chris wasn't a spring chicken either, but Nigel must be nearly ninety.

"You've done a remarkable job keeping Tamburlaine going all these years. Don't let yourself begin to believe you haven't fulfilled your debt to him. That has been paid in full, with interest over and over; the paper has been burned to ash. You have to know that." Nigel kissed Chris' hands.

Elmer blurted out: "We think the...younger Folgate has something to do with all or at least some of the attempts on Chris' life."

"I didn't want to get you involved," said Chris to Nigel. "I was hoping you weren't going to be in your office today. But, you've always been here."

"Every day, seven days a week, like clockwork. Now, finish your drink. And, then you and your friend will go and I will find out what I will find out."

Chris begrudgingly tossed back the bourbon, the ice cubes tinkled playfully against the crystal. He stood. "Thank you, Nigel."

"No. Never. No thanks required. Never. You are the one to be thanked." He led them back to the elevator. Marcie waited to take them down to the lobby.

Chris stopped, kissed Nigel's cheek, rubbed at the lipstick left behind.

Nigel raised his hand to his cheek, and for a moment, he held Chris' fingers. "This color has always looked good on me." Nigel's smile now included tears.

Chris walked through the door Elmer held open for him. The sun spied down from its zenith, bringing every pane of glass into luster, blinding anyone caught walking on the street at that hour. This, Chris believed, was, in fact, that harsh light of day so many spoke of. He had, for decades, avoided this light: too many pores were visible; no foundation covered cleverly enough; no walk of shame was worthy of that light.

"What was that?" Elmer hissed. "Why didn't you tell me first that there were several Mr. Folgates and second you knew one of them intimately."

"This is not an appealing side you're showing." Chris shoved his hands into his pockets, hoping for a pair of sunglasses to be hiding there among the butterscotch candies and wadded up tissues.

"Not an appealing side of me? Chris, you've got to tell me what's going on. Things are happening so fast, but yet seem to be moving in very slow motion."

"Here," said Chris as he opened a dark door and entered, not exactly holding the door for Elmer. It took Chris' eyes a moment to adjust.

"Here?"

"Oh, Liz, you just have to trust me every once in a while." Chris shaded his eyes for another moment. "They have great food here. One of the lesser known secrets in our little neighborhood."

"Chris!" An old man, short, stout, apron up to his white-shirted chest, a clean towel over his arm, tripped over himself to meet Chris where he stood.

"Mario!" The two kissed each other's cheeks. "Can you squeeze us in for lunch?"

"Of course, of course." Mario led Chris and Elmer to a round booth in a far corner. He lit the candle and placed a small hurricane glass over it.

Elmer remained stunned, although he sat and scooched into the booth.

Mario, without a pad or pen in hand, asked: "What can I bring you and your friend?"

"Two glasses of the house red and whatever pasta the chef creates for us." Chris didn't bother to take notice that Elmer might want something different. "And, some of that wonderful bread. Still Mama's recipe?"

"Of course. Of course." Mario, a good Italian Catholic, grouped his right fingers and thumb together and touched his forehead, chest, and then his left and right shoulders, making a sign of the cross. "May she rest in peace." He kissed his still gathered finger tips. He smiled at Chris. "We've missed you, Mr. Marlowe. We're like you, holding out. If you can do it, so can we."

Chris smiled toward Mario; the man turned and headed through the swinging doors into the kitchen.

"I've never noticed this place before," said Elmer. "There's no sign or anything."

"No, there's no sign. Only certain people know about Mario's."

Chris's eyes finally, fully adjusted. There, in the corner, a small bar without a bartender, a mirror ball, still and without sparkle, at the ceiling's center; an upright piano, beat up a bit, stood against a far wall. Chris had played that piano, back in the beginning, before he'd headlined, played that piano in men's clothing, at first, and later in women's. Mario had barely flinched. He'd met them, those men with connections, those men who ran the city from their various fields. Some thought of them as "Family" others as "Gangsters." Chris thought of them as men, strong men, with connections and fidelity.

There were no other patrons now, but Chris always thought of Mario's filled to the brim with old men, movers and shakers, making smoky deals over two-martini lunches.

"Chris, talk to me." Elmer took Chris' hand.

Chris allowed his hand to be taken, but still, he didn't look at Elmer. He didn't want to cry any more. He'd been so tearful these past weeks.

What he wanted...What did he want? There weren't answers to those questions now, not that he could easily share with Elmer. He disliked that name. He preferred to call his friend, his lover, Liz.

"Chris?"

Without a word, Mario set a bread basket on the table. He nudged a tall, filled wine glass in front of Chris and another near Elmer.

Chris smelled the warm garlic bread, retrieved his hand from Elmer, and took a large slice from the basket. He pulled off a bit of bread and popped it in his mouth, avoiding his lips. "Mmm." He ripped another piece off the slice and ate that one. Next, still avoiding any form of eye contact with Elmer, Chris drank a large swallow of Chianti. Those old days now washed over him. The stories those men had told; the truth those men told; the lies. Jimmy got him the job when Chris wanted extra money for a trip to Paris. He'd only been the piano player, not much different than the kid who now played at Tamburlaine between Chris' sets. Chris tinkled the keys, listened to the conversations, and kept his mouth shut about what he saw and heard.

No one had ever been murdered in front of him, although many had been scared to the point of wetting their pants. He'd never seen a gun, or even the bulge of one. There were never any of those things you see about the Family on television. Instead, there were those who belonged, those who didn't, and those who sought favor one way or the other. Those men, they had all been solid. Nigel had been solid. But, Chris couldn't talk about this, not to anyone, not to Elmer, not even to Liz.

"I can't tell you any of it," Chris said before another long swallow of wine that emptied his glass. Just as the empty hit the table, Mario replaced it with another full glass. He took the empty and silently reentered the club's shadows.

"How could you not tell me about Nigel before we walked into that building? How could you not trust me?"

It was Chris' turn to take up Elmer's hand. "Oh, dear Liz. I hoped beyond all hope that Nigel would be out and the snot-nosed kid would be there."

At last Chris looked into Elmer's eyes; Elmer whispered: "It felt like a slap across the face."

"Oh, dear, that was never, never my intention."

A long silence enveloped them. Chris felt awkward holding Elmer's hand at the odd angle their hands had come together.

Mario solved the issue by bringing two heaping plates. "Pasta primavera in an Alfredo sauce." Again, he stepped away and virtually vanished from sight.

Chris knew what Mario knew. Wait for the moment, use it, let it go.

"If you knew Nigel could help you with this, why hadn't you gone to him before?" Elmer focused on his food.

"I didn't know if he was still alive." Chris felt the tears rise and he pushed them back down. He had to stop all this crying. "I hadn't heard of his death, but you saw how old he is, how frail, how.... Let's just eat, okay?"

Elmer played with his food.

"Okay?" Chris pushed.

"Okay."

The juke box came to life, an ancient machine that played records. Louis Prima sang: "A Good Man is Hard to Find." Chris turned his head to see who had played the song; he had sung it many times, but with a much different connotation than Mr. Prima. The younger Folgate stood in the unsettling yellow glow. He cracked his knuckles, eyes boring into Chris.

"Should I do something? Call the precinct?" Elmer asked.

Whatever arguments or differences they had dissipated in a flash. They were together; they were one.

"No," said Chris. "There's no longer anything to fear."

Elmer whispered: "Do you mean because of Nigel?"

"You, boy, what are you doing in here?" Mario crossed the room. With poise, the waiter had Folgate's arm behind his back propelled him toward the door.

"Watch your back old man, and you, too, Marlowe."

The waiter gave one final shove and Folgate flew out onto the street. Into the bright light, Mario yelled, "Never come in here again." His actions as deft as Tamburlaine's Rocko.

Chris applauded quietly with appreciation. "My hero."

"Sorry for the disruption, Mr. Marlowe. That damn kid is trying to close my business. He's called the health department several times, the police department, the liquor board. It's been one battle after another for nearly a year."

"I know it. He's after Tamburlaine, too." Chris wiped the corners of his mouth with the cloth napkin.

"Lousy *bischero*," Mario muttered on his way back into the shadows. He returned with two very small cups of very strong coffee, a piece of cheesecake, and two forks. He placed these in front of his guests. "On the house."

"Thank you," said Chris. "My favorite." He took a small sip of the coffee.

Elmer remained silent, not touching his cup or the dessert.

"Well, you wanted to know the story, right?" Chris kept his eyes on the cheesecake. "So, here goes. Oh, we were all so young—"

Christopher Marlowe, in very high heels and short everything else, stopped center stage, alone in the spotlight. He opened his perfectly lip-sticked lips and, to the great surprise of everyone sang Puccini's "O Mio Babbino Caro," a Capella; perhaps not as well as Maria Callas, but incredibly well. The entranced audience in the Tamburlaine Theater applauded nearly seven minutes at the conclusion. All the while, Chris performed deep curtsies in the manner of an opera singer.

The next evening's performance sold out. Again, at the show's conclusion, the audience stomped their feet and applauded long and loudly. As Chris performed his deep curtsies, that night dressed as Callas with a chignon and a flowing gown, a handsome man handed him a bouquet of yellow roses. Chris liked that the flowers were yellow and not red. He preferred the lighter colors. He sank his nose into the bouquet, all the while connecting visually with the man who'd given them.

That man waited for Chris near the hallway that led backstage. When Chris appeared, in flared slacks and a gauzy blouse, his face makeup softened, his hair still in its knot, the man approached; without warning, he kissed Chris with passion. Around them, as the cast walked past, they sent out catcalls and crude remarks; Chris kissed the man back for a long while.

He breathlessly introduced himself: "I'm Nigel."

"You should buy me a drink or something. It will never do to make out here in the hallway like children as the world watches."

"Oh, I can't do that," said Nigel. His eyes, the palest blue, bore into Chris'.

Chris wanted to make a joke. People loved his jokes. Nothing came into his quick-witted head. "Why not?"

"I belong to another."

With a flick of his wrist, his fan opened. Chris flashed it back and forth, closed it with a snap, and pushed Nigel away with the fan's tip. No word spoken, he made his way into the bar. At the sight of him, the crowd went wild. He sat at the end of the bar, playing the role of queen, allowing others to kiss his hand and buy him drinks.

"That is how we met," Chris said. With the cheesecake gone, he motioned to Mario for the check.

"Wait, there must be more," said Elmer.

"Well, of course there's more." Mario brought the check; Chris placed a hundred-dollar bill in the leather folder. "Keep the change."

"Very kind of you, Mr. Marlowe. Don't be a stranger." Mario offered his hand to Chris, who allowed the assistance as he slipped out of the booth and headed for the door. Elmer did his best to keep up.

Forty-two

"So, what happened after that? Who was the other person?" Elmer asked.

Chris drank a swallow of bourbon while Elmer rubbed his feet. It felt good to be home; to have had a great meal, to be here with a new lover who he really liked, a good glass of booze in hand.

"Chris, who was the other person?" Elmer grabbed Chris's foot with a bit of pressure.

"Oh, Nigel?"

"Yes, Nigel. You never finished the story."

"Jimmy, that's who. I'm not sure how they met; probably at Tamburlaine. Older man, young guy. But, that's where the Picasso came from. The *Streetwalkers* have been up in the office ever since then. That would've been sometime in the late '70s, just before Jimmy got sick." Chris drank more bourbon.

"Okay, so why is Nigel so supportive of you? The two of you had an intimate moment this morning."

"Was that just this morning? It's been a very long day." Chris nudged Elmer, who switched feet. "No, we never kissed or had sex or anything like that. Jimmy hung on for a very long time. He survived thrush and the sarcoma's and everything else that horrible disease threw at him. We were in and out of the hospital for more than eighteen months. Along the journey, Nigel never wavered; he kept cash flowing at Tamburlaine; he brought in an accountant; and, more importantly, he did all he could to make Jimmy happy. That's where the Jasper Johns and the Warhol and—"

"We're sleeping in a dead man's bed?" Elmer stopped rubbing Chris' feet.

"This was forty years ago; I've had several beds since then."

"But, all the paintings in there? Those are all gifts to Jimmy from Nigel?"

"Yes." Chris stared into space, remembering the smell of paint. "The artists were trying to break in and working hard to make a living. Jimmy loved the energy of those paintings. There were many nights I lay in bed with Jimmy, sometimes with Jimmy and Nigel both, getting stoned or eating shrooms and getting lost inside those paintings."

"And, that's why you've never sold those, right?"

"Right," said Chris; more bourbon, but no tears. "So, Nigel and I have a great respect for one another. And, after Jimmy was gone, it was Nigel who financed Tamburlaine and this loft for me at very favorable terms."

"But, you said it was family who financed…"

Chris watched Elmer process what he'd been told.

"Oh. Family. Got it. We can scratch Nigel off the list."

"As far as I'm concerned, he's never been on the list." Chris sat up, pulled the clicker off the table, and changed the CD to Ruth Etting.

"Do you ever listen to anything from this century?" Elmer stood and stretched, exposing his little potbelly as his shirt rose. He scratched that belly before heading into the kitchen. He returned a moment later with a freshly opened beer.

"Only when the children bring music into the bar for me to play. I don't care for it, it's not the same as these great old torch songs about love and angst."

"You know, CDs are quite passé. Everyone is streaming; listening to digital downloads."

"I moved from records to cassettes. Cassettes to eight tracks; back to cassettes. Then to CDs. I feel like I'm done upgrading over and over. The CDs play just fine. And, I've got nearly a hundred of them loaded into the player. I like it, like a miniature juke box."

After a long pause, Elmer asked: "So, who do you think is on the list?"

Remembering the juke box from the afternoon: "Hmm. The younger Folgate."

"Who is new in your life?" Elmer had his small notebook and a pencil out. Chris watched him, waiting to see if he'd lick the pencil tip again like the old-time reporters, but he didn't.

"Are you serious? We've done this a dozen times," Chris said. "There're all these people, the actors, the kitchen staff, the bartenders. All of them are new to me. There are hundreds of people passing through the doors every night." A sigh escaped. "Sorry, I don't mean to get testy. I don't like to think that there's someone out to kill me."

"Chris, I'm sorry, but you have to face this. There have been five attempts at your life. Five. There's no coincidence here. Someone is trying to kill you. Maybe more than one someone."

Chris thought about his life. He thought about the changes and the re-found success of the club. He'd recently bought a small Da Vinci sketch with some of the profits. "I know." He rewound events in his mind. "We know that Benny was connected to the two poisonings; we just don't know why or who might've been behind him. Benny had been around for four or five years. I just don't think he'd been plotting for that long. Hell, most of those nights, it was just the two of us. He could have easily offed me and left my body in the basement to rot."

"Do you think Folgate could have gotten to him?"

"Not likely. The two of them never appeared to get along." Chris went to take another sip of bourbon, but set the glass back down without drinking. "All of this really started right after Ingram showed up."

"Ingram? He's been a rock of support." Elmer made a note as he spoke.

"Yes, he has. But, with his arrival everything changed. I got back in touch with Jerry. The club came back to life—"

"Those are good things, though." He did it, Elmer licked the tip of his pencil.

Chris felt a warm smile spread through his whole being. "They are." This time he did drink. "The fires happened after Nancy Ann came onto the scene."

"But, with Nancy Ann came two dozen actors, Jerry, light guys, the kitchen staff."

"We're just repeating ourselves."

"Who else was in that newspaper photo? Where is it?"

That newspaper photo did have a group of people in it. "It's in my office at the club." Chris yawned. "Why don't we call it a night, Nancy Drew? I'm bushed."

Forty-three

Chris didn't go with Liz to run errands. He couldn't remember the last time he'd been alone. Just him and Rusty. As she crooned and prattled, he cleaned.

Wearing a ratty nightshirt, and nothing else, Chris Swiffered the floors, enjoying the smell of the spray liquid, scoured the kitchen table and counters, and finally emptied the refrigerator of leftovers, before removing the shelves and washing everything there with hot water and bleach.

Chores. He'd never really minded them. He liked when his home smelled of Pine Sol, Lemon Pledge, and Fabreze—how had they lived before the invention of Fabreze? Crisp sheets, clean and pressed, now that remained Chris' idea of luxury and refinement.

Weekly tasks completed, he showered, put on makeup, shiny dress, heels, and wig. He wanted to be at the club early to pay the bills and walk the place. Since the scrim falling and nearly killing him, he hadn't been walking the club nightly, but he missed it. Knowing what went on in the place saved him money over the years, catching leaking pipes, dead lightbulbs, and occasionally the odd rodent. Better to catch symptoms of decay before they took you down.

Dressed and ready, he walked to the club. The sky still held a hint of sunset color, although it was getting darker and colder earlier and earlier. He pulled his wrap close and walked the rest of the block. He enjoyed the click of his heels on the pavement; he'd missed that while recovering.

New thoughts. Happy thoughts. I am happy and well, he said to himself.

The front door remained locked and there were several guys hanging out, smoking on the street.

"Just a moment, fellas." Chris ducked into the alley; that door was open. He stepped inside. "Hello?" No one answered. There should be people here, actors warming up or smoking in the alley; Matilda and her crew chopping and prepping. He hit the light switch. Nothing happened. "Hello!" he called out louder; again, no response.

Chris made his way out of the kitchen, through the dining room, down the hall, and to his office door. It was open, unlocked. In the dim light from the high window, the clean spot on the wall verily glowed. The *Streetwalkers* were gone. The safe: locked. The desk: untouched. The room neat. Chills ran through him. Alone. Who could he turn to?

"Chris!" Liz shouted. "Are you here? What's going on?"

He rushed toward her voice. "My hero!" he hugged her tight. "I don't know what's happened."

"Are you okay?" Liz whispered.

"Why are you whispering?" Chris whispered back.

"It feels like that part in the movie where we should whisper. I don't hear any music though, so we should be fine for a bit."

Chris laughed and so did Liz. He wanted to tell her about the painting, about the unlocked door.

"Where is your staff? Where are the actors?"

"I don't know," he said. "There isn't any power, either." He led the way back into the kitchen; tried the door to the basement, locked. "Liz, in that drawer there, there should be a ring of keys."

Liz opened the metal drawer, the keys rattled. "No wonder people come and go here like they own the place, you leave the keys to the castle laying around like this." She shook the keys toward Chris.

"Not the time." He took the ring.

"Sorry. There should be people here. Something has happened," said Liz.

Chris fumbled through the dozen or so keys, found the one he wanted, and pushed it into the lock. A twist of the key and a turn of the knob and the door flung open. "Hello?"

"Do you hear that?" Liz whispered. The former detective took the lead and ran down the stairs. The door between the kitchen prep area and the rest of the basement was closed and locked.

Pounding echoed through the door.

Chris rushed to it, tried two keys before he found the right one. Finally, it opened. There were cheers and tears and then silence.

"What the hell happened?" Liz asked.

Nancy Ann stepped forward. We were all doing our prep. Three guys with rubber Nixon masks wielding machine guns—"

"Assault rifles. Like the M-16, sort of—"

She cut the actor off. "They were loud, aggressive, forced us down here, took out the big fuse, and locked the doors."

"Sweet Jesus, Mother of God, Buddha, Allah, Mary, Joseph, John Travolta! Is anyone hurt?" Chris asked; a catch in his throat. It was one thing to come after him, but a very different thing to come after the young people—his friends and staff.

"No. No one fought back. No one did anything stupid." As she spoke, she patted the back of the actor who knew about guns.

"Why didn't you call someone? Everyone here has one of those cell phone contraptions."

"They collected them as we were hustled down here," said one of the guys.

"Okay, everyone up and out of here." Chris headed deeper into the basement. The folding file cabinet had not been touched or moved. From the top drawer of a nearby dusty cabinet, Chris pulled out a fuse. He took it to the box, put on the gloves, positioned the fuse in the tool, and shoved it into place in a light shower of sparks. Lights and sounds burst from all over the club.

"Sometimes, you're so butch," said Liz as Chris pulled off the oversized black rubber gloves and then raised his arms and showed off muscles that he didn't have.

"I have to tell you something," Chris whispered.

Liz moved closer.

"It's gone." Tears welled into Chris' eyes.

"What?" Liz shouted.

"It's got to be what they were after. Everyone is okay, the club is okay. The *Streetwalkers* seems to be the only thing that's missing."

"The Picasso?" Liz pulled Chris into a hug. The two stood there, embracing, supporting each other.

Finally, still clenched together, Chris whispered: "I'm sorry I haven't been taking all of this more seriously. You've been trying for weeks..." The tears spilled and turned into sobs.

"We'll get through this. We'll figure it out together."

Forty-four

Chris paced the loft. Into the living room, into the kitchen, into the bedroom, storage room, and office at the other end, and back again he walked, his bare feet slapping off his steps against the old floors. As he paced, he wracked his brain for anyone who might have something against him, anyone he knew of, at least. Being an old, performing drag queen, there were certainly a lot of people over the many years who weren't thrilled Chris was on the planet. Not only bigots, but disappointed tricks, heartbroken boyfriends, the exes of men who'd dropped their lovers to be with Chris. There were parents of the guys who came out; those who worked at Tamburlaine over the years, too. And, spouses of... Anger mixed with fear mixed with anxiety as he explored his past in random images and bursts of memory.

He stopped in the kitchen. Elmer sat at the table, his feet up on a chair, a half-finished beer in front of him next to a legal pad. He'd scribbled names and doodles on the pad.

Chris poured more bourbon into a glass, downed the shot, poured more, sat with Elmer. "I wish I had a cigarette." The mumbled words weren't a request, but another random thought that connected this moment back into his past. "I think we'll have to do it."

"Do what," asked Elmer. "Start smoking again?"

He smiled with tight lips. "Stroll through my entire past. Right? It could be anyone from my entire life, right?" He slumped into a kitchen chair, sighed.

"I don't think a blow-by-blow meander through your sordid past will lead us to the answer." Elmer nudged Chris with a foot.

Chris took hold of that foot. "You should put on slippers or socks, your toes are cold. He rubbed with both hands. "Why not?"

"Hmm, that feels great. I think that the major incidents are going to stick out. I think that whoever is out to get you wants more than just your demise. They want material things. If that weren't the case, I don't think they would have stolen the painting."

"But, they didn't steal the painting until they'd failed many times at bumping me off." Chris released Elmer's foot and picked up the other one. "People think they know what that painting means to me..."

Elmer put aside his pad. "What does it mean to you?"

"Nigel wanted Jimmy to have security. The painting—"

"No, that's not it."

Chris looked at his friend. "No. That's not it. It was a joke—Jimmy tricked for cash. That's how he raised the funds to originally buy Tamburlaine. Nigel owned the building and was a client."

"Who stands to benefit from your death? Who does the bar go to? The artwork?" Elmer flipped to a clean sheet of yellow paper, drank more beer, held a pen at the ready.

Frustration mounted; Chris held back a scream. "Hell, just about everyone knew about the Picasso, whether they'd seen it or not. I should have listened. So many people said the paintings should be donated or sold to a museum or something. But, Jimmy..."

Elmer wrote "Jimmy" on his pad and drew a circle around the name. "When Jimmy died—"

"I'm sorry, but you don't know anything about that time in my life, about Jimmy." Elmer's foot went rigid. "Sorry." He released the foot. "When he died those paintings were there, they were his. I just haven't been able to bring myself to move them."

"Chris, when Jimmy died, more than thirty years ago, those paintings weren't worth much. A few thousand dollars, ten thousand? Right? He'd gotten those paintings cheap because no one knew the artists, well, beyond Picasso, right?"

He didn't want to give an inch, but Elmer was correct. Chris nodded.

"Now, Jimmy's been gone nearly four decades. Those paintings have all appreciated beyond his or anyone else's wildest dreams."

Another nod.

"It's amazing to me that something like this hasn't happened long before now." Elmer scribbled figures on his pad. "I think it's time to admit all this and to find a better home for the paintings, even if it's temperature-controlled storage."

"No, not storage. Jimmy always said there was no point to storing art.

It should be seen, even if only by one person who loved the work. Art should be seen."

Elmer added that phrase to his pad. "Chris, Jimmy's dead. You don't owe.... Who benefits from your death?"

He resisted a long moment. He'd never told anyone this; no one knew Jimmy's desires except for Chris and the attorney.

"Chris, tell me." Elmer's voice, so soft and tender, resounded inside Chris' head.

"Okay. Okay."

Elmer flipped to another fresh page.

"Jimmy had a nephew. His name is, well, was, Anthony."

"Was?"

"Anthony died in the late eighties from a cocaine addiction." Chris looked up to find Elmer glued to his every word. "Anthony married when he came into some money. He'd invested well, you remember the eighties? Everyone who had any cash got rich, easy. The woman, pregnant before the marriage, had twins. A month or so later, Anthony is found dead in a hotel room with lipstick on his dick."

"So graphic."

"The twins, Mary Alice and Brenda Lee—"

"The Brenda Lee?" Elmer's eyes skeptical, his penciled eyebrows raised high.

"Silly." Chris slapped Elmer's foot. "They had a pretty good life—inherited their dad's money, went to good schools, you know. Brenda Lee died in a car crash, but Mary Alice met a guy, married, and they had a daughter."

"How do you know all this?" Elmer drew a naked tree and added the names Chris recited to the different branches.

"The way my will is written, whoever is the youngest member of that lineage gets everything. All of what Jimmy left to me, and all that I've created. The only clause from Jimmy was to leave his artwork to the youngest. I added my own stuff because I don't have anyone to leave anything to. There is no family. I am the last of my own line. No cousins, no nieces or nephews. There is the slightest possibility that I have a child, but that's very remote."

"What? You have a child?"

"I don't know. I fucked a woman. The only woman I ever had sex with in my life. She played me for a while, said she'd be having my baby, but the woman turned out to be nuts, crazy as a loon." Chris bit off a hangnail, tasted bitter nail polish, spit the particle out of the side of his mouth. "No one has ever told me or come to me or informed me I was a daddy. Nancy Ann showed me how to do a Google search. I've done that for names, but haven't found anything."

"How do you know about, what's her na...Mary Alice?"

"Every year, I send a Christmas card to them. Each year I receive a card in return. They know me because I was their Uncle Jimmy's business partner. The generations have grown kinder over the years."

"That's it? Christmas cards?"

"They're a Christmas newsletter family. Lots of details about their family and kids. For several generations now."

"Is it possible that they know about their inheritance?" Elmer added mounds of snow around the base of his tree.

"I don't think so, but who knows what others really think or know."

"Okay, so far we've got Jimmy's kin, your possible illegitimate child, and a crazy real estate developer. They've all got motives to whack you."

Chris smiled at Elmer's enthusiasm. "Hey now, this is my life we're talking about." He laughed into his glass before downing the swallow of bourbon from inside.

"Sorry, but I do get excited about figuring out cases. That's why my success rate was so high."

"I'm tired of talking. Can't we go cuddle on the couch and watch a movie? *A Chorus Line* came from Netflix today."

"Popcorn?" Elmer stood up from the table; he stretched his arms high toward the ceiling.

"Of course!"

Together, the two retrieved the fixings: hot air popper, bowl, butter, corn. As the machine whirred and blew hot air and the occasional un-popped kernel, Chris thought once more about the possible son or daughter he may or may not have. They'd be thirty-six or thirty-seven by now.

Forty-five

Chris paused the movie. "*A Chorus Line* would be perfect for Tamburlaine."

"Sure," said Elmer through a yawn.

At least he continued to agree with him from that place of near unconsciousness. Chris wanted to call Jerry, but they hadn't spoken face to face since the director had walked out of rehearsal a few days earlier. Actually, they hadn't really talked, not like civilized people, since the fight over Nancy Ann. He brushed popcorn crumbs off his blouse and slacks. Elmer let out a little snore. Chris got up, collected their glasses, bottles, and bowls and took them into the kitchen.

He washed dishes, setting them in the rack to dry. Without thought Chris dampened a dishrag and wiped down the counters, the appliances, just as he had done a million times before. His mind's vision recreated the thankful and fearful and angry faces of his staff and the actors and crew at Tamburlaine when he finally got the door opened. What had been happening?

The phone rang, its volume intense after the long period of silence. Chris picked up the pink princess phone before the first ring subsided, hoping it hadn't awoken Elmer. Lately, when he thought of Elmer, said his name in his head, Chris had started to hear the musical refrain from *Funny Girl*, "Nicky Arnstein. Nicky Arnstein," every moment another opportunity for musical theater trivia. Without plan, he answered: "Hello gorgeous."

"Shouldn't I say that to you?"

Chris smiled. "No, I should say it to myself in a mirror." He waited for a moment, a slight crackle over the land line. "Elmer and I watched *A Chorus Line.*"

"Horrible movie."

"It would be great at Tamburlaine." Chris hung the rag over the edge of the sink.

"Hm. Who is all ginger and jazz? Maybe."

"Hey Mr. Producer, here I am."

"Oh, Chris. I'm sorry."

"Hm?" That apology could be good for a lot of offenses.

"I heard about the Picasso, about the gunmen."

Chris moved the rag, straightened it, re-squared the corners. "I still don't have a response to that." He realized he missed Jericho. He'd gotten used to seeing him, to talking to him. Was he still that much in love with Jericho Taylor? Well, of course he was. He had something, some hook or something. Once he got into your heart you could never expel him, like heartworm.

"Are you there?"

That lost voice. That lonely man; the loneliest man Chris had ever met. And that said something.

"I'm here, Jerry. I just…"

"I know, kid."

"Kid. Hah. Those days are long gone. For both of us. We know too much, have been broken too badly, have broken others so horribly." Were they breaking up again? Really? Coming back together again? Really? No, neither were realistic.

"Are you still with me?"

"Jerry, where are you?"

"At your door."

Chris turned on the monitor. "Hi."

Jericho waved. "Hi."

"Are you alone? I want you to be alone and sad and lost."

"I'm some of those."

"Not good enough. You're not alone."

"Jerry, we're not kids anymore. You can't show up at my door at all hours and expect to be allowed into my bed again and again. Your days of slapping my ass, of pounding my ass with that marvelous cock of yours, those days are done. We're not that anymore. You may be that still; but I'm not." Chris turned from the screen. He thought he might rearrange the towel again, or have a staring contest with the blue cat. But, when he turned and raised his head he never made it to the clock; instead, he found a different pair of eyes to stare into.

"No? We're not all that?"

Chris knew he should hang up. He pleaded for forgiveness with his eyes. Elmer's may have been too tear-filled to notice that pleading. Chris sighed, took up a paper napkin, walked to Elmer and wiped away those tears. While he pulled Elmer into a strong, honest hug, he said into the phone. "Not tonight, Jerry. Hail a cab. Go home. Sleep. We'll talk tomorrow after the sun goes down." And, with that, he ended the call. It felt so right, hugging Elmer, looking toward the future through a few cloudy tears. Letting go of that part of the past, well, could anyone really let go of the past. Accept it? Perhaps. Allow it to be the past? Perhaps.

Chris leaned harder into Elmer. "I love you, Baby." There, he'd said it. He moved a step further into the future, or at least a step further into the present.

"What was that call about?" Elmer asked.

It didn't bother him that Elmer hadn't responded with his own "I love you." This all felt good, right. "I don't really know. But, he's back. He's his old self. And, I told him I thought *A Chorus Line* would be a good show for the club." For the club, not for us. A small, but important shift had occurred. "What do you want to do now?"

"Sleep. It's the end of a very long day."

Forty-six

Chris folded shut the *Times* arts section. "Still no *Little Shop* review."

"By God!"

"What?"

Elmer shoved the open paper toward Chris. "They found your Picasso."

"Stolen at gunpoint from Tamburlaine, a downtown night club, the *Streetwalkers*, believed to be a study by Picasso for a larger work by the same name, was recovered late last night in a warehouse in New Jersey filled with hundreds of stolen objects including art, cars, and—"

"Stolen art is rarely recovered." Elmer added two spoons of sugar to his coffee cup. "Rarely."

"Shouldn't someone have called me? The police or something?"

"They should." Elmer took the paper back. "It doesn't say how or why they were at that warehouse."

"I'm thinking I should do something with the painting. Loan it to the Met or something." Chris leaned into the table, trying to view the upside down picture of his painting.

"That's a very good idea." Elmer turned the page.

The doorbell rang.

"Put a robe on. I might think your jingle and jangles are cute, but..."

Elmer stood, jingled his jangles in Chris' direction, and left the kitchen.

Chris pulled up the video screen with the exterior shot. Two policemen stood squared at the camera. One of them picked his teeth with his hand practically inside his mouth.

"Yes?" Chris asked into the receiver.

"Mr. Marlowe?"

"Yes," said Chris.

The speaking policeman flashed his badge toward the camera. "Can we come in and speak to you?"

Chris contemplated the question for a moment. "I've been having some trouble lately and frankly, I don't know you. Anyone can get a badge on the interweb or Canal Street or Coney Island."

"The interweb?" the teeth-picking cop asked.

"He means the Internet. The guy is like a hundred."

"Oh, I'm not all that old." Chris didn't offer his actual age.

"Sir, we are from the police department. And, we have questions."

"What are you doing, Chris. Let them in." Elmer had dressed; he stood next to Chris and looked at the screen. "They really do look legit."

"Okay, I'm going to buzz you in. But I have a very strict rule about no guns in my house, so we'll have to talk outside." Chris hit the three button and heard the buzzer. He watched the police ram open the door. He took a shawl from the chair and wrapped it tight around him and opened the door. A chilly blast hit him.

Again the police flashed their badges. "Elmer? Is that you?"

Elmer held out his hand. "Nice to see you again. Officer Leander?"

"Yes, that's correct. And this is Officer Hero."

"Chris, you should let them in. It's too cold for you to talk to them with this door open." Elmer took Chris' elbow. "Officer Leander was at Tamburlaine the night you were poisoned the second time. He's the one who got me for you, to translate all that eye blinking."

He didn't trust these men. Police or street thugs, they had an agenda and they carried guns. Chris had never liked the energy related to guns or the residue of energy that lingered on people who carried them. But, he acquiesced to Elmer who seemed to know these men. "Fine." He stepped back, looked them over, and sat down at the table, focusing on his cooling cup of coffee.

"Why don't you boys sit? Can I get you some coffee?" Elmer as hausfrau cleared a few dishes and returned with coffee cups.

Frustrated, Chris asked: "You said you have questions?"

Leander opened a notebook. He pointed to the newspaper on the table. "So, you've seen that they've found your painting? Thanks, cream for me, if you've got it."

"Yes, my painting" said Chris. He nodded as Elmer warmed up his cup of coffee.

"The warehouse is leased by a Folgate Foundation. It isn't a registered entity, but there is a Folgate Corporation just around the corner from here."

"Yes, I know the Folgate family."

"Family? No, there's only one that we could find. Nigel Folgate. But, strangely, the credit card and lease agreement weren't signed by him."

"There are three. Nigel Folgate, who I believe to be an honest man, mostly. His nephew, Norton Folgate. He's the one who has been harassing me for months. And, Nigel has a sister. I can't remember her name."

"We have no records at all of a Norton Folgate." Leander punched his finger at the screen of his tablet. There are no business entities registered to him, no driver's license, no Social Security number." Leander continued to stab at the screen. "If the sister married, she'd have a different name."

"Have you seen all these shows?" Hero asked. He touched several warping *Playbills* on the wall.

"Yes, of course." Chris snapped at the man.

"Sorry," said the youthful officer.

"How can there be no younger Folgate?" Chris asked. "Elmer, you were there with me. You've seen him. You heard Nigel speak of him."

"I was with you when that man harassed you. I'd never seen him before that."

Chris' head swam. "You said you had questions?"

"Yes." Leander pushed his screen several times. "Can you tell us again how you discovered the painting was missing?"

"I've told and retold this story."

"Chris, just tell them again." Elmer said.

"Why do you guys ask the same questions over and over?" He wanted these two men out of his house, make that three. Perhaps because he was a cop for so many years, Elmer seemed to have aligned up with his brothers too easily. Chris retold the story, arriving at Tamburlaine, the missing staff found in the basement, story of the masked gunmen, office broken into, painting missing. As he spoke, Leander typed and pushed at his screen. It felt like a Sci-Fi novel he'd read. In that story, those questioned ended up the next dead.

"Your painting will be held for a bit, as evidence, until we complete our investigation. That was really why we stopped by today."

"That, and to hear your story again," added the baby-faced cop who didn't make eye contact, but instead watched the cat clock swishing its blue tail.

Leander stood, Hero followed. Everyone shook hands and the cops left.

"I don't like any of this," said Chris. "Something is off about those two. I don't believe they're cops at all."

"Chris, Leander was the guy that helped the night you were poisoned."

"That doesn't make him a good guy; it just makes him a guy who was there." Elmer was also a guy who was there that night.

Forty-seven

Chris pushed through the doors into the lobby of the Folgate Building. He tapped his foot on the marble floor in time with his manicured, red lacquered fingernail on the marble counter. "I'm here to see Nigel Folgate."

The assistant eyed Chris with a smirk. "He's not seeing anyone today."

Chris wanted to slap that look off her face; he wanted to throw some shade about her bad dye job, uneven roots, and knockoff dress. Instead, he said: "Please tell him Chris Marlowe is here. He'll see me." He held the woman's gaze until she blinked. "You know he'll see me."

She picked up the phone, spoke Chris' name, and hung up. "Follow me."

He wanted to snap his fingers. He didn't gloat, or tried not to, but those shoes of hers were bargain basement, too. As the elevator opened on the top floor, Nigel met Chris.

"Alone?" Folgate asked.

"Yes. I had to see you. I want to talk to you."

He steered Chris into the office and closed the doors behind them. "I was just pouring coffee for myself, will you join me?"

Chris chose a comfortable chair; Nigel poured him coffee and handed him a white porcelain cup on a wafer-thin saucer. He poured another for himself and sat opposite his guest. Chris tasted the hot coffee, enjoying everything about it, the aroma, the perfect, drinkable temperature. He left behind a lipstick mark, but did nothing to remove it.

"What can I do for you my dear friend?"

After a moment's hesitation, Chris began: "The Picasso has been found."

"Yes, I saw the papers."

"It was found in your warehouse in New Jersey."

"Yes, it was."

"I was informed you have no nephew, but even your secretary, the last time I was here, asked which Folgate."

"Chris, what are you accusing me of?" Norton set down his coffee cup and saucer.

"I'm not casting accusations. I suspect the police will be filing charges, issuing warrants. But, I'm just so confused. Who is the evil boy?"

"My nephew."

"But the police say there is no nephew. He doesn't exist." The cup on its saucer offered the faintest of rattles before Chris placed them on the table. "Your sister's boy?"

"No, there is no nephew."

"Norton, you talked about him. He's been harassing me for weeks. Who is this man impersonating your nephew."

"I really don't know what to tell you."

"Nigel!" Chris sat back, exhausted, flummoxed. "First you tell me you'll protect me and then my painting was stolen. Why?"

"He wanted to prove that he could do it. After you were here we talked about you, about Jimmy…about the art. Do you still have that big Jasper Johns?"

"Who? Prove to whom?" Chris took out a handkerchief and tapped it along his neck.

"The boy wanted to prove to me that he could run the neighborhood. You and those Jews and that old Wop, you three are the only holdouts. We own the rest of the neighborhood. An entire neighborhood. We can turn it into anything. The boy has a vision and it doesn't include ancient dives hanging on by a thread. So, what do you do? You up the ante. You get your place hopping. Now, the Wop doesn't want to sell. The Jews never did want to sell, third generation. They're making money again from all your drunks."

"You're making no sense."

Nigel sipped coffee. He wiped his lips with a linen napkin, a white "F" embroidered in its corner.

"Well?" Chris asked.

"The boy is my lover."

A quick laugh escaped Chris' mouth before his mental editor could catch up. "He's a quarter of your age, Nigel."

"We're married. He's taken my name. When I die, it's all his."

"Well, this just gets better and better." Chris felt the room spin. "Why is there no record of him? Son, husband, there's got to be records."

"Perhaps they haven't caught up yet."

"So, that's how he knew how to break into the office. Jimmy taught you the lock."

"Taught me? I built that lock. I taught Jimmy. And, I taught the boy."

"Why? Why would you steal Jimmy's painting? What was your connection to Franz?"

"We were lovers. I helped him get those paintings into the country."

"Were they…are they…stolen?" Chris felt the heat rise to the roots of his curls. It would have been the late '60s. No connection to World War II. But, Franz did have a German name.

"No. They weren't stolen. He just didn't want to report them. Most of those pieces were from a collection in France. No documentation. Franz did what Jimmy did. Bought work from young, unknown painters. Where do you think Jimmy learned to do that? Is the Jasper Johns still in Jimmy's bedroom?"

Chris leaned forward and filled a glass on the tray with water, he drank a few sips, and then pressed the glass to his cheek.

"Not feeling well?"

He hated the memory of Nigel and him in bed with Jimmy when he was dying. "Just flushed. Unless you've poisoned me again?"

"Chris, I've never harmed you. And, the boy never harmed your staff. He shouldn't have done it, shouldn't have stolen the painting. But, he was trying to prove to me he would do anything. It just, well, got out of hand."

"Got out of hand? I've been poisoned, there have been several attacks with fire and gas. My staff robbed at gunpoint…"

"Chris, I've had nothing to do with any of those things."

"What about your boy?"

"As far as I know, he's only responsible for the painting."

"Why does he tell people he's your nephew? Why not your husband, or your lover?"

"Our ages. People assumed he was my grandson; he thought nephew was a better title."

The two sat for an elongated moment. Nigel held Chris' gaze, keeping an amused look on his face.

"I'm so tired." Chris leaned forward. "The police told me I'd get my painting back. And, it is *my* painting. Jimmy owned it and he left it to me. My club is a success right now. You can't have it. And, he can't have it either." Chris stood up. "I don't know what kind of cat and mouse game you thought you were playing at, but the rules have just changed. I will never, ever give up my club to you or anyone else." Chris strode toward the door. The wheels inside his head spun. He wasn't going to lie down for this anymore, that was for sure. "Tamburlaine is mine and you can't have it." He opened the door. "And that goes double for your boy!" He stepped out and slammed the door shut.

The elevator was open, the box unattended. He strode in, pulled the grill closed, and grabbed the handle. He guided the elevator down to the ground floor in a herky-jerky manor; it arrived in the lobby with a hard bump.

"Mr. Folgate—" started the secretary.

"Can kiss my ass," finished Chris as he shoved the two doors open onto the street and a great wind tore into the building.

He walked a block, cleared the Folgate Building, and his knees went weak. Chris propped himself against a dirty gate blocking a broken-glassed doorway into a long-closed shop. Wops, Jews, Spics, Fags. That's what this neighborhood had always been; a strong, working-class neighborhood; hard working meat packers and shop owners. A vision began to form in Chris' mind of what the neighborhood had been all those years ago and what it could be again. He felt more excited than he had in years. He also felt lonelier than he'd ever felt. How could those emotions reside so closely together inside of him?

With his footing regained, Chris walked toward home. The late fall chill went head-to-head with the great sunlit sky: A battle that would now rage until spring.

Forty-eight

Chris stopped at the corner. There ahead of him, at his front door, a gaggle of people waited in the streetlight's illuminated circle. Someone held a television camera, another smoked, the red ember of the cigarette glowing red and hot at even intervals. He debated turning and walking back to the club, but he needed to change clothes before his set at Tamburlaine.

"Mr. Marlowe! Mr. Marlowe!" came the shouts as he drew closer.

Chris wished he'd taken a moment to freshen his lipstick.

"Mr. Marlowe! How long have you owned the painting?"

"What were you doing with a Picasso in your bar?"

"Mr. Marlowe!"

The reporters, he assumed they were reporters, blocked his door. Keys in hand, he found himself in the middle of them, all men, all pushing him with their shouted words and aggressive body language.

Chris inhaled through his adrenaline spike. In the middle, he couldn't do much. "The painting was a gift. I'm so glad it's been recovered," he said.

A volley of questions from all directions.

"Boys, boys, one at a time." He flirted, treated it like being heckled on stage.

The handsome man, the one from *New York 1 News*, chuckled. "Chris, do you think the painting was stolen because of the recent success at Tamburlaine?"

"Success at Tamburlaine is an ongoing thing, has been for more than forty years. But, you know that." Chris winked at the television reporter. "You're there all the time, aren't you? You look so familiar." Chris took another step toward his door; the gaggle shifted around him. "I don't know why the club was targeted or the painting stolen. It's been there for a very long time."

"How did you end up with a Picasso?" someone asked.

"Well, no need to be rude," said Chris. "The painting was a gift. Pablo was still alive when Jimmy got it. When Jimmy died, it was gifted to me."

"The police say the painting was found in a warehouse leased by the Folgates. Do you think…"

He didn't know how to attack Nigel and his protégé yet, so refrained from saying anything about them. "That's what the *Times* said." He shuffled another few inches toward his door, held the key ready. "The *Times* hasn't reviewed a single show at Tamburlaine, so I have nothing to say about the *Times*."

"You have a lot of expensive paintings, don't you Mr. Marlowe?"

How did he know that? Chris spoke with caution, his mental editor on high. "I do have a small collection, but when they were acquired, they weren't worth much at all. I've always supported artists, artists of all mediums. I still do. Money is like manure, it's not worth a damn unless it's spread around, encouraging young things to grow." Nothing wrong with a Dolly Levi moment.

Several of the guys groaned.

"There have been lots of strange incidents for you recently, haven't there? Who do you think is harassing you? Do you think it's the Folgates?"

"Well, I don't know. There have been a few difficult moments. I'm just happy that Tamburlaine keeps bouncing back. You should come see *Little Shop of Horrors* or *Ain't Misbehavin'*." He felt the cool metal of the door, found the lock, thrust the key in, turned it, pushed with his whole body; the door creaked open. "Bring that camera to the club if you want more from me." He slipped into the darkness and pushed hard on the door. It resisted. Chris feared the reporters wouldn't let it close, but they did. He could hear the chuckles and crude comments, but said nothing. He stood for a long moment, letting his knees strengthen before walking down the alley.

He entered the kitchen to a ringing cell phone and doorbell. He pushed the button on the security monitor as he picked up the phone. "Yes?"

"Chris, just checking on you. Just so you know, there are a group of reporters at your door."

"Yes, Frank, I've just spoken with them."

"Well, I was walking by your place on the way into work and…"

"The painting. They want to know more about *Streetwalkers*."

On the monitor, one of the reporters repeatedly pushed the buzzer.

"What is that noise?" Frank asked.

"There's an asshole laying on my bell."

Chris pushed the button to speak: "Please stop that." The noise stopped.

"Are you okay?" Frank asked. "I could be back over there in a minute with my baseball bat."

The buzzing started again.

"Aren't you sweet? No, it's fine. I'll be in early." He hung up the phone and walked out of the kitchen. The buzzer echoed through the loft. In the bedroom, he stripped down to his boxers. He looked at the Jasper Johns, then the Jackson Pollack, worried for the first time that something might happen to them while he was out of the house. He rummaged through his fallen slacks for his cell phone and punched in his lawyer's number.

"Peter Pfizer's office," answered a receptionist.

"Christopher Marlowe for Mr. Pfizer."

"Please hold."

Chris swayed to "Girl from Ipanema."

"Chris! What can I do for you? I saw you got your painting back." Peter had been Chris' attorney for more than two decades. He knew more about Chris' affairs than Chris did.

"They still have it, for a bit, anyway."

"Do you need my help with that?"

"No. Not yet. But, I do need your help. Reporters are asking about the art. People know about it, or will. It's time to do something with it."

"Are you sure?"

Chris could sense Peter holding his breath. "Yes."

Peter exhaled. "Storage? Auction? Maybe a gift to the Met or MOMA?"

"No. I don't know. I want to still own it, but I don't see the point of storage. I'll never see it there."

"Let me make some calls. I know a lot of people."

"Well, don't go telling every Tom, Dick, and Mary about it. I'll come home and it'll be gone. Or, someone will slit my throat."

After an elongated pause, Peter said. "First, I'm putting a security guard at your front door."

Chris breathed to protest.

"Not a word about it." Peter laughed heartily. "And, while I'm at it, there'll be security guards at the front and rear of Tamburlaine by tonight, too. I'm worried about you and your people. Something is going on."

They'd met late one night at the club. Chris owned it already. Peter came in, tall and handsome, covered with brown, curly hair. His small dick didn't matter. They talked, a lot. They played chess in the nude. They drank bottle after bottle of bourbon together, even though Peter preferred 30-year-old Scotch. They lounged naked: in bed, on the couch, in the kitchen. They kissed for hours. They went to Greece, laid naked on the beaches—Peter liked to be naked—drank ouzo until they passed out. Chris never did know why they'd stopped being together, it just sort of petered off: he'd always attributed that phrase, petered off, to that relationship.

Ignoring the direction Peter had the conversation headed and the memories of sun-crisped skin in linen suits, Chris said, "I want you to see what we could get for the Jasper Johns. One of those flag paintings of his just sold for a mountain of cash."

"I'm sure we could find a buyer without going to auction. Take a picture of it with your phone and email it to me. Is there anything else?"

"Peter, the collection is pretty big now. Close to two-hundred works."

"And they're all there?...Of course they are. Let's get off the phone so I can get some security over there. Sorry, it's going to feel like you're being watched for a bit."

"There are reporters outside my door right now."

"Chris, are you okay? I mean really. Are you okay?"

He didn't know how to respond to that.

"I'm going to make a few calls and then I'm coming over there. What time are you leaving for the club?"

"No later than six," said Chris. "I'll be here if you arrive before then."

He did remember why they'd stopped seeing each other. They hadn't broken up, but drifted apart. They'd argued about the art collection. Chris had wanted Peter to take a small notebook page, a study by Chagall. It had only been a few thousand dollars at an auction. Peter liked it so well. He'd sat stoned in front of the thing for hour upon hour. He said he could enter the sketch. But, he wouldn't take it. They'd argued. The only time they'd ever fought, ever. Peter left that night. He continued to be Chris' attorney, but they were never together again.

Forty-nine

The Picasso was returned without ceremony. The police handed Chris the painting wrapped in clear, thick plastic marked with codes and numbers. Chris unwrapped it in his office. There did seem to be a nick in the top corner of the painted surface, but otherwise, all was well with his garish women. He wanted to return them to their hallowed home, but just rested them on the couch.

"Chris?" Nancy Ann stood in the doorway.

Chris turned to her.

"I'm glad you got your painting back."

"Me, too. Here, come sit with me." He pointed with manicured finger at the leather sofa. She did as told. "The girls are back."

"Yes."

"And, I've decided to give them to you." Chris swallowed back his emotions.

"No! You can't. They belong here."

"They aren't safe here. Everyone knows about them. They were Jimmy's. You're part of Jimmy. Don't protest too much or I'll change my mind." He held her eyes and smiled. "I know that the success here has a lot to do with you." He pointed toward his desk. "There's a folder there with all the papers and legal stuff that shows the transfer of property to you. Because it's a gift, there are tax consequences, and I've written you a check that should cover those, too."

He could tell she wanted to say something, but he didn't press her.

"What should I do with this? My apartment isn't the right place for it either. I live in a pretty rough neighborhood."

"Well, I've made arrangements and my collection is being moved to a safer place. We could certainly include this with those, for now."

"Where? Where is it all going?" Nancy Ann's eyes were wide, horrified. "How can you let it all go?"

Chris tried to put the painting back inside the plastic, but couldn't get the angle right. Nancy Ann helped him.

"Well, there are still details to work out, but my attorney has made arrangements for MOMA to house them. There's going to be a show in a bit." Chris brightened and they safely rewrapped the painting.

"The Modern Museum of Art? That's…. I don't know. I still feel like it should be here."

"Are you worried it's like Sampson's hair? If the painting is gone, Tamburlaine will fall?" He watched her head nod. Chris took a finger to her cheek and raised her head until she saw him. "Trust me, we had decades with the painting on the wall and no success at all."

Nancy Ann smiled through tears. "I love you. I can't believe how generous you are." She hugged Chris and held on to him for a long moment.

He liked the touch and smell of her: youth, vibrancy, future. "Okay. Don't you have a show to run?"

"Oh, I do." Nancy Ann released him and stood. "So, you'll make the arrangements with MOMA to include this with the collection."

"I will call my attorney." Chris didn't stand. "Leave the paperwork here until you're done for the night."

Nancy Ann turned back, the office door framing her. "I really do love you, Chris. Not because of the painting."

"Yes, I know, dear." He waved her away and he was alone again. He sat back deeper into the leather of the old sofa. There should be a picture of Jimmy here, but there wasn't. There weren't many pictures of Jimmy. The newspaper picture: What would those men think of the painting going to Nancy Ann?

"Well girls," he said to the *Streetwalkers*, our run is finished. You'll have to find others to inspire in the nighttime." Chris stood, leaned the artwork against the side of the couch, and left his office. There was time for a bourbon before his set.

Fifty

Chris walked with his hand and wrist in the crook of Liz's arm. The two were headed from an early supper at Mario's to the club. The chill of the nearly winter air blew in from the river in a gust. Chris tried to pull closer to Liz for warmth.

"Any closer and you'll be inside me."

Like a teenager, Chris giggled. "We did that last night," he whispered.

"It was nice." Liz put his gloved hand atop Chris' bare one. "I don't know why you won't wear gloves?"

"Don't nag me. We're having a nice moment and you nag me."

"Sorry. I just want you to be warm and comfortable and happy." Liz gripped Chris' hand tighter.

"I am happy." Chris wasn't convinced of those words, but he said them. It's what Liz expected. It's what everyone expected. He missed the paintings; their removal made him sad.

They turned the corner; people milled around the front door, mostly smokers, mostly male. Several of them applauded as Chris approached. He loosened himself from Liz, without fully releasing their bond, and curtsied, which brought more applause and a catcall from the small crowd.

"You boys are so kind."

One of the men opened and held the door for Chris. The Tamburlaine stools had butts on them, the tables were mostly full.

"Coffee," said Liz to Frank through the patrons before she headed to her reserved, high-top table in the corner, next to the window, where she could watch the room.

"You got it. Boss, there are messages for you." Frank finished filling a third shot glass and placed them in front of the guys nearest him.

Chris immediately went into the routine: he took off his wrap, grabbed the pink message slips, and headed to his office without care for anyone around him. His room held no charm now. It needed to be painted to remove the faded rectangle on the wall, a constant reminder of his good deed. Maybe it was time for new furniture, too.

He read and tossed two of the messages in the trash. The third was from Jericho. He sat, poured a few fingers of bourbon in a glass, and dialed Jerry's number. It rang and rang and rang before finally going to voice mail: "Hi. It's Chris." He didn't know what else to say. "Returning your call."

They hadn't had a serious conversation since the late-night phone call. Yes, he continued to rehearse the shows and give notes to the actors, but he'd avoided Chris for weeks. He replayed their fight over Nancy Ann again in his mind.

A knock at the door brought him back. "Chris?"

Ingram stood, ruddy faced and handsome. Slightly thinner, but more solid in his frame hugging shirt: rehearsals were good for dancers.

"My boy! Come give mother a kiss." Mother? Where had that come from?

He laughed and glided to Chris and kissed his cheek. "I have something for you." Ingram pushed an envelope toward Chris. "I really want you to be there."

Chris took the envelope and opened it, revealing a single ticket.

"For opening night of *Godspell*. I don't have anyone else and you helped me get my foot in the door and…"

"It's tomorrow! And, only one?"

"Yes. I know it's really short notice. I have to admit I wasn't going to invite anyone. I didn't realize they'd held tickets for me. So, today, they were on my dressing table. There should have been two, I know, but the guy next to me needed a ticket for his boyfriend, and since I wasn't going to ask anyone…"

"I'll be there."

"Great." He quickly kissed Chris on the cheek again. "I've got to run. There's a party tonight."

"Don't drink, too much. You've got an important show tomorrow."

Ingram backed out of the office, facing Chris, smiling broadly. "Yes, Mother!" He laughed and bolted from the room.

The ticket proclaimed *Godspell*! The seat number was orchestra center. He'd always hated being in the middle, preferring the safety of the back. But, for the boy, of course he'd go. Chris absently picked up his cell and redialed Jerry's number. Again, he got voicemail. He hung up without leaving another message.

He tossed off the last of the bourbon in his glass and contemplated a refill. He could hear the buzz of conversation punctuated with forks on china in the dining room. *Nunsense* would start in ten minutes. The dining room would be mostly empty then. Fifteen minutes later, he'd start his first set. Chris felt tired. He poured more liquor into his glass, contemplated it for a moment, tossed it back. He thumbed the lipstick on the glass and looked again at the faded spot on the wall. Success, he thought, would help him feel better, help him feel happier. It hadn't. Not really. A boyfriend, Elmer, it was nice to have someone in his life again, but old man sex wasn't a fantasy fulfiller. All that combined wrinkled skin, like two old Shar-Pei fighting under the sheets. At least he wasn't alone.

He pushed the ticket around on his desk. Listened to the sudden, near silence. Chris applied a fresh coat of lipstick without the benefit of a mirror, and headed out to the barroom stage.

Fifty-one

The packed theater frightened Chris. He'd been alone in theaters of all sorts, of course. This felt different. He'd grown used to being with Liz, or Elmer, whoever he decided to be on any given day. The alternating personalities felt strange and odd to Chris, who had, for a lifetime, strived to be just Chris, not a transvestite, but a drag queen, a man with a woman's flair.

He drank a glass of bourbon on the rocks at the lobby bar, enjoying the cool liquid on his tongue with its slight burn as it traveled down his throat. He took in the audience, some in tuxedos, others with their pants so low Chris wondered why they even bothered to wear them. The op-eds harped about the poor state of dress at the Broadway theaters these days; Chris loved it. He loved the personal expression of these men. True, he didn't fully understand the evolution from gangsta to exhibitionist, but he loved it all the same.

The house lights blinked.

Inside, Chris found his aisle and waited for the people to stand so he could wriggle his way to the center seat. Once he arrived and began situating himself, he discovered he sat next to Nigel Folgate. The old man turned toward him, tried to engage him. His heart beat so hard he thought it might burst.

How could Ingram have done this to him? More important: how did Ingram even know Nigel?

Chris kept his focus on the stage. No grand drape: instead, a simple set with playground equipment and a back wall of chain-link fence, broken side walls covered with colorful, spray-painted tags and graffiti. A breeze ruffled the trash on the stage, explaining why it felt so cold in the theater.

"Chris," whispered Nigel.

The man touched Chris's arm. Chris pulled it away, tighter to his side.

The opening night of *Godspell* began with soft music, piano and guitar. The audience settled. It shifted to harder rock, electric guitar, loud for a moment, and then words over synthesizer: Man arrives on God's newly created earth as gardener.

Chris pulled tighter into his seat, torn between the action on stage and knowing Nigel sat next to him. Disjointed, disjunctive, disconnected. Actors sang "Tower of Babble." They were all over the stage, singing, cleaning up the trash, shoving papers into cans. The colors of costumes, lights, moving pieces of set. It all felt like a music video. Tension formed in Chris' neck. His heart beat harder. He felt trapped. He looked at the people on stage; there went Ingram, mixed in with others of all sizes and races. "Each of us, a Child of God."

With eyes closed, he focused on the songs: "Prepare ye the way of the Lord. Prepare ye the way of the Lord." Light came up slightly in the house. People in the audience, not actors, were singing along. The world of stage and viewer merged for an uncomfortable moment. Ingram at the front of the stage, he looked so good, so solid, so in his element.

Chris was thankful they ran the show without an intermission. Time had stopped for him as he listened to his heartbeat, felt the heat coming from Nigel, watched them sing and move on stage. He'd seen the original cast, and later, the revival; Jericho had updated the show, slightly, it held its ground. And, it sounded good, really good. Time had obviously been spent on vocals, on musical rehearsals. Of course. He wasn't The Great Jericho Taylor for nothing. Yet, Chris longed for the end, for the death of Christ, so that he might escape his own current hell.

And, as with all scripted ends, this show's demise came. Thankfully, they didn't carry the dead Christ through the theater. The cast carried him out through the wings. A great wind erupted and once again trash and paper caught in the chain link. The set looked as it had when the audience had arrived. Full circle.

The rows stood, began emptying into the aisles.

"Chris." Nigel grabbed Chris' arm, tight. "We have to talk."

He breathed deep. "No, we don't."

"We do."

Chris turned to his accoster. "How did you get this seat? How did you end up next to me?"

"Norton. Ingram gave Norton the ticket."

Confusion. "Ingram?" Was this what a swoon felt like? "How. But. Are."

"Chris, sit."

People slowly shuffled out of the theater.

"I don't understand," said Chris.

"Ingram and Norton. They've been…seeing each other."

"Norton has been cheating on you with Ingram?" Chris sat back into the soft chair.

"Yes. They've been living together for months."

The boyfriend. It wasn't a fellow actor's boyfriend, it was his boyfriend. Ingram had set him up so that he'd be sitting next to Nigel for two hours. "So, he's been found? He's turned up again?"

"Found?" Nigel asked. "He wasn't lost."

"But, you…the police."

"There's so much you don't know." Nigel placed his hand on Chris'.

Chris pulled his hand away. With effort, he propelled himself out of his seat. He wanted to be gone, to be at his club, to be drinking a bourbon. "I don't want to see you again."

"Chris, what have you done?"

He knew what Nigel spoke of, but didn't say anything.

"You've taken over my company!"

He had. He'd taken the proceeds from selling the paintings, because that's what he'd done, sold the paintings. Once they'd been reviewed by the curator, they'd offered a king's ransom. He'd taken it. Sold everything, except the Picasso—not his to sell—and the Pollack, which he truly loved more than all the rest. He took those proceeds and bought every share of the Folgate Company he could get his hands on. "Your sister hates you." Because of her, he now owned sixty percent of that company. "You and Norton, or whoever he is, will never take away Tamburlaine, now. You two will never tear down my neighborhood."

Nigel went pale. "What are you going to do with the company?"

"I haven't decided, yet. What I do know is that I'll be asking the board for your removal as CEO. I've spoken to the police about Norton. He'll be in the system as soon as they find him."

"What have you done? You don't know this boy, what he's capable of."

Chris turned and walked down the aisle, leaving Nigel where he stood. The theater's orchestra, now empty of patrons, offered a red glow from soft light reflecting off the seats, walls, and rich carpet. He knew he looked good in this light and took his time walking to the back of the room.

An usher, a young woman, very skinny, smiled at him. She moved forward and pressed her hand to his. "I'm a huge fan," she said with a seductively, husky voice. She was a boy.

"Me, too." Chris checked his hand for patches or poison as he walked out the door. All looked good. He raised that hand and a cab pulled up. "Tamburlaine."

"Chris!"

He turned. Jericho stood near the open cab door.

"You're leaving? Without saying anything?"

"I..."

"You're not coming to the party? The opening night party. Ingram will be hurt if you don't come. It's down the street, at Sardis."

Chris took a twenty from his pocket. He handed it toward the driver who waved it away.

"No harm, no foul," said the grizzly old man. "You can buy me a drink next time I'm in your club."

"Of course." Chris pocketed the money. He took Jericho's hand and stepped out of the cab. The two men stood for a long moment. They were alone on the busy street, looking deep into the other's eyes. Breaking the silence, Chris said: "Very nice show. I like the updates."

"You hated it." Jericho broke their eye contact. He turned away.

Chris touched his upper arm. "No, Jerry, I didn't hate it. The cast sounded amazing. I'm so pleased you spent the time with them. The harmonies were wonderful. There wasn't any of that horrible chaos that often happens during this show."

Jericho turned back and faced him. "Thank you." After a pause, "I'm sorry."

"There's nothing—"

"There is. And, I'm sorry. I was hurt. You'd taken something from me I wanted, just like before. Just like Jimmy and the club."

"I didn't take anything. Not then and not now." Chris firmly stood, feeling his feet plant and body square. "We both know you couldn't have done it." He raised a hand to stave off Jericho's protest. "You couldn't have, wouldn't have buried them all. Stayed behind to buy all of them." Chris took a deep breath. "I'm tired of this."

He ignored what Chris had said. "No, that's not what I meant. It's cold. Come with me." Jericho took his elbow, but Chris didn't budge. "Chris, come with me for a moment." He smiled through glistening eyes.

They walked down the side alley, into the theater, around several quick turns. Jericho unlocked a door and they were inside an office.

"I didn't want to have this conversation in public. Sit."

Chris sat in a chair and watched as Jericho took out two glasses and a half-empty bottle of bourbon. He poured the brown liquid, tossed off his own, and refilled his glass. Chris sipped.

"What I wanted to say...what I meant to say..."

Chris opened his mouth to speak.

In a harsh, reprimanding tone, Jericho said: "No, let me do this." He cast his eyes to the floor. Quieter, "Sorry. You do something to me, Christopher Marlowe. You always have. I have been in love with you my whole life. I worry about what you think or what you might think. I..."

"Jerry, I love you, too. But—"

"It's not that I want to be with you. I know you're happy with Elmer. I know we'd never be a successful couple. That's not what I'm saying. Wait." He drank off more bourbon. "When Nancy Ann decided to leave me and work for you, I was hurt in the same way as when you chose Jimmy over me."

"But, I didn't choose Jimmy. You left me. You left the club. No one heard from you again. We tried to find you when Jimmy was sick and you were having success and you never returned our calls. I didn't choose you over someone else. I couldn't choose. You gave me no options." Chris sipped his drink. There was no urgency for him any longer. He was speaking to a spoiled, selfish, petulant child. And, he wasn't this child's mother. "Jerry, you do know that Nancy Ann is Jimmy's niece, right?"

"Jimmy's what? They're related?"

Chris smiled. "You are Peter Pan, aren't you? Yes, they are related. When you introduced her to Tamburlaine, you introduced her to an uncle she never knew. You invited her into our inner circle. You did that."

"I would never have..."

"But, you did."

They both drank for a moment. Jericho added more to both their glasses and they drank some more. All the time, they looked at each other, speaking through their eyes and hearts instead of their mouths.

Finally, because he had to say it; after all these many years it needed to be said aloud. "You have always been in love with Jimmy. It was Jimmy you wanted then and Jimmy you want now. When he died it scared the hell out of you. Yes, that could have been you. When so many of our generation died, and the generations around us, it could have been you. But, you didn't come to care with us, to mourn with us. You avoided it all. Well, Jimmy is dead. We burned him to ash and dumped that ash into the Hudson. I kept his club going because he asked me to—so there'd be somewhere for the others who needed to be buried. I've put in my time. I've paid the price. Those were my choices. I did that because I wanted to. But, you." Chris wiped spittle from the corner of his mouth with his thumb. He pointed his index finger at Jericho. "You no longer get to hold his death over me. I didn't kill him; I only helped him die. And, I kept his legacy going until someone showed up. He knew one of his family would show up. He thought it would be one of the boys, but it turned out to be Nancy Ann."

"I heard you gave her the painting."

Was that contempt? Jealousy? "I did. And, she doesn't know it yet, but Tamburlaine belongs to her, too. It's what he wanted, what Jimmy wanted."

"But, Chris!"

"Our contract, the Tamburlaine Players, that's still ours." Chris finished his drink. Jericho reached to fill it again, but Chris shook his head. "No, I think I've had enough. Have you said all you wanted to say? Are we finished?"

"Finished? That's melodramatic."

How could he not smile at the charming man sitting before him? "I meant this conversation. Is this conversation finished?"

"If you'd like." Jericho stood and offered his hand to help Chris. "I'm sorry. I don't think that's enough; it doesn't feel like enough."

Chris stood, centered his body, touched Jericho's cheek. "You're a sweet man, Jerry."

Jericho stepped in and kissed Chris on the lips. Not a romantic kiss, although for a moment it felt like it might be a Hollywood ending. Instead, something changed during the approach and the two simply kissed. They held their lips together for a bit, but it was friendship, not romance that kiss sealed.

Fifty-two

He'd always loved Sardis, with its round banquette tables, heavy draper-ies, and, of course, the famous caricatures. Jericho held the door for him to enter. Chris stopped at the bar.

"The party is in the main room." Jericho tugged at Chris' sleeve.

"I'm not ready for that. And, I think you should enter on your own. We aren't a couple. Go, take your bow."

"You're sure? I'm happy to escort you inside."

"Go." Chris watched the handsome, tuxedo-clad man walk through the red draped archway where applause greeted him. Chris turned to the bar, took up the one empty seat, and ordered a bottle of water.

In that room, with its clatter of voices and silver and crystal and walls covered with colorful pictures was Ingram, and probably Nigel. Chris thought he might sneak away, just slip out. He'd never be missed by them.

"What did you think of the show?" asked the man sitting next to him at the bar.

"Hmm?" Chris turned a bit toward someone he didn't know making conversation.

"The show. You came in with The Great Jericho Taylor so I assume you saw the show."

"I did see it." Chris drank some water. "I think the music and singing were wonderful." He almost added "I really enjoyed it," but he hadn't enjoyed it and didn't want to lie. Instead, he said: "And, you?"

"Well, I have to love it. My granddaughter is in it." He held up his glass in a cheers sort of motion before downing his drink, placing the glass on the bar, and pointing toward it for the bartender to see. "Can I get you another?" He looked toward the water bottle. "Another?"

"I would love a bourbon." Chris made a cheers motion with his water bottle.

Once the drinks were poured, they raised them silently and clinked them together.

"You look so familiar," said the man.

"I have a club downtown. Tam—"

"Tamburlaine!" He looked around and then laughed a nervous laugh. "Oh, I remember it well. Jerry and I were dancers back then, together."

Chris tried to place this man. He turned and squared off with him.

"You don't remember me?" The man smiled and drank. "It was a long time ago. Sam Samuel."

Chris wracked his brain, running images of the past quickly through his mind. "Sam?" More images, more stalling. He drank bourbon. A switch flipped. "Sam! You and Jerry." Now he had it. "The boy who got Jericho the tour. I remember. And, you've got a daughter in this show?"

"Granddaughter. Well, that's a very long story. Aren't they all long stories?"

Another one who Chris wished he'd never see again. Another person who had brought him grief in the past and now had drudged up that memory, that pain. He tossed off the last of his drink.

"Another round," Sam said to the bartender.

"No." Chris stood. His legs weak, he almost fell, but caught himself. "I have to go."

Before he could take another step, Ingram sidled up beside him. "Chris! Why don't you come inside? There's food and champagne in there. I'm so glad you came. Did you like the show? Does it compare to the others you've seen?"

"Breathe, dear boy." Chris, bolstered his balance by hugging Ingram. "You were wonderful." He pressed his cheek to Ingram's, breathed deep of his youth and cologne over sweat smell, made a kissing sound. He flashed on their first night together. He was sad they'd never had sex, but, thinking of Sam sitting there, glad too that that wasn't a memory for them, either. Chris released the boy.

"You've met Sam. He said he knew you."

"Yes. Another man who has a sordid past that I play a role in."

Sam and Ingram both chuckled at Chris' joke.

Chris smiled at the boy. "Like Nigel. How did he end up next to me?"

"Who? Oh, he's the father of my roommate. Norton couldn't come tonight; he asked if I minded if he passed the ticket on. I told you, I hadn't planned on asking anyone."

"I thought you said you gave it to another actor for their boyfriend?"

"I did, but they gave the ticket back because he couldn't come tonight. What does it matter who you sat next to?"

"No, of course it doesn't matter." Chris realized Ingram knew nothing about what was happening with the Folgates, or, perhaps he actually was a great actor. Chris now believed the former to be the truth; Ingram knew nothing. "I'm going to slip out. I'm glad I got to see you, but I'm not feeling... I thought I'd stop by the club, make sure everything is going well, and then head home."

"No, you have to come in. You just have to." Ingram stepped closer to Chris again. "I wouldn't have gotten this job if you hadn't called Jericho. I owe you my life."

"Don't be melodramatic. You got the job because you're talented."

Even in the soft light, Chris could see the flush that rose on Ingram's face.

"Now," said Chris, "go back inside. You should be with your friends. You should have your picture taken. You should enjoy this moment and remember it." Chris again pressed his cheek to Ingram's, kissed him softly. For some reason, he felt he'd never see this boy again.

Without another word to Ingram or Sam, Chris steered out of Sardis, back into the mid-town streets. He hailed a cab. He got in, but before he said "Tamburlaine," he felt exhausted. So, he gave his home address instead and sank back into the depths of the cab, drunk, overwhelmed with emotions, and pushing the past as far out of his head as he could.

Fifty-three

First, clogged traffic. Next, sirens. Now, fire trucks. The sound deafening. The cab could go no further.

Chris paid the fare. He walked, smelling smoke. Hearing shouts he couldn't understand. He walked faster, heels clacking on the pavement.

The corner blazed. His corner. Tamburlaine.

Rushing forward, wanting to get there, a policeman grabbed Chris, stopped him, using his whole body as a block.

"I have to get there. It's my club," Chris wailed over the cop's shoulder. "I'm the owner. Is anyone hurt? What's happened?"

"Miss. I can't let you pass. It's too dangerous." As the policeman said those words an explosion rocked the ground under their feet. He shifted from blocking Chris, to holding him up.

In front of him, flames roared out of the broken front window. Firemen blasted water at the building from several directions.

"When did it start?" Chris asked. He clung to the policeman as his stomach sank into his knees.

"About an hour ago."

Chris moved to the street and leaned against the hood of a parked car. He watched the men work to put out the blaze. People watched from a half-block distance, he assumed some had been inside. *Little Shop of Horrors* would have just been letting out. Hundreds of people would have been in the hallway, the bar, the showroom, finishing dinner.

"Chris? Is that you? Oh, thank, God." Frank rushed at him, his face and white shirt covered in soot, a gash on his forehead dripped blood.

"Frank! You're hurt. What's happened? How did this start?"

Frank hugged tight to Chris. "Oh, Mommy." As he held him, he said into Chris' ear: "A brick burst through the big window. I was over the bar quick. Two guys were sitting right there. They got cut up. I was helping them up and away, toward the bar, when three flaming bottles came fast through the window. They crashed on the floor and flames were everywhere. It was chaos."

Chris moved his lips, tried to push air through them: "Were people hurt?"

"Yes." Frank began to sob.

"Who? How many?"

Frank shook and sobbed. Through tears and gasps for breath he said: "I did my best to get people out. It was chaos. I pushed and shoved as many as I could through the front door and on to the street. Flames everywhere. People on fire. Drinks spilled adding more fuel."

"Oh my God." He held Frank, let him cry.

"The piano and stage went up in slow motion. The Piano Player, he got out, I didn't see him. That wall blazed; that took it into the theater, I'm sure. People were running and screaming and shoving and pushing and falling into the gasoline fueled flames. Everything smelled of gasoline."

"Was Liz there? In her spot?" He felt guilty not asking about Liz first. Liz in her corner keeping an eye on things.

"She was there. I don't know what happened to her. I remember bringing her a coffee just before the show let out. Just before the brick came through the window. But, I don't know what happened to her."

"Think! Think!"

"I'm sorry, Mommy. I don't know what happened to her. I don't remember anything about her after the brick. It was chaos in there."

"We need to get someone to look at your temple." Chris touched the cop's arm. "Are there paramedics? He's hurt."

"There," he pointed to some flashing lights. "You really are the owner?"

"Yes."

Chris helped Frank toward the flashing red and blue lights the policeman indicated. Once paramedics started helping Frank, Chris walked down the sidewalk: people were covered in black, burnt clothes, stark white bandages. He studied their faces, looking for cast members, staff, but everyone looked the same, with soot-stained faces and stunned, wide eyes. No one paid any attention to him. All around lights flashed, rivers of water rushed through the street, sirens blared. None of those on the street were Liz.

Closer to the club, he scanned the crowd watching the fire; he looked for Liz's big tits sticking out, but he didn't see them, didn't see her. "Liz!"

he shouted; sirens and other shouts drowned him out.

Someone grabbed his arm. "You can't go any further. You'll have to go around. Chris? Chris! Oh, thank God you're okay."

He didn't register who spoke. He stopped walking. He looked down and there stood Matilda. Chris crushed the malformed woman to him, tight and close. She smelled of grease and chicken and smoke and gasoline. "You're okay. You got out."

"The whole kitchen and dining room staff are safe." Her voice muffled against Chris' chest. "The cast and crew are safe, except for...well..."

Chris released her, looking into her face.

Matilda finished: "No one has seen Nancy Ann."

"What? We have to get in there."

"Chris, we can't. One of the guys said they were swapping the sets, putting Audrey Two away in the basement."

"The basement? Nancy Ann was in the basement?"

"Yes. What? Yes, putting away the giant Audrey Two, the plant..."

Chris took off, running as best he could in heels toward home. He fought with the door, but it finally opened. He pulled it tight behind him with a bang and ran into the house. He kicked off his shoes as he ran through the loft to the door under the stairs. It opened with a woosh of air and smoke. Down the stairs, through the dusty passage, to the dead-end wall. He felt it, surprisingly cool. He pushed, it didn't budge. He pushed again with everything he had and it opened, water splashed and gurgled around his ankles.

"Nancy Ann!" he called into the smoky darkness. Chris fumbled along the top of the cabinet next to the door, found the flashlight, turned it on. The room was empty. He moved to the door. "Nancy Ann!"

Pounding on the door. A muffled: "Here!"

With the turn of the lock, the door opened hard as it fought with the dirty water. She fell into him, gasping for breath.

"I've got you. I've got you." He held her for the briefest moment. "Come on." They shut the door, exited through the passage. As they made their way toward Chris' loft, a huge crash followed by a muffled explosion cast a cloud of smoke and debris toward them. Nancy Ann helped Chris up the stairs and out of harm's way.

Chris' cell phone rang; he ignored it. He helped Nancy Ann into the bathroom. She started to breathe more normally. She went to the

sink and saw herself in the mirror: drenched, hair and face and clothes
covered in black soot and muck. Without words she stripped out of her
clothes, leaving them in a muddy, dirty heap on the floor. She got in the
shower.

He turned away from the naked girl. Not out of modesty, but out of
sorrow. "I'm here," he whispered. It was all he could think to say. He
walked into the bedroom and rummaged around a drawer. Elmer had left
sweatshirts and sweatpants there. He slept in them and lounged in them.
He preferred them because he was always cold. Chris placed them on the
counter in the bathroom.

His cell rang. "Yes," he answered, hearing the shock in his voice,
feeling it in his body.

"Where are you?"

Chris didn't recognize the voice. "I'm at home. I got Nancy Ann out.
I saved her." The words mechanical.

Frank, that's who spoke. "Chris, Liz—"

Chris snapped his phone shut. "Liz! She got out." Chris shouted
toward the shower. "I've got to go back to Tamburlaine. I've left clothes
for you."

"No! Chris!" Nancy Ann flew from the shower and wrapped her long,
dripping arms around Chris, holding him. "You can't. Tamburlaine is gone."

"They've found Liz. They got her out." He pulled himself free from
Nancy Ann. "Clothes." He pointed at the counter.

"Shoes!" Nancy Ann shouted, "Put on some shoes."

Chris slipped into a pair of flats and raced for the door. He pushed
on the outer door and it didn't open.

"Fuck!" he shouted. He pushed and banged on the door, but it didn't
budge. He stopped and heard pounding. It came from the opposite
side. "It opens out!" he shouted to whoever was out there. The racket
stopped. Chris again pushed desperately at the door, but it didn't move.
He pulled out his key, tried to slide it under the door, but the industrial
metal weatherstripping, flush against the ground, stopped him. He beat
his hand against the door, pushing his whole body into the panic lock. It
wouldn't give, not an inkling.

"I've come for you!" A shout from behind the door. Gun shots rang out.

First, one, then two, then six metal mounds formed from Chris' stomach
to head. He pulled back against the bricks. A tugging: at his hand, his arm.

"Chris, move away. Come back," said Nancy Ann, dressed in Elmer's sweat suit, which hung on her, so much fabric around her small frame, her hair wet, her feet bare.

"You'll catch your..."

More shots fired into the door, the door again stopped them.

Nancy Ann dragged Chris back further until they were on the patio. "Phone?"

"Your feet. Nancy Ann, you'll be ill. It's too cold. Get inside the—"

"Phone," she repeated.

"What?" Chris said.

"Give me your phone." She held out her hand in anticipation.

Chris rooted in his pocket, brought out the phone, handed it to her. Light enveloped them from the device. "Chris, he's called you."

"Who?"

She held it up for him to see Liz's picture on the screen. Chris fumbled and slid his finger over Liz's face. He pushed the message and held the phone to his ear.

"I love you, Baby. I'm not going to—" In the background, cutting off his words, a deafening explosion.

Chris replayed it.

"I love you, Baby. I'm not going to—"

"Chris," Nancy Ann said softly as she took the phone. She dialed a number. "Frank. Thank God. Listen. We're at Chris'. Can't get the door open. Someone has been shooting at the door. Yes. Shooting." She listened and then ended the call. "Help is on the way."

More gun shots rang out at random moments. Chris could feel the shooter's frustration.

The two moved around the corner, back into the apartment. The blue cat watched over them, wagging his never ceasing tail.

Chris and Nancy Ann turned on the street video cam. "It's Norton Folgate," said Chris. "Norton!" he shouted into the intercom. "What are you doing?"

The man turned toward the sound. "Where are you, Marlowe? Come out here where I can see you, get a better shot at you." His words slurred; tears streamed down his dirty cheeks. "You were supposed to be in there." Norton wandered out of the small street image and came back into it. He aimed at the camera, pulled the trigger.

Chris winced.

Nothing happened.

The kid pulled the trigger again and again, but he'd run out of ammunition. He threw the gun toward the camera. "Why can't I just kill you and be done with this?"

"Done with what?" Chris asked.

"You. My past. Everything."

Nancy Ann touched Chris' arm. "That's good. Keep him talking," she whispered.

Chris nodded. "What are you talking about?"

"You. My mother. That horrible old man…" he wiped at his eyes with his hands.

"Who is your mother?" Chris asked studying the youth on the screen. Who are you?

"Oh, you know my mother. You fucked her."

"I what?" he said. There had only been one woman, ever. One drunken night. One of the drag queens, Eleonore, what was her last name? Bull. That's it. Elly Bull. Wonderful stage name: Eligible. Turned out she wasn't a queen, but a woman pulling a Victor/Victoria. A woman, pretending to be a man, pretending to be a woman. Things had progressed so far, to the point of no return, that Chris sampled a real vagina. Like a science experiment gone wrong. But, oh, how they had laughed and drank. Chris kept Elly's secret for months, but then she just disappeared, as so many of the queens had.

"Is your real name Norton Bull?"

The guy looked hard into the camera. Blue and red lights flashed all around him. He never answered. Cops slammed him up against the brick wall. Handcuffed him. Out of the picture.

"Chris?" asked Nancy Ann, touching his hand. "You've gone white. Like you've seen a ghost."

"Not seen one," he said. "Am one."

"Not yet, Mr. Marlowe."

His buzzer sounded. "Yes?" Chris asked into the video screen where two police officers waited.

"Can you let us in, Mr. Marlowe?" one of the officers asked.

"I'm sorry, but the door is stuck. It won't open."

After a long pause, the policeman said, "I'm sending two officers up the fire escape. We'll get you out of there."

"Okay," said Chris. "Dear, go to the gallery. In the far corner is a ladder up to the ceiling. Unlock the latch so they can get in.

She ran from the room, her bare feet slapping up the stairs. He and Eligible had a son?

"I'm a father? And, my psychotic son has been trying to murder me? How Greek."

Nancy Ann returned. "Chris, all the paintings, they're gone."

"I know."

Two policeman, Leander and Hero, tall and solid and stern, followed her into the kitchen. They questioned him about the door and the shooting and the shooter. Chris answered their questions, wanting more bourbon, but afraid to reach for the glass. That's what had gotten him into all this, being drunk on a bottle of bourbon and discovering his date wasn't a man in woman's clothing, but a woman in…well, woman's clothing.

Before long, a crew of firemen had the old metal door opened. Chris and Nancy Ann, now free, walked back to Tamburlaine. Nancy Ann tried to get him to go to a hotel, to leave his home. But, the sun had begun to color the dark, morning sky. Just a glint. They got coffee from a corner cart.

Tamburlaine was gone, nothing now but a burnt-out brick shell: massive, ancient, hand-hewn charred timbers protruding from a smoldering hole. The ambulances were gone. One crew of firemen remained, hoses lined out straight and empty on the wet street as they coiled them back into their truck. The police or the city or the firemen or whoever takes care of such things had already circled the building and alley with metal stanchions like they use for crowd control on Gay Pride. Yellow police tape fluttering the message "Do Not Cross" flapped in the cold morning wind.

Fifty-four

Chris and Nancy Ann called the hospitals. Chris whispered, "He's not at St. Vincent."

No one had a Liz or an Elmer or a Nashe, or any unnamed patient fitting his description. No one knew what had happened to Liz. Frank's call the previous night wasn't that they'd found her, but that they hadn't.

"There's something I haven't told you," he said.

She turned, looked at Chris. He watched her face, blotchy from tears, eyes puffy from a lack of sleep. She poured more tea into his cup, added a lump of sugar, then a second.

"I should have told you," he said.

"What?" she sat and placed her hand atop his. "Chris, what is it?"

"You own Tamburlaine. Owned."

"What?"

"When I found out you are Jimmy's niece, when I transferred the *Streetwalkers* to you, I had the lawyer transfer Tamburlaine to you, too."

There were only looks between them for a long moment. Chris placed his free hand atop of hers. "I thought you should have it. Someone needed to take the place over if I died, which isn't out of the realm of possibilities considering all that has happened. Jimmy said someone from his family would show up. I wanted someone who cared about it to take it over and run it."

"Like *Charlie and the Chocolate Factory*."

"Not so much of a prize today as it would have been yesterday." He patted her hand several times and thought, not realizing he said the words aloud: "You know what happened to the man who suddenly got everything he ever wanted?" He didn't finish the quote, but said instead: "At least, there's the insurance."

"Insurance?"

"Yes, of course. Years ago, I met a man, very handsome, very hairy, very very big dick. He sold insurance. Boy, did I buy insurance. I've kept those policies going for years and years. Now, I'm glad I did."

"You can rebuild. That's what insurance money is for." She slipped her hand free and drank more tea. "A new place with—"

"Oh, that's a nice dream, but only a dream."

"No, you must. You have to rebuild it." Her eyes bore into Chris until he looked away. "We don't have to make any decisions today." She picked up the list of hospitals. Each one now crossed off. "He might have gotten out."

A great, overwhelming sense of sadness washed over and through him. Tears didn't come this time. Perhaps, he was finally all cried out. "I don't think so. If he'd gotten out, he'd be sitting here with me and we'd be reading the paper together." As an afterthought, Chris pointed to the list she held. "Or, he'd be at one of the hospitals."

"What do we do now?" Nancy Ann asked.

"You should go home. Feed your cat. Get some sleep."

"I don't have a cat," she said, a soft smile overtook her mouth and eyes. "Chris, what are you going to do?"

"I do not know, my dear. Sleep. Get on with it somehow." Buying all those shares of Folgate's company flashed through his mind. The idea of forcing him out, coming up against him, it felt overwhelming. What had he been thinking? If he'd just sold.... No, Norton Bull wouldn't have been satisfied with that.

"Where are you?" she asked.

"Oh, thinking about what I might want next."

"No decisions today." She braced her long, thin arms on the table edge. The muscles pulsed under the clear, lightly haired skin. "Would you mind terribly if I slept on your couch for a bit. I just don't think I have the energy to get home."

Chris stood and held out his hand. She took it, stood up, and he led her to his bedroom. "It's a very comfortable bed. You should sleep there. No protest." He helped her take off her shoes and tucked her under the soft sheets and thick quilt. Her eyes closed and she slept.

He wandered the place, touched the door that led to the tunnel. He thought about going back down there, but knew there was no point. The smell of smoke caught up in his nostrils again. He didn't know if it was real or imagined, if it came from without or within. He pulled a shawl around himself and went outside, down the alley. The door now gaped open, the firemen broke the lock to free them. The bullets had ripped the metal in places, but kept death outside, away. Chris touched a hole about four feet from the ground. His breath caught and he turned his head away.

He walked.

At the Jewish deli he bought a whole chicken and coleslaw. They'd have that later, when Nancy Ann woke. He ordered a corned beef sandwich, thought of eating the last one with Liz, and changed his order to turkey. He might never be able to face another corned beef sandwich again. Who would wipe the mustard from his chin?

While he ate, sitting in the overly-warm room with the smells of soup and pickles dancing around him, Chris wished for a moment he'd done it earlier, years ago; wished he'd gotten out, sold to Folgate, walked off the pier. What had been the point of keeping Tamburlaine open, of sitting there night after night for all those years, only to have everything come back together and then ripped away from him? There it was again, that wave of sadness and nausea he'd been feeling all night. He swallowed the turkey and drank a bit of coffee. No tears came.

He had a son—an angry, miserable, murderer of a son. Why hadn't she told him? Everyone knew where to find Christopher Marlowe. But, that boy chose acting out, revenge, instead of talking. He could have offered him so many advantages: money, education, time. Chris had always had a lot of time.

Then again, the kid looked more like Folgate than he looked like Chris. Was it possible that Nigel and Eligible had...

What would become of that boy, now? People had been hurt because of his actions. Liz was missing. He clung to the idea. No. Dead. But, no one is dead until there's a body, right?

"Chris?"

Ingram.

He didn't know what to say.

"Chris? Can I sit with you? I was coming to see you and looked in the window as I passed and here you are."

Still Chris said nothing. The boy sat down. "Coffee," he said toward the counter. "I don't know what to say except I'm sorry. And, I am sorry. I had no idea who he was or what he was planning. He..."

Chris raised his hand and shook his head. "No. Please don't make excuses or tell me stories about him." He reached for the coffee cup, but didn't raise it. "I trusted you."

"It wasn't me."

The old waiter set a cup in front of Ingram, filled it with coffee, and topped off Chris' cup. He watched them, but said nothing.

"No. Stop. I can't be with you; can't talk to you." Chris stood, picked up his to-go order off the counter. "No." Again he shook his head and placed a hand on the door. "No."

The afternoon held grey clouds and shadows. The neighborhood, silent, dark, the dank smell of wet smoke clung to the cobblestones and pitted bricks. He owned most of this now, these crumbling, boarded up buildings. Saving it, restoring it, seemed stupid and ill-advised. Chris turned the corner to find Jericho standing at his door, fingering the bullet damage. Chris walked home and without words the two men hugged and then walked down the alley to the kitchen door.

"There's nothing to say," said Chris as he entered the kitchen and tossed off his wrap. He put the bag on the counter, pulled out the coleslaw, and put that into the refrigerator. He busied himself making coffee. The bourbon called to him from its shelf, but he ignored the desire, pouring water into the coffeemaker.

"Chris, look at me."

"Jerry, I can't."

The coffee dripped into the carafe as wisps of steam escaped from the top of the machine. It needed to be replaced. Liz kept saying "Let's go shopping today," every time she made a pot of coffee.

"Chris, you had nothing to do with this. Some crazy person throws fire, you get out of the way. If I hadn't dragged you into Sardis last night, you would have been there. You'd just told the cab driver to take you to Tamburlaine when I made you get out."

He turned and faced Jericho: "You're some fucking savior now? You've saved the old queen? Is that it? Fine. You've fulfilled your mission." He wiped the spittle from his lips.

"Chris. No." Jericho pulled Chris to him.

Chris resisted, but felt himself softening, giving in, feeling those strong, lithe arms enfolding him, smelling Jericho: Ivory soap and sweat and cigarettes? No, smoke and char.

"You are here. You have survived," said Jericho.

A rush of emotions, mixed with tears and snot and words flowed from him. He told Jericho everything in a flood, into his ear, while Jerry rubbed his back and squeezed him toward him. Ingram. Nancy Ann. Liz to Elmer to Liz. The Folgates. Eleonore Bull. His Son. The Paintings. The Stock. The *Streetwalkers*. The Insurance. The pain of Jericho walking out again. All the while, Jericho held him, hugged him, let him be until finally, after a moment of heaving silence, Jericho created a bit of distance between them. With a dishtowel, he wiped away the tears and snot and makeup. His face held a sympathetic smile.

"You have survived. All the details are just details. You are here. You have survived. You are exactly where you're supposed to be."

Chris turned away, took out mugs, poured coffee, and placed the mugs on the table. He sank into a chair, a long, lung-emptying sigh escaped his parted lips. "I have survived. For what?"

"No one ever knows the answer to that question." Jericho sat, took a sip of hot coffee. "Some say they know, but no one knows. Not really."

They drank coffee.

Nancy Ann came into the kitchen. "Oh, hello."

"Hi," said Jericho.

She filled a coffee cup and took a seat at the table. "You said I owned the place? Tamburlaine?"

"Yes," said Chris.

"So, we rebuild. Are you in, Chris?"

After the briefest of hesitations, he answered, resigned: "Yes."

"Jericho?" she asked.

"As you wish."

Nancy Ann held up her mug to toast. "To Liz."

Chris didn't raise his mug. "No. If we do this, we do it for us. No promises to the dead. No commitments to the past. If we rebuild, we do it for the future."

Jericho smiled. Nancy Ann raised her cup again. The three clinked their mugs. "To Tamburlaine."

About Rusty Warren

Knockers Up!
Rusty Warren is lusty, gutsy, and r-r-r-r-r-Rusty!

Rusty graduated from high school in Milton, Massachusetts, a suburb of Boston, and went on to study classical piano and voice at the New England Conservatory of Music. As one of their outstanding students, Rusty performed under the baton of Arthur Fiedler. Rusty Warren started with "Moonlighting" gigs in small niteries in the Boston area and in the "Borscht Belt" hotels in the Catskill Mountains during the summer.

In 1954 in Chicago, Rusty got around to the raw and raucous. Her material came from the naught to naughty. It was hot and hilarious entertainment. Rusty opened her show with "I Wish I Could Shimmy Like My Sister Kate" and supplied some inside information on the saga of "Frankie and Johnny." Rusty and her entire company of audience then marched and sang and rose their "Knockers Up!" A commentary ran right through the entire performance. No comment. Each song was done in a manner that can only be described as r-r-r-r-r-Rusty and she closed with "You're Nobody 'til Somebody Loves You."

"If you're queasy or uneasy, if you like your comments breezy, Knockers Up! If you're thinking what I'm thinking, if you're winking or just blinking, Knockers Up! If you think this all will rock you, even socks you where it shocks you, you're right!"

If you are anything like the cult that gathered to hear her every night, you'll laugh and laugh and laugh. If you've heard "Songs for Sinners," you know. If you haven't, well then?

Basically, Rusty's act was designed for the women in the audience. Her favorite targets were young, dating couples. "Look, sweetie, take my advice. Don't give him any before you get married. Don't give him any at all. Just give it to his friends and let them tell him how good it was."

Inevitably, the men in the audience came in with their escorts for their share of her barbed one-liners. "A few nights ago, a fellow ran into the club and said to me, 'Rusty, I want you in the worst way.' The worst way I know is standing up in a hammock. Have you tried it?"

While she can call herself "a brazen broad with no boobs who likes to joke about sex and expound my theories on the floor of the house," there is a serious side to Rusty, as well. "I like helping inhibited females enjoy themselves and I don't say anything at night that people don't do in the daytime. I'm not an intellectual or a 'sickie.' Maybe the thing that some people object to the most is that I'm too healthy. Well, it's all in fun and usually I get as much of a kick out of it as the audience."

The late Sophie Tucker advised the copper-haired Rusty many years ago: "Always have the courage to say what you want to say. Few women do." It was a time when Tucker reigned as a singing queen of America's nightclubs and Warren was just getting started. Rusty's first album came in 1958, *Songs for Sinners*. Three years later she taped *Knockers Up!* and had a hit. "My purpose," she said demurely, "is to get Mr. and Mrs. America rolling on the floor." Some of the titles of Rusty's 15 big-selling albums include *Knockers Up!*, *Rusty Rides Again*, *Banned In Boston*, *SIN-Sational*, *In Orbit*, *Rusty Warren Bounces Back*, *Sexplosion*, *Bottoms Up!*, *Songs for Sinners*, *Knockers Up '76*, and *Sex-X-Ponent*.

Rusty, now age 87, is retired and spends her time between sunny California and tropical Hawaii. She does interviews and comes out of retirement for special appearances. She personally autographs the items sold on her website and emails her fans through the website and her Facebook page. She is still known as the "Mother of the Sexual Revolution" because she was one of the brave women who spoke out at a time when woman were trying to break out of their stereotypical roles and demand equality with men. She was the voice for women encouraging them to stand up for equality. She used her humor to educate, illuminate, and make us laugh at ourselves. It was a time of sexual freedom and exploration and saying out loud that "women liked sex." Today, Rusty can still be heard saying, "Everybody get your Knockers Up!!" and promotes love and laughter.

Learn even more (and shop!): http://rustywarren.com.

Acknowledgements

No man walks alone. So many have helped me pursue and improve my craft. Love and thanks to Todd Isbell, you make all things possible. Thanks go to my editor, Leslie Hoffman. You make everything I write look better. I appreciate the critiques received from members of the Henderson Writers' Group. Further thanks for critique and feedback go to Paul Atriedes, Roger Storkamp, Bill Walles, Darlien C. Breeze, Tonya Todd, Nancy Sansone, Ellen Dugan, and Bonnie Apple. A very special thanks to Liz Rizzo (for all you do!) and Rusty Warren.

This project is funded, in part, by a grant from the Nevada Arts Council, a state agency, and the National Endowment for the Arts, a federal agency.

About the Author

Gay-Contemporary author, Gregory A. Kompes (MFA, MS Ed.) writes and teaches writing in Las Vegas, Nevada, where he lives with his husband. Learn more at Kompes.com.

www.ingramcontent.com/pod-product-compliance
Lightning Source LLC
Chambersburg PA
CBHW060311260626
47160CB00007B/2573